D0847264

OUT OF TIME

ALSO BY MATTHEW MATHER

THE DELTA DEVLIN NOVELS

The Dreaming Tree

Meet Your Maker

THE ATOPIA SERIES

The Atopia Chronicles

The Dystopia Chronicles

The Utopia Chronicles

THE CYBERSTORM SERIES

CyberStorm

CyberSpace

CyberWar

THE NOMAD SERIES

Nomad

Sanctuary

Resistance

Destiny

STANDALONE NOVELS

The Darknet

The Robot Chronicles

Polar Vortex

OUT OF TIME

MATTHEW MATHER

BLACK STONE
PUBLISHING

Published in 2021 by Blackstone Publishing
Cover design by Alejandro Cruz Castillo
Book design by K. Jones

Printed in the United States of America

First edition: 2021
ISBN 978-1-5385-8947-2
Fiction / Mystery & Detective / General

Version 1

CIP data for this book is available
from the Library of Congress

Blackstone Publishing
31 Mistletoe Rd.
Ashland, OR 97520

www.BlackstonePublishing.com

For Maya Merrick

1

Large Hadron Collider, Meyrin, Switzerland
April 19th, 3:59 a.m.

"Now I am become Death, the destroyer of worlds," a hooded figure whispered.

From this height, five stories up on the blue metal gantries, the eye at the center of the metal monster loomed from the middle of eight great tentacles that snaked outward and wrapped back on themselves. Massive aluminum I beams ringed and supported the structure in an octagonal web. The last of the scaffolding had almost been removed now that the rework was completed, readying the world's largest machine for its final journey into the unknown.

The figure checked a digital device attached to its wrist. 4:00 a.m. exactly.

A lone person remained in view. A grad student on their hands and knees, scouring the cement floor underneath a mass of red and yellow wiring, performing a manual search for any stray fragments of debris.

Grooming the beast.

The hooded figure glided past the student, soundless and unseen. The same way it had evaded the sleepy, blue-cloaked guards and remained invisible to dozens of webcams and security devices, as if guided by a preternatural agility or precognition of each obstacle. Down and down the figure had descended, through the convoluted maze of doorways, locks, passages, and elevators that led into the beating heart of the greatest device humanity had ever created.

And one that would forever alter its future.

The hooded figure deftly slipped over a green guardrail and slid down an eight-foot supporting H beam to the lowest concrete walkway. Glanced left and right and stole away under the cover of a metal walkway. Raised a hand and slipped a security badge past a detector. The final doorway clicked open.

This close, the vast machine thrummed.

The figure slipped open a black backpack, and in careful, practiced motions unscrewed a manifold cover. A warm yellow glow spilled out as a metal sheath was removed.

"So it begins, and so it ends . . ." the figure whispered, and reached in to take the prize.

2

Marina Bay Sands Hotel, City Area, Singapore
April 21st, 9:24 p.m.

"Where is he now?" US Deputy Marshal Delta Devlin gasped the words into her wrist mic.

She was sprinting, sucking wind and pumping her arms. Going as full out as she could. Her stiletto-heeled Louboutins clacked against the ribbed concrete floor of the parking structure. She should have put on her Nikes. Her lurching gait attracted the attention of a family getting out of their car. The mother held her two children back protectively.

One of the kids held up her phone like she was taking a picture. So much for stealth.

Del shrugged an apology as she clattered past.

"Second-floor flyover," came Zoya's reply in her earpiece. The Israeli agent was on comms and tactical support, tracking the target. "They're heading for the elevators. You're better off going straight into the lobby from ground level."

Del burst from the cool, temperature-controlled garage into a wall of humid air. Honking cars and mopeds sped between walls of pedestrians mobbing both sides of the two-lane road outside. The highway divider was lined by a row of handkerchief trees, their white petals flowing in the vortices of passing cars. Neon lights burst in greens and purples and hyper-iridescent blues that glowed in shades Del knew only she could see.

A detonation overhead, and fireworks splashed across the sky between the fronds of sugar palms.

Del cursed as she edged through the mass of people and glanced up at the second-floor skywalk connecting the parking structure to the hotel. A trio of curved glass walls arced overhead to support a vast oblong structure a thousand feet high, lit by spotlights that blotted out the night.

The Hari Raya festival in Singapore. The conclusion of Ramadan, and the end of fasting. A time to ask forgiveness and to sacrifice.

Also, the busiest night of the year.

She hadn't realized how crowded it would be.

Del had left the sleek glass-and-steel towers of the Interpol Global Complex for Innovation headquarters in a taxi nearly two hours ago, which had been a miscalculation, to say the least. Normally it was a fifteen-minute drive into the city center, and her goal was hard to miss. She headed toward the thing you could see from almost everywhere in the city—the glittering megalith of the Marina Bay Sands Hotel. Three knobby uprights topped with a slab that seemed to be melting, as though sizzled by the heat of the fireworks that pinballed from east to west and back again.

Families in matching outfits thronged around stalls selling sweet treats, all of it laced over with cat's cradles of green lights and diamonds and crescent moons. Clothes hanging row on row higher than the longest arm could reach. Del apologized between more curses as she elbowed her way through and into the lobby of the hotel.

"Third level," Zoya said in the earpiece. "To your right. I just got a hit on a security camera. Do you see him?"

The lobby was massive, twenty sloping stories of gold-and-glass walkways making an interior ziggurat of entrances to rooms on every side. A gigantic wire mesh sculpture hung suspended in the gulf of air above Del. People milled about the oversized circular reception desk, greeting each other, smiling, hugging. Del looked right and up and counted three levels. Squinted.

There.

Was it the man she was looking for? Just a glimpse, but enough. It looked like him—the same dark hair and bearlike build as the man in her files. The man she had been secretly chasing for two years now, ever since she found out he existed, ever since he had changed her life forever. She had kept the real reason behind tracking this gang secret, but it would soon be out in the open. Maybe.

Behind him was another man, unfamiliar to her. Equally burly and wearing an eye patch.

"I see him," Del said into her wrist mic. She pushed forward through the crowd, glancing up and right as the man disappeared around a corner.

"He's in the west wing elevators," Zoya replied. "Go right."

As she tried to squeeze through the endless stream of people, a woman blocked Del's path, dressed all in green. Her face was obscured by a headscarf, but Del could see a dead zone splashing its way across the woman's left cheek and up toward her eye, the skin there bloodless. Cold. She extended a small packet in her outstretched hand. "Take, take."

Del smiled and shook her head.

The woman persisted, blocking her as the crowd slid past. "Take, take," she repeated. Smiling. "For you. For lucky."

Del had read up on the festival on the flight in. These packets were like the red envelopes exchanged at Chinese Lunar New Year. They held lucky money and were given by adults to children and friends to friends, or sometimes as gifts to strangers. She accepted the offering to get the woman out of her way. The woman melted away into the crowd.

Del shoved the packet in her purse.

Burst back into a sprint through an opening in the pack. "What floor?"

"Top," came the reply.

Del flashed one hand into an already packed closing elevator. A few of the smiling partygoers inside frowned, but Del just apologized and squeezed herself in. The instant it pinged open to the top floor, Zoya said, "Go right."

The woman had to be watching her on the elevator camera.

An inferno of explosions in glittering red and gold crackled over the swaying branches of a forest of palm trees stretching along the interior of the SkyPark a thousand feet above street level. Pushing patrons left and right, Del advanced to the edge of the enormous, sweeping infinity pool that lined the eastern edge.

"Past the pool," said Zoya in Del's ear. "Jump off the edge. Beyond that, I can't see them. No cameras. They looked like they were heading for the fireworks battery."

Hundreds of people lounged in the massive pool, wading about, most of them with drinks in hand. The glittering skyline of Singapore stretched beyond the edge of the water, but it was a thousand-foot drop onto the parking garage past that.

"*Jump off the what?*"

A man in a tuxedo with a martini sloshing in one hand turned to look at Del. She must have said that louder than she'd meant to. Some undercover op she was.

"There's a . . . below," Zoya replied.

It was hard to hear her over the music pumping from loudspeakers and the crowd shrieking as fireworks flared and burst around the SkyPark like it was under attack by an artillery brigade. Zoya had to mean there was a ledge or ladder, not a thousand-foot drop off the edge of a pool. She hoped.

Hopping from one foot to the other, she pulled off her heels and jumped past a waiter heading toward the pool with a tray of drinks. A set of stepping-stones lay sprinkled across the pool, and Del darted from one to the next, waves from revelers splashing across her naked feet. Arms windmilling, Del stopped at the edge. Peered over.

Ten feet below was a metal gantry. She knelt, wished her heels a soft landing, and dropped them. Putting her hands on the wet ceramic rim of the pool, she slid over the edge. Explosions left and right in the sky. Her right knee slammed into the grating, a zing of pain sizzling along her leg, mirrored by a spike of pressure behind her eyes. From the fireworks? Or the change in lighting?

The world had gone from dazzling brightness to pitch-black the second she dropped over the edge. Del righted herself and began to get up, squinting into the darkness.

"Zoya," she whispered, "which way—"

A crunching blow straight into her left cheek snapped her head back. The impact lifted Del clear off her feet, her arms flailing.

Two powerful hands grabbed her. They pulled her back from the fall she'd been in, then pushed her down to the ground. She tucked and rolled herself over, aimed her right foot, and kicked as hard as she could. The man staggered back, and Del sprang to her feet. An uppercut into his ribs sent him sprawling.

The man's weapon clattered onto the metal grating.

She scanned the shadows. From behind her, someone grabbed her and pushed her face against the plexiglass wall. A thousand feet to the sidewalk below. Cheerful people dancing, lights, music. She'd make one hell of an entrance.

She turned and kneed the man in the groin. He backed off, panting. A darting punch from the man with the eye patch snagged her cheek. He wrapped his hands around her wrists and arms, and held her tight. Even in the darkness, she recognized the familiar build and face.

"Johnny." Her voice was reedy, the wind knocked from her.

"Who the bloody hell are you?" the man asked. "My name's Patrick."

"I know who you are."

"You're one up on me, then. You best tell me, lest you want the last thing to go through your head to be your arse. It's a long way down, lass."

"Let go of me, you idiot."

"Not exactly the answer I was hoping for."

He joined the man with the eye patch. Together they lifted her as she struggled, her arm sockets lancing in pain, and dangled her over the edge into the yawning blackness of a thousand feet of space.

Through the pain, Del gasped, "I'm your niece, asshole. Sean's daughter. Your brother—remember him?"

3

15th Arrondissement, Paris, France
April 24th, 7:00 a.m.

Streaming sunshine laid stripes along the buttery pine floorboards of Del's apartment. A breeze blew down from the ceiling fan in the dogleg nook by the back that made up her bedroom. She'd left the shutters open again, which Jacques always tutted at her for. You will let in all the heat, he'd say. Even in early May, the temperature would be suffocating by noon.

She didn't care.

Opening her eyes to a morning of rosy gold sunlight filtered through the flowering red nasturtiums in the window box made something uncoil lazily within her when she awoke. She stretched under the light duvet; the white sheets still crisp. Heels clicked by on the cobblestones below, pigeons called each other from street to street. Deep ringing church bells counted to seven.

The flight back from Singapore the day before had given her a lot of time to think, especially after meeting the elusive uncle she'd been hunting. The past few years had been the best of her life, what she'd always dreamed of—living abroad, chasing international criminals, working with some of the best in the field of forensics and crime.

And now this.

She stroked Jacques's shoulder.

They had been dating—if she could call it that—for almost a year. It was hard to say how long, since there wasn't an exact start. Their relationship had warmed like they were in a pot of water, the temperature rising until it was suddenly at a full boil before they noticed it. She smiled. He was her frog.

She kissed his shoulder this time.

For her, it started back when he showed up in no-man's-land in southern Ukraine, like the proverbial knight, dashing in to rescue her—even though she had saved herself already. It was the look in his eye, the protectiveness she sensed. She hadn't felt that from a man in years, and it felt nice for someone to be willing to risk themselves for her.

Really, though, it began in Paris, as all beautiful romances should. When she decided to move here, he offered to show her around. The friendship blossomed. Del was lonely, if she was being honest. For the first time, she was away from her family. By herself in a foreign country, with a dashing Frenchman who wasn't hard to look at and who'd tried to save her life—as much as they tried to keep it professional, it ended up here, in bed. Which wasn't a bad thing. But they still hadn't fully accepted the reality of it.

At least, she hadn't.

Even so, day by day, it felt like the distance between Del and Jacques halved as they became closer—but that final threshold felt impossible to step across, as a half of a half of a half became a progression stretching to infinity that would never quite close all the way.

Maybe it was better not to overthink it. She kissed his cheek this time.

They'd only made it to bed at 2:00 a.m., yet he had risen at 4:30 for his prayers. She had pretended to remain asleep, part of the game in which she acted as though she didn't notice that he tried to hide his five-a-day sessions with Allah.

Jacques rolled to face her, answering her unspoken question. He smiled the smile she remembered from the first time they'd met at Interpol. "Good morning, *chérie*."

She returned his sly grin, but gently removed the hands that slid against the bare skin on the small of her back. He tugged. She resisted. Message received, Jacques released her and rose from the warm nest of blankets to pull on gray linen pajama bottoms—part of the growing collection of his clothes that had found a home in her dresser.

A toothbrush in the bathroom.

Other things kept drifting from his life into hers, too—a copy of the Bhagavad Gita in French, a fountain pen, tiny espresso cups. Each time he stayed, the incoming tide of Jacques Galloul left bits of flotsam and jetsam in its wake when he retreated. She never stayed overnight at his place, and not even one hair band had mysteriously strayed.

He strode off purposefully and disappeared from her view.

She remained still, warm under the covers.

A few bars of Nina Simone's "Sinnerman" played in the other room, then Jacques changed the channel. The soothing tones of the BBC, quickly muted. Jacques liked to jump into the news of the day right away. She preferred quiet. This was their compromise.

Clinking sounds came from across the studio apartment, then running water and a jingling spoon. Jacques's other morning ritual—making the coffee. He liked to do it, as he told her every time she protested and tried to take over. What he really meant was that he couldn't stand the American swill she made.

Decision made that sleep was done, Del swung her feet over the edge of the bed, rolled a kink from her neck, and reached down to her toes. A little tight in the back, her ribs still sore from that jab to her kidneys.

She'd fit in some time with Mickey later today to punch back.

Del lifted a rose-patterned robe from its hook beside the bed and wrapped herself up in it. A wild garden printed on it against a background of Paris green. She'd bought it to match the wall of her kitchen. The color was an approximation—real Paris green didn't exist anymore, as much as she tried to find it. It was a beautiful shade, just this side of apple.

"Helloooo," Jacques called from the kitchen. "*Dans la lune* again. I asked you how it went."

Del tied tight the robe's belt and padded barefoot thirty feet to the other end of the apartment to join him. She didn't reply but rolled her eyes and made sure he saw it.

"You study too hard." Jacques stroked her cheek. Lightly kissed her forehead. "It will give you wrinkles."

Del stepped back from his touch. Wrinkles? Seriously? "You think I'm the one who works too hard? I'm not the one who sleeps at my desk." She sometimes wondered why he even kept an apartment.

The top of the hour headlines came on: tensions increasing between the US and Iran, spurred by social media posts by Governor Guthrie in his senatorial race. The crawl beneath the newscaster posed a question: "Could This Lead to War?" Del leaned on the counter, watching footage of an antiwar demonstration in Washington, DC, the night before. It reminded her of Ukraine during its own election two years ago—a powder keg, ready to be ignited.

"*Et voilà*, coffee. Too much milk in yours, as you like it. And I am teasing. Your buttons are too easy to press. I am"—he paused, and then elongated the next word—"*kidding*. Please."

She wrapped her hands around the offered oversized mug and let the heat seep into her fingertips as she leaned against the kitchen island. Del loved mornings, that time when the day was still perfect, before the jumbled puzzle pieces of life came into focus. She didn't like being baited this early.

Jacques sipped his espresso. He placed his cup carefully in its saucer with a light clink. "Did you find your Lucknow gang? Are they based out of India? Because Lucknow is the capital of—"

"Uttar Pradesh. I know. I know. And no, they're not Indian. Didn't you read the report?"

"*Bien sûr*, of course. But all the way to Singapore for this?"

"Yes. Anyway, where were you while I was there? I called you twice, even called the office. No one had any idea where you were." It wasn't the first time he'd disappeared.

"I was busy. There are things that I need to do that I cannot tell you about. You understand. It is your way of life also."

"Of course I understand. But—"

"Please, go on. Tell me about Singapore."

"IGCI"—she pronounced the acronym for the Interpol Global Innovation Center as *ig-see*—"is the cybercrime HQ. Two years and I hadn't been. I was due. I am studying to be a Treasury Agent, right? Financial cybercrimes?"

Jacques fixed her with that look. His interrogation gaze. Eyes steady, no smile.

Just because she could detect lies didn't mean she was any good at coming up with them. She knew what he wanted to ask.

What really happened? What wasn't in the report? And how would she answer—I was tailing my uncle, the terrorist? The man certainly wasn't a freedom fighter anymore. Common criminal was a more apt description. Bile rose into the back of her throat. A kneading pressure grew behind her eyes.

Finally, she said, "We didn't make the contact."

"Security cameras saw you were close. If this man is with Lucknow, you must be careful. It is an international operation—"

"Can we do this later?"

He shrugged that Gallic flick of the shoulders she found so infuriating. It said, whatever you like, and also, why should I care?

"You flew back with your new friend, Zoya? You like to make friends with the nerds, yes? Is that a good word?"

"It's a bad word."

"I thought Americans liked the nerds."

"She's the deputy head of digital forensics at the Interpol Global Center for Innovation. She's one of the leaders in the field." A tough spot for the only woman in the male-dominated space. Del had bonded immediately with Zoya after the blond agent had rolled her eyes during a particularly egregious meeting. Zoya had bought coffee after, and they'd talked for a couple of hours.

"As I said, a nerd, no? Like Suweil? You seem to make friends with them."

Del rolled her eyes again.

"And what did you two discuss on the plane?"

"Work stuff. What do you talk about with your coworkers?"

"I don't know, this and that."

"You think we talk about boys and hair and makeup, is that it?" They *had* spent a few minutes talking about shoes, but there was no way Del was going to let on about that.

"I was just curious. I wondered if she told you anything interesting."

Del took a sip of her coffee. The questioning was a bit odd, but Jacques's handsome face showed no signs of stress, no blood rushing to his cheeks. "Nothing that would interest you." She went to take another sip, but then winced. Her stomach knotted.

"Are you okay?"

The pressure grew. Her saliva glands watered. "Maybe a little jet-lagged."

"You don't look well, *chérie*."

"I told you, I'm fine."

"I might be French, but I know this word does not mean what you Americans say it means." He eyed her, but let it go. "Did you have news about your father? How is he?"

She almost spat a mouthful of coffee back up into her mug. *What the hell was going on with her stomach?* "Don't you think you should get ready to leave?"

"I think one day it will be possible for us to arrive at the office together. I am sure this is no secret anymore. A year we have been together now. You do realize we work in an office of detectives."

"Who did you tell?"

"I am not stupid."

"Pierre? I bet you told him, right?" Del stalked past her suitcase, still on the floor, and flung open her closet doors to loudly slide hangers back and forth. She pulled out a jacket and pants with a cream blouse and dropped them on a chair.

"I said nothing to anyone. As agreed," Jacques said.

Del headed to the bathroom and closed the door.

The tiny bathroom's halogen lights made the pressure behind her eyes increase. She pushed the dimmer down as far as she could, then sat on the only available surface, the closed lid of the toilet. Put her head in her hands and took slow breaths.

The air in the little room still carried the scents from his products—earthy and warm, cardamom and clove. She let out a long breath. Why did cops always end up with cops? It seemed like Jacques should be able to understand—but maybe that was the problem. She wasn't really a cop anymore.

What exactly was she?

Not a Long Island policewoman. Not working for Interpol, even though that was who she reported to. Her monthly paycheck came from the US Department of Justice, but even that was temporary. She was in no-man's-land. Not even that. More of a Purgatory of some kind.

Del dry heaved into the sink before regaining control of her stomach. *Food poisoning?* More likely the twelve-plus hours in cattle class on the flight back, plus the six-hour time difference. She brushed her teeth and splashed some water on her face. Then changed, put her hair in a ponytail, washed and dried her hands. Lip gloss, mascara, and unscented hand cream. Done.

She exited the bathroom and closed the door with a light click.

Jacques was already dressed and waiting by the front door. Suit the color of sand, the jacket lined in sky blue. Everything perfectly pressed, though she never saw him iron. So handsome. So calm. She felt herself soften, wanted him to wrap his arms around her. *No. Not now. Get it together.*

"I'll see you later?" He took two steps toward her, leaned in and kissed her on the cheek. She hesitated but pulled him in for a proper kiss. Then he was out the door. She closed it behind him.

Del crossed the apartment, walking past the kitchen with its green wall, past the items Jacques had left scattered about, past her paintings, white on white. She stopped in front of one of them. The Pegnini.

To everyone else the image was a mottled white without form. Only her unique vision, which separated out tens of millions of colors other humans couldn't see, formed the apparition. The spinach-essence paint she mixed herself fluoresced in the sunlight at the center of the canvas.

It was her rendering of that dark night on one of her first cases as a Long Island detective, of a bookie named Pegnini squirming and impaled on a stake, suspended high in the air, after trying to jump from a second-story balcony in the dark. The poor soul had landed on an iron fence post. It made her skin crawl every time she remembered it, but the painting reminded her of the need to look before jumping, the kind of prudence she always had a problem with.

She pushed the image of that night away and took a lungful of air.

The space was airy and bright, the pale curtains skirting circles in the breeze. But she missed her old place, her mother's old place, and she missed New York.

Most of all, she missed her father.

He had seemed tired at her birthday party.

Her thirty-first, which they had celebrated together days before she'd packed up the last of her things and had them shipped here. Maybe he was just settling into retirement—it had been two years since then. But there had been something in his eyes, in the careful way he walked and moved, something she'd never seen in him before.

A creakiness. A fear.

And now she knew why.

She sighed. What was she doing here?

Del pushed aside the curtains and leaned out the window. The shutters were open, the flowers were blooming, and she leaned out as far as she could. She spotted Jacques below, crossing the cobbled street. She raised her head and looked out over the rooftops, the gabled eaves, the glinting windows, all the way to the twinkling Seine.

In the distance, the Eiffel Tower loomed over Paris.

4

St. Denis, Paris, France

April 24th, 9:45 a.m.

The doctor asked, "Do you see anything at all?"

"I do," Del replied.

"Read row by—"

"C . . . B . . . Z . . . W . . ."

"Amazing." The doctor whispered, not to her, but to a notepad he scribbled in.

Del continued reading the next line, but the one after that was fuzzy. The bottom two a total blur.

"Still, this is remarkable," the doctor said when she complained about not being able to see the last of the letters. He switched off the lights, dousing the room in pitch blackness. A click in the dark, and faint red letters glowed in the distance.

Del began reading them out again.

A few days before in Singapore, she had started having terrible headaches. Blurry vision. She had been working in the cybercrime forensics lab with Zoya when the pain had started again, and the woman had suggested going to see her old doctor in Paris if the headaches had not stopped by the time she returned.

Now they were compounded by nausea—she'd almost thrown up, again, when she arrived at the clinic this morning.

"Extraordinary." The doctor flicked on the overhead lights. "Has anyone ever tested the limits of your vision? I mean, really pushed—"

"It's kind of a private thing."

"Would you let me write a case study of—"

"No."

Del blinked as her eyes adjusted to the halogens.

They'd made her headache worse when she had first sat down with the doctor. Too bright, they cast a skim-milk sheen over the little room's immaculate walls and made the doctor in his mask, goggles, and surgical cap look otherworldly.

White walls. Antiseptic fumes.

A flash of her father in his hospital bed, the last place she had smelled this mix of bleach and steel—and that other hospital smell, one harder to name. The underlying whiff of the things excreted from bodies, cleaned away, scrubbed off, but still lingering. As a detective used to morgues, the smell was familiar, and Del always secretly liked it—like the toxic sweet smell of gasoline—while still being repulsed.

The scent of this room was similar but different. Too clean. Unused. No bodies had decayed or died in this place.

She breathed deeply, counted to ten, and then released. Always return to the breath when stress reared, that's what her dad had taught her. She was annoyed at the doctor, this poking and prying, but then her father had also said, when you feel like someone's getting under your skin, best to look to see what's under there before they find it.

It wasn't the doctor.

It was Del.

The doctor had gone out of his way to purchase special ultraviolet and infrared light sources and jerry-rig an eye test to display the images projected by them onto the walls. The images would be invisible to someone with "normal" sight, but Del, a tetrachromat with extra cones in her retinas, could see things in wavelengths beyond the limits of average human eyes.

But Del didn't like being treated like a lab rat. It wasn't his fault—she had asked for the tests—but still, she didn't like people prodding her.

After a few seconds of silence, the doctor said, "Please, do not worry. I understand."

He must have sensed her discomfort.

The doctor reached for a paper file folder the color of onion skin and flicked it open. Glanced up at her. His eyes small and blue, no blossoms of stress or flashes of dishonesty. "Everything in this room is confidential. We are very strict on this doctor-patient relationship in Europe. And also, my own code. *S'il vous plâit*, go ahead."

"I want to know why I've been having these headaches," Del said. A pressure mounted behind her eyes. "Would they really have anything to do with me being a tetrachromat? I had cataracts as a child."

The doctor's eyebrows went up, and he leaned in close to her, as though hoping to see them. "What was the treatment?"

"Artificial lenses. Surgical implants. They don't cut the ultraviolet wavelengths, so I can still see into the near UV range. Like Monet."

"As I recall, he had cataract surgery later in life. Changed how he saw colors. How did it affect your vision? Do you remember?"

"I see the near UV range as shades of white-purple. And other colors I have my own names for." *Ishma* was one of those names, but she wasn't going to share that if she didn't have to. "I didn't realize other people couldn't see black light until I was in college."

"How would you describe it? The way it looks to you?"

"Like a deep purple. Flowers have iridescent canvases of colors in sunlight. I took some photos of these beautiful lavender flowers the other day, and they turned out to be white when I looked at them on my camera."

"Screens cannot reproduce the same spectrum of color you see. You see more than the technology allows for." He paused, then asked, "And the sky?"

"Looks hazy and white most days."

"Not blue?"

"No."

"This is an effect called Rayleigh scattering. Only affects ultraviolet wavelengths."

Of course, Del knew about this effect. She had had to deal with her awkward vision her whole life. In fact, since her last case, she had decided to try and begin ignoring the colors she saw that were different from everyone else.

Two years ago, she had been targeted for being a human lie detector, so she preferred not to tell anyone about her special abilities anymore. And she tried, as much as she could, to ignore the special aspects of her vision.

She just wanted to be normal.

***

The doctor nodded, wrote down some more notes. Del had been in here an hour already.

"Can we get back to my headaches? I've never had them before. Not like this."

"This we do not know for the moment. You must please answer my questions, as there are many elements that may very well be important."

He asked about her headaches—how often, how painful, how long did they last? Any photosensitivity? And how would she describe the vision problems she'd been having? And the nausea she had mentioned—again, how often? Did it seem to be triggered by smells? Del answered all of these as well as she could, the doctor making notes every time she spoke. The metal point of his fine-tipped pen made noises like a tiny creature clawing at a wall.

Then he asked about her parents—were they alive, where did they come from, any diseases or chronic conditions? She answered yes, Louisiana, Ireland, and yes.

"Could you elaborate on that? Which conditions?"

Del paused. Another flash of her father, in a hospital bed. Could her headaches be related to what he was going through? The pain behind Del's eyes coiled in on itself, became a dull lump of pressure behind her eyes.

"Cancer," she said. "My father has lymphatic cancer."

For two years after the initial rounds of chemo and radiation, her father had earned a clean bill of health. Nothing in the PET scans, no angry red dots to indicate active tumors, all his blood work clean. Every three months the same thing. They'd thought they'd had it beat. And then, at her birthday party, he had been distant, his usually easy jokes and banter forced.

The cancer had returned, and now the options were limited.

The doctor scratched something in her file and continued. "And could you tell me about your grandparents and extended family? Are there perhaps any conditions further back we should be aware of?"

She explained that her mother was healthy, had arthritis digging into her joints that flared up when it rained. On her mother's side, there was diabetes, some history of heart conditions, but Del chalked that up to the rich Louisiana diet.

On her father's side?

Her family tree was stunted to that side, cut off where her father had excised himself. No branches there for her to follow, not until last week, but that hadn't seemed like the time to ask her terrorist uncle about his medical history.

"Are we about done here?" Del smoothed her skirt over her lap. "I have meetings all afternoon. I should really be going."

The doctor raised his eyes to hers, nodded, and closed the file folder. "A few more tests while your blood work is processed?"

"Can't you text me? Email the results?"

"There are confidentiality concerns. And also, if there is a treatment for us to follow, it should be initiated right away."

"I see."

Del had walked through an empty mall to get to the clinic, past boarded-up shops and waterless fountains. Zoya had told her it would seem odd, but had said the building was so new that no one had really moved in yet. But there had been garbage in the waste bins and plaster dust on the surfaces. Del had been the only person on the elevator.

Del watched the doctor's face as she spoke. "Can you tell me again how you know Zoya?"

Even behind his goggles, Del saw the area around the doctor's eyes light up with a bloom of stress-response blood flow. Like he'd been put on the spot. He turned quickly and left the room. When he returned, wheeling another new-looking machine ahead of him, the area around his eyes appeared cool. Normal. Yet he averted his eyes from Del's and bent over the fiddly knobs of the new contraption.

"Zoya. She referred me to you," Del said. "I wondered how the two of you knew each other."

"She was my patient, of course." The doctor raised a limb from the new machine and angled it at the wall.

"That's not what she told me." Zoya hadn't told her anything about the doctor—but Del's bluff worked. The stress response blushed deep around the doctor's eyes as they darted up to hers. She saw him seeing her, knew he knew how she was seeing him. He looked away.

"We had a—how do you say?—relationship."

He turned and walked to the light switch on the wall. Flicked the lights off. Darkness.

Then, on the wall, two colors. He asked Del questions about what she could see. Then two different colors. More questions.

But when he had Del read a simple eye chart, the kind with the letters that got smaller and smaller, he made little clucking sounds. Finally, he examined her under one of those medieval-looking crown things with eye holes, switching lenses until he let out a long murmuring tone. Nodded. Rolled back on his chair and turned on the lights.

"Well, Ms. Devlin." He peeled off his gloves and pedaled them into a stainless-steel waste bin. "While your tetrachromacy is most impressive, you will need to buy some glasses. Or contact lenses, if you prefer. I will make a prescription."

"I've been feeling nauseous the last few days."

As though on cue, a light tapping came at the door. The doctor opened it and accepted another paper folder from a nurse Del barely caught a glimpse of. Was she the same woman from the reception desk?

The doctor didn't make any noises as he read. Closed the file. "All of this could also be related to your pregnancy, of course. You didn't mention this to me."

The headaches were bothering her so much that right after she landed from Singapore, the day before, she had come in to give a blood sample. It took a beat or two for the words to process in Del's brain.

The nausea . . . she had had it before. She had missed her last period, but that happened sometimes when she was stressed, then add to that the flying back and forth from Europe to America to Asia, and all the time changes. She hadn't experienced headaches before, but the nausea now felt sickeningly familiar. *Pregnant.*

"Ms. Devlin?"

"Of course. I should have mentioned it."

Some detective she was. She couldn't even see the signs screaming from inside her own body. Her hands involuntarily went to her stomach. Something was growing inside of her. Not some*thing,* but *someone.* She had taken all the precautions, had not missed a day of her pill.

"Are you okay, Ms. Devlin? Should I call someone? Is someone waiting for you outside? Did you drive here? Is the father here?"

"The father?"

Del's phone buzzed. *Jacques.*

5

Meyrin, Switzerland
April 24th, 4:05 p.m.

"This magnificent beast is the CRONUS detector, the beating heart of the new high-luminosity phase of the Large Hadron Collider," Dr. Breedlove said.

Rake thin, with glasses and a gaunt, angular face, he had introduced himself as "please, just call me Pete." He explained that the CERN team had just reached the end of the Long Shutdown 3—as if it were the end of an epoch in time after a mass extinction and new life was finally arising once again.

To Del, it looked like the eight tentacles reaching out from the center of the "beast" were trying to claw their way out through the surrounding earth. Ventilation ducts, Dr. Breedlove explained, that pulled heat from the refrigeration devices that cooled the most sensitive parts of the detector to near absolute zero. Minus four hundred sixty Fahrenheit, he added, the temperature at which everything stopped moving.

His eyes certainly never did.

They darted around, up at the massive machine looming over them, then back at the door, then to the rows of displays along the walls, never stopping to contact either Del's or Jacques's. Even when he said, "This is the biggest machine humanity has ever created. Did you know that?"

"I've always wanted to see it in person," Del said.

It was one thing to see a massive object over and over again in a picture—like the Golden Gate Bridge or the Taj Mahal—but another thing altogether to see it live, and the LHC hadn't disappointed. This detector cavern was over ten stories high, the top level buried over four hundred feet below street level.

They'd navigated a maze of security checkpoints, stairways, elevators, and tunnels to get down here. How on Earth someone got into this place to commit a theft, Del had no idea. It had to be an inside job, Jacques had mused on the drive in.

It wasn't the first time things had disappeared from CERN. Jacques had been here twice already in the past year, and when it came up again this morning, Del had been tasked to join him. She tried to refuse, but an official request for assistance had already been filed.

An odd request, one that had the suffocating feeling of his trying to use work to keep close to her. She had just finished at the doctor's office and wanted to keep as far away from Jacques as she could, but he just pulled her closer. She needed to think. But he gave her no space, no time.

Breathe. Just breathe.

The walls felt like they were closing in around her, both literally and figuratively. Even this vast cavern didn't do much to push back her creeping claustrophobia. She hated confined spaces, and the air seemed to get thinner and thinner the deeper they descended.

Jacques knew she was claustrophobic and yet had forced her to come to this place.

The CERN thefts were his case, but he had made a request with Interpol for her to accompany him when this alert came in over the wires. Then again, he knew she was a fan of the LHC project. At first, it had excited her to come—until she realized she had to burrow four hundred feet underground to see it.

Del took a deep breath, let it out, and smiled at the professor—he had explained earlier that he still taught advanced physics at Cornell—in the middle of another one of his monologues. She was here for the job. She was a professional. Focus.

She looked straight at Dr. Breedlove.

Peter turned his gaze away and made a point of looking further afield when he noticed she was putting all her focus on him. "This detector replaces ATLAS and uses scintillating fiber trackers. SciFi for short. Detection is five hundred times faster than with the original LHC and packs a hundred times the brute power."

Del's undergrad art history courses bubbled to the surface. "Cronus was the mightiest of the Titans, wasn't he? The ruler of the universe, master of time and space?"

His eyes caught hers for an instant, then darted away. "That's right."

Another half memory surfaced. "Cronus devoured his children, didn't he? To prevent a prophecy from becoming truth?"

"Correct again."

The dark center of the detector seemed to stare back at her. The black core, the blue wires and steel plates ringing it. Del realized she had gotten the scale all wrong—*this* wasn't the Titan. This was just his iris. His skull crackled forth, shattering the room, his body growing as she watched in her mind's eye, unfolding with tubular limbs, strung with wire veins and muscles torn from the walls of the caverns.

Carved out of the earth, this machine stretched for miles into the surrounding bedrock. It was hard not to feel a sense of awe akin to a sacred experience.

Which brought Del's mind back to Jacques sneaking out of bed to pray at 4:00 a.m. His religion had felt vaguely alien to her at first, but less so now, and she had a deep respect for his faith. When had she last been to a Catholic church, and not just to gawk at the architecture? This place had that same feeling of a cathedral, although one to a different god.

"Is it possible to skip the mythology?" Jacques addressed the question to Dr. Breedlove, but looked at Del. He then mouthed "*Hello*?" at her.

To get here, Jacques had requisitioned a sleek black Mercedes from the carpool, slapped on the siren and lights, and zipped along the highway at a stomach-lurching speed, the radio blaring the latest updates on the tensions between the US and Iran. He drove so fast, it was impossible for Del to think, let alone speak. But the blood patterns in his face told her everything she needed to know. They pulsed through his cheeks and lit up around his eyes. Like he was mad, but about what?

She asked him, but he knew better than to lie to her, so stayed silent. She felt for him—it must be a pain in the ass to date a human lie detector. When Jacques sped between two semis and bile spilled into the back of her throat, Del finally asked him to stop. Raced into a rest stop bathroom to throw up.

"We need more details about the item that was stolen. We also need access to the area it was removed from," Del said to Peter. She turned slightly so Jacques was out of her field of view. "Can you take us there?"

Peter stopped in the middle of another story, his eyes flitting from one side of the cavern to the other. He blinked a few times. Then nodded in quick, birdlike jabs, his lips moving as though he was counting something. One last nod. "Yes, yes, of course. That is why you are here. Yes. Please follow me."

He led them down a long tunnel lined with tubes and panels, like the one they had walked down to reach the detector. But the wires here were mostly blue, while those in the other tunnel had been orange. Some of the tubes were swaddled with what appeared to be tinfoil. The rounded cement walls were covered with chipped paint in a bland gray-white even Del couldn't see more colors in.

The air smelled trapped but electric. Like the fresh wind after a storm had been bottled. Peter spoke as they walked, shooting rapid-fire details over his shoulder. Del slowed her pace. Jacques strode ahead, nearly keeping pace with the physicist.

"The stolen device was a transition radiation tracker with forty million readout channels." Dr. Breedlove's voice echoed off the curved walls of the tunnel. "Basic detector element is a carbon nanotube with five hundred thousand straws in each barrel, each straw one hundred and forty-four centimeters long. The ends of each straw are read out separately. Five hundred thousand straws in each of two endcaps. Each straw is thirty-nine centimeters long. Precision measurement of ten nanometers, particle track to wire."

"What is it used for?" Jacques asked.

"It provides additional information on the particle types in the detector. That is, it can tell us whether a given particle is an electron or a pion."

Del tried to keep her mind on why they were there. Jacques held out a hand, but not to try to hold hers—to try to slow her down.

"Delta," Jacques said in a low voice. "What's wrong?"

Del tried to keep her voice mellow. "I love being driven around by a crazy person. Do you even *know* how fast you were going?"

"If I go too slow, I am hit by the one behind me."

"You're completely irresponsible."

Jacques's face registered bewilderment.

"Dr. Breedlove," Del said in a louder voice, "what about the cameras in this tunnel?"

He blinked a few times, a small blue-and-silver pin on his jacket catching the light as he turned toward her. "Of course. I can show you on the map. Or I can take you to see the data repository itself, where we can download the videos." He pointed ahead of them, along the tunnel. "And there are a few more cameras back the way we came."

"The map will be fine." Another headache bloomed in her skull. Her legs ached. And her stomach was raw and empty.

"No, in fact," Jacques swept past Del, "we would like to see all the physical locations. We will also need to know who had access to the area. And what the stolen device might be used for, if not used here."

Del sighed as quietly as she could. The pain in her head expanded. She nodded her agreement, and Peter turned and sped away down the tunnel.

Peter was mid-speech again when she caught up: "We are delving into the very fabric of reality. Reproducing the conditions at the start of the universe, maybe tearing open gaps in time, even creating tiny black holes."

"Isn't that dangerous?" Del asked.

"At the size we might create black holes, the Hawking radiation would dissipate their formation within nanoseconds, if we were even creating them at all. What is perhaps riskier is pulling open rifts in time. My experiments are producing vast quantities of antiparticles, more commonly referred to as antimatter, that I believe travel back in time—"

"Time travel?" Jacques interrupted. "You cannot be serious."

"As cancer."

The attempt at a joke fell flat. Jacques glanced at Del, but her smile didn't falter. The physicist was obviously socially awkward. That sort of joke required knowing your audience, and from the look on his face, he must have sensed he had tripped up.

She moved the conversation along. "So, time travel is possible? Is this the implication?"

"For subatomic particles, yes. There is nothing in physics that dictates time needs to flow in one specific direction. But physical time travel may not be possible, or at least would be exceedingly difficult. It would require the creation of negative energy and wormholes, but at the speeds we would need to travel to even entertain such a journey, just encountering a photon would be catastrophic to the integrity of a physical being."

"Some kind of virtual time travel, then?"

"Not just virtual. Gödel had a theory—"

"The incompleteness theorem?" Del said. That had been the topic of one of her philosophy classes. "That there will always be a set of questions that cannot be answered. How does that apply to time travel?"

Jacques looked impressed.

"That's very good, Marshal," Dr. Breedlove said. "But no, not that one. In 1949, Gödel discovered an exact solution of Einstein's relativity field equations that allows particles to follow loops that traveled into their own past. It's—"

"Professor, perhaps we should stick to the theft?" Jacques said.

"Maybe this has something to do with it," Del said.

Jacques raised his eyebrows. "*Time* travel?"

Peter smiled at Del and caught her eye for a moment before looking away. "I knew you would like this," he said. "All the books and movies are dead wrong about it. But *data* time travel—using anti-particles—might be possible. SciFi is the focus of my research—part of the reason we built CRONUS, to collect and use antimatter."

"You mentioned this 'SciFi' is the name of this detector's technology?"

Del asked. *He knew she would like this? That was an odd thing to say. How did he know anything about her?*

"SciFi—scintillating fiber. Right again. I knew you would get this."

Again, the odd choice of words. "What's wrong with all the time travel movies?" Del had become a bit of a buff lately—especially after her last two cases, when science fiction seemed to have moved to the nonfiction aisle.

"Time travel requires *space* travel. Time is a fourth dimension, but if you voyage across it, you're not traveling in the other three at the same time. If we went back a year in time, we wouldn't end up in the same place."

Peter stopped in the middle of the tunnel. "We feel like we are not moving right now, but we are. The Earth is rotating on its axis at about sixteen hundred kilometers per hour, depending how far from the poles you are. We make one full revolution around the Earth's forty-thousand-kilometer circumference every twenty-four hours.

"The Earth is traveling around the sun at over a hundred thousand kilometers an hour, and the sun is rotating around the galactic core of the Milky Way at over eight hundred thousand kilometers an hour. The Milky Way around the Local Group of galaxies and the Local Group around our local Supercluster at over two million kilometers per hour. While we feel like we are not moving"—he paused, then waved his arms around—"our bodies are actually speeding through space at about a thousand kilometers each *second*."

"*Wow*," said Jacques.

And he wasn't easily impressed.

"If you went back a year in *time*, like they do in sci-fi films, you would not end up in this underground cavern—you would end up at a point in space thirty billion kilometers away, back where the Earth was a year before. This is seven times further than Neptune, our most distant planet. You would literally be deposited into interstellar space."

Del said, "So, if you travel in time, you need to travel in space as well. You would need a spaceship."

"If you want to end up on Earth. It would be incredibly hard to transport an entire spaceship and passenger back in time—not impossible, but difficult. But the rifts in space-time we create here? We already squeeze through a few anti-photons at a time. In fact"—Peter's eyes seemed to twinkle, and for the first time, he looked straight at Del—"I *know* that it is possible."

He smiled an awkward smile. The moment, whatever it was, passed, and he led on.

Jacques followed, but turned to Del and made a face before he did.

Peter, ahead of them, said, "Please, this way. We are about to start a test. I'll show you where the transition radiation detector was stolen."

"How much would one of those cost?" Jacques asked.

"Incalculable. This is a custom piece of equipment, handmade, like an exquisite watch. Four million read-out channels, each composed of carbon nanotube clusters of wires—"

The two men advanced down the hallway.

A flickering in her peripheral vision, up above her head. A low thrumming came up through the metal grating into the bones in her feet, up through her tibia and joints, and shook her body. CRONUS was coming alive. A crackling ultraviolet light snaked through the air, invisible to anyone but her. And lights and colors she had never seen before. She stood, transfixed. The hair on her arms prickled to attention.

Someone jerked on her elbow.

Jacques pulled her into the tunnel. "They are starting the machine. We need to clear the area."

The door closed behind them.

She turned to Peter. "You said you suspected someone of the break-in?"

"That's right."

"Who exactly do you suspect?"

6

Lyon, France
April 27th, 8:08 a.m.

Spring was melting into summer as Del walked from her hotel through the Tête d'Or botanical gardens, just like she had when she first came to Lyon. It seemed like another life, a long time ago, yet only two years had gone past.

What would she do if she could travel back in time?

Dr. Peter Breedlove was an odd fish, but his technical credentials were beyond impeccable, teaching at Cornell, a PhD from the ETH Zurich, and winner of the Breakthrough Prize in Fundamental Physics.

On their drive back, Jacques had commented that the physicist seemed to fancy her a little more than was professional. *Fancy* her, a British expression. He was implying that Breedlove was attracted to Del. Like Jacques was jealous. Part of her felt offended, but part kinda liked it.

At least he'd driven back at a more leisurely pace. His temper was like hers, darted out quick as a viper and retreated just as fast.

The gravel path led her past orderly beds of blushing azaleas spiked with hot mango birds of paradise and pruned rose bushes alive with tiny bees. Butterflies darted in and out, sparkling in lime green and fuchsia. The air was warm, smelled of clipped grass and the earthy wetness of a storm that morning, the sky now cloudless and blue. Laughter from somewhere, children playing.

On her right stood the greenhouse, an arced and turreted giant birdcage. To the left a lake lay just out of sight. She stopped where the path split. Regarded the cone-sculpted conifers on either side of the doors of the great glass house. Legend had it that the Crusaders had buried a golden head of Christ somewhere in this park, hundreds of years ago.

What would that have meant to someone then—someone who truly believed? It had to be something worthy of a pilgrimage.

And what would it mean to someone now? Someone like her?

She'd grown up going to church with her father, but the cold stones and suffering saints had left her with more questions than answers. This park, like other green spaces, reminded her more of her mother's faith. She felt the loa around her, in the air, in the sky. Waiting to ride.

From beneath a bush near her right foot, a spined tail arced its barb over a flat, armored body. Front pincers reached for her, grasping. Six legs bent in a spiky chorus line, bright patterns of fluorescence kaleidoscoping off them.

She watched the tiny scorpion scurry across the dirt and disappear into a hiding spot.

Just like Del had done the last two nights.

She had spent them alone, avoiding Jacques's phone calls, studying, trying to put things out of mind. At least she thought she had. Now that she was here in the perfect French sunshine, she wasn't so sure.

The gardens had been laid out in the nineteenth century, when the western model of the universe was clockwork and the general feeling was that nature could be ordered as humans saw fit. How could she make the cluttered parts of her life this tidy, this rational, this uncluttered, straightforward, and clean? Somehow, she always seemed to move from one mess to another, although it wasn't quite fair to call a new life a mess. Being pregnant with a coworker was the tricky part.

She turned, crossed the park, and approached the mirrored cube of the Interpol offices. Jacques stood at the entrance. Her vision was improving, though still slightly blurry—but she knew it was him. Impeccable trousers, jacket swung gracefully over one arm, the low-rise Nehru collar of his ivory Egyptian cotton shirt setting off the olive tones of his skin. Even at a distance, she felt like she could smell him—clove and jasmine and cardamom so faint you could only get a hint of it up close. When they'd returned to Paris two days ago, she'd let him know she needed some alone time. She'd taken the TGV into Lyon that morning.

He stepped aside to let her go through the automatic door ahead of him. No kiss, not even a polite cheek peck hello. She walked past him, paused, and said, "Thank you."

***

The door to the Deputy Marshal's office was open, embodying Boston Justice's oft-repeated policy.

He'd made some changes.

Where Katherine's personalization had consisted of a withered jade plant and a Soda Stream, Justice aimed for man-cave vibe. Against the glass wall, deep plum leather armchairs stood on either side of an oversized faux parchment globe, which Del suspected opened to reveal bottles and shakers. A wall of cherrywood bookshelves was poised behind Boston's leather-topped desk, a silver eagle in flight raising its wings above his head. A two-foot-high Blind Justice raised her scales over the desk, next to a glass inkwell that held no ink.

Subtle, Del thought, but out loud she said, "Good morning, sir."

Justice grinned. "Morning, Devlin."

He stood to shake her hand, then waved her into one of the two wishbone chairs across the desk from him. While it looked comfortable, it nevertheless forced her to sit upright and at attention. She guessed the armchairs were reserved for victory celebrations.

"You about ready for your big exam?"

Del's cheeks flushed as she wondered for a second how he knew about her pregnancy. Then reminded herself that *she* barely knew about it. "The Treasury Officer exam. Getting there, sir."

"The only sir is my father. Boston. Everybody calls me Bos."

This felt like a forced attempt at informality. Being here popped a question into her mind. She resisted for a moment, but then relented. He wanted informal. "So, Bos, what happened to Katherine?"

"She left government. Not because she *had to*, but because she had to. And she's paying for it in private industry with a fat salary and a government contract, I'd wager."

Didn't sound like much blood had been spilled, but neither did it sound like Justice was on Katherine's side. Still, it was hard to tell with people like this—which Del had learned the hard way. She didn't know where to start, but she did know she had to get the parts of her life in some kind of order. She took a deep breath. "I need to go to New York."

"For the case?"

"For my family." She needed to see her father, to sit down with his doctors and understand what was happening with his new cancer diagnosis. More than that, though—she wanted him to meet his brother, Johnny, to force some kind of family reunion. She had arranged for Johnny to enter the United States, and she needed to be there when he did.

"No can do, I'm afraid. Need you here."

"I do have information for the case."

"I'm listening."

She told him what Peter had said as she'd left CERN.

***

Del took the elevator to the top floor, crossed the common area with the same lilac walls and impressionist prints that had been here two years ago, and walked down the hall to the windowless forensics lab. Tables strewn with papers and microscopes and machines, the whole chaotic operation kept humming by sunny Suweil.

"Miss Delta!" He smiled as soon as he caught sight of her. Put down whatever he was working on and scurried over to the door. "You have made it! Wonderful to see you. Come in, come in!"

Suweil escorted her through the room, pointing out new acquisitions and pieces of evidence as they went, chatting all the while.

Across the wide table, Jacques was examining a pile of fluff that looked like hair. He glanced at Del as she came in, gave her a quick nod, and went back to it. Had she pushed him too far away? Or was he just doing what she should be doing and keeping his mind on work?

His skin looked cool to her, no heat around his eyes or cheeks. She nodded back to him and continued through the room, propelled by the unstoppable force of Suweil's portly frame.

"My apologies, everyone." Zoya slinked into the room and dropped her Hermès Birkin bag down on the table. Her sapphire-blue jumpsuit offset the new gold highlights in her long surfer-blond hair, and her teeth shone white against her olive skin. Suweil, still smiling, set to tidying up the items she had just disturbed. "It takes me so long to walk anywhere in France—a shop on every corner."

Del smiled at Zoya. Gave a quick nod, not really wanting to talk about shoes at work. But there was a lightness about Zoya that made her feel it was okay—like they could be girly and still expect to be taken seriously. Like they were a team.

Jacques looked up at Zoya, his eyes narrowing. "Detective Abramov, I was not aware you would be joining us."

"Deputy Marshal Justice put in a request. There is a strong link to financial cybercrime, perhaps related to the Lucknow Gang, which Marshal Devlin has been investigating."

A deep crimson flared up Jacques's cheeks. He didn't say another word, just went back to his work. He'd never had a problem working with a woman before, to Del's knowledge. Had Zoya stepped on his toes? What was up here?

Del walked over to the Israeli woman and lowered her voice. Enough that Jacques would not be able to hear. "I wanted to say thank you."

"For what?"

"Singapore. I know I left some details out of the report."

"Sometimes this is necessary. If you have a moment, I have a question for you."

Del waited.

Zoya said, "The Lucknow leader? Any identification?"

Del paused a beat before replying, "I'll keep you updated. I—"

"Are you ready to go, Deputy Marshal Devlin?" Jacques opened his laptop on the table, not looking up.

Del pulled her own laptop from her briefcase. "Whenever you are."

Jacques swept his arm wide, indicating that she could take the floor and begin.

"The item stolen from CERN is a transition radiation tracker." Del paused to let everyone around the table get ready, while Suweil lowered the lights and clicked on a screen that took up the entire far wall. Details about the tracker's materials appeared. "Inspector Galloul and I spoke to Dr. Breedlove, the team leader on the project."

"We also obtained samples from the affected areas of CERN," Jacques said as a color-coded map of the facility popped up on the display. "Officer Jatt and his team are looking at them now."

"And Dr. Breedlove volunteered a possible lead—the name of a physicist who had recently left the project under less-than-ideal conditions. Breedlove believes this person may have been motivated to sabotage the project."

Zoya snorted. "Always suspect anyone who gives you a name."

"This kind of simplistic thinking can initiate misleading conjecture," Jacques said.

A flash of heat rushed to Zoya's cheeks and forehead. Why? Jacques's comment was a bit sarcastic, but it wasn't quite as biting to elicit so much stress.

Boston Justice arrived, said a goodbye into his phone, tucked it into his jacket's inner pocket, and surveyed the faces around the table. "That was Reginald Turner over in Lawrence Livermore's. They've had a theft as well."

Suweil said, "Is there a connection?"

"That place is surrounded by Gatling guns." Justice sighed and leaned over the table. "Each one with the firepower of twenty officers armed with automatic weapons. It was like a ghost got in and out. We don't know if these incidents are connected, but—let's hand this over to our lead." He inclined his head toward Jacques. "Inspector Galloul here is the Interpol point person for the investigation into any suspected crime network."

"Breedlove estimates the radiation tracker stolen from CERN might be worth fifty million dollars," Jacques said. "I think we need to start with this. It could be broken down into parts. There is an exceedingly small list of organizations, and more likely rogue nation-state operations, who might be potential clients for items such as these."

Suweil said, "Carbon nanotubes like this are difficult to come by."

Zoya said, "What if this person, or this group, is not stripping the parts down and selling the components? What if they are building something?"

Suweil asked, "Do you have an idea?"

"Money is one question, but mine would be—*what* could they be building with this kind of equipment?"

***

The meeting broke up.

Justice got back on the phone, and Suweil returned to the evidence he had been examining earlier. Zoya closed her file and picked up her purse and waved Del over.

"Here." Zoya handed her a small cardboard box, about the same dimensions as the box a Chanel lipstick would come in. "Arnica. For your headaches. Put six drops under your tongue when you feel one come on. Gwyneth swears by it."

"Thanks," Del said.

"Inspector." Zoya nodded toward Jacques as she walked past him.

He shot her a look, then leaned in and spoke quietly to her. She pulled away from him and shook her head. He responded with the ghost of a nod before packing up his papers. He didn't look at Del but avoided her gaze.

Del was on the other side of the room and didn't hear what they exchanged. What was that about?

Jacques didn't look like he wanted to share, so Del exited the room after waving goodbye to Suweil. Jacques followed but didn't say a word until they were in the elevator. As they stood in the closed box, empty but for the two of them, he spoke without looking at her. "You and Detective Abramov have become close."

"What did you just ask her?"

"Something about an old case."

He looked away from her as he said it. She didn't need to see his face to know he was lying. She sensed something else, though. He was angry again, but she wasn't in the mood.

"Listen. I'm going to New York. To interview the physicist Dr. Breedlove named."

"Then I should be coming." Jacques still spoke without looking at her.

"This is also a personal trip. Missy texted me the other day. My father's cancer is more aggressive. They're talking about surgery."

7

Lyon, France
April 27th, 7:32 p.m.

From their table, Del watched the light change on the river as the sun set. The stone walls of the town glimmered a dusky pink as the winding streets came alive with groups of young people out for drinks, families going for dinner, and couples strolling along the banks of the Rhône. The evening was warm, though an occasional breeze blew in with a little chill from the water.

Despite Lyon being crowded with bistros, bouchons, and wine bars, Zoya had directed their taxi here—to a sprawling open-air patio on the riverbank spotted with stark white tables and glass-walled fire towers. Pergolas wound with yards of cherry-red cotton protected some tables from the sun, while others were presided over by matching umbrellas. At Zoya's request, they had been seated as close to the water as possible, a deep-green hedge as their only protection from the elements.

"Do you need a pashmina?" Zoya asked. "I don't need mine."

Del shook her head.

Zoya looked her up and down, then arched a perfectly plucked eyebrow at her. Leaned close and lowered her voice. "You still look a little . . . meh. Did you go? My doctor friend?"

"I wanted to say thank you."

"Was it helpful?"

Helpful? Finding out she was pregnant was like getting hit by a truck loaded with bricks. Del should have recognized the signs, but . . . Finally, she said after a pause, "He was."

"Maybe he even told you something you did not know before."

Del felt herself blushing. She was sure Zoya couldn't know, but that comment hit a little too close to an uncomfortable truth she had been trying her best to pretend didn't exist.

Her friend smiled, her teeth glowing bright white. "I mean only that he always seems to know me better than I know myself. I was wondering if you had the same experience? He is a wonderful man."

A waitress arrived and set down a bottle of white wine and two glasses. Poured for them, then set the bottle in a steel wine bucket at the foot of their table.

Zoya raised her glass. "*Salut!*"

Del eyed her own. The wine looked crisp and cold, little beads of condensation already collecting. She could have one glass of wine, no matter what she decided to do about the pregnancy. One would be fine. That she was even thinking this way crossed her mind in tight knots.

She returned Zoya's toast and took a sip.

Delicious.

Zoya said, "The only place in town with organic wine. The food is all local—nothing shipped from the other side of the world." She leaned in lowered her voice again. "Why don't you tell me what in the world you did to those Louboutins in Singapore? The red soles looked like they were attacked by a cat."

Zoya was one of the world's leading cybercrime forensics investigators, but she somehow found the time to also run an online boutique specializing in high-end fashion. A hobby, she had explained to Del when they first met, and one that immediately fascinated Del.

Zoya had lent her the shoes and the Marchesa dress she'd worn in Singapore. The stilettos had been ruined when she'd chased down Johnny at the Marina Sands Hotel. "Sorry, I took them off as quickly as I could."

"And I am sorry I had to partially charge you for them, but my business partner—"

"It's fine. I love them, even all banged up. At least you were able to take back the dress."

"A little tear under one arm. I charged the rest to Interpol. It was an official operation, yes?" Zoya raised her glass and cheered again.

Del took another sip, thinking again about whether she should be drinking.

The tables around them filled with chattering groups of people out to enjoy the evening. Staff went from one fire tower to another, flicking them on as the twilight deepened. The trapped flames licked electric blue and lime green at their edges, almost black in the center. Del was more relaxed. She took another sip of wine.

"It is all make-believe, you know." Zoya looked down her narrow nose at the crowd.

"What is?"

She waved her arm, her gold bangles clinking. "Dressing up, going out, having fun. It means nothing. Real life is nothing like this."

"I'm not following."

"Tell me about your life," Zoya said, swatting away her previous remark. "How was it for you growing up?"

"About as American as apple pie."

"I will guess you have a nice family, graduated first in your class, went to college, got the job you had always wanted. I have not befriended an American before. That is how it goes in your country? Yes?"

Was Del's family nice? Most of them. She nodded, sure, yeah, and took another sip of wine.

"School, then marriage, then babies and a house and one job for the rest of your life. The United States dream and a white picket fence? My experience growing up was different."

"Me, too," Del said.

"I doubt like mine."

Del put down her glass. "What happened?"

"Things that never should. Families ripped apart, people killed."

The conversation was interrupted by the arrival of dinner. Soup arrived first, a thick carrot butternut squash puree with leek. Beef carpaccio followed, with roasted eggplant, and then cheese and charcuterie, one small plate after the other. Del found herself gobbling everything down as though she hadn't had a proper meal in days. Come to think of it, she hadn't. Her nausea was easing off—for good, she hoped.

"Is this a business dinner? We can charge to Interpol?" Zoya laughed and raised her glass. "Which means I will ask you about the leader of this Lucknow Gang again. What do we know about him?"

"Not much on my end." Which was true, really. Del wasn't about to share her family secrets with Zoya just yet. "Is there any more information coming through digital forensics?"

"We are always looking, you know, for the exceptionally large deposits that follow illicit sales. Monitoring crypto assets. Correlating bank details to see if anything might lead us to the stolen equipment. If you like, I can run searches of this kind on your Lucknow leader."

"I'm doing all that already."

Whatever her uncle Johnny was up to, he was family. Whatever came to light about him, Del wanted to be the first to know. At least, for now.

"Let me know if anything changes."

"Do you know about this area?" Del asked.

They were in the Croix-Rousse, which had been a major route for silk trading for hundreds of years. Del had learned this when she first moved here—her long walks had led her here, and she'd spent many hours investigating the neighborhood.

Zoya replied, "I have done the walking tours when I first arrived. Crazy. How the women kept the economy afloat when the men were busy waging wars and dying of syphilis. Running through the tunnels around here to deliver beautiful silk to rotten men."

She gestured with her fork, sweeping it over the general area. "This is how it is to be women sometimes. Underfoot, unseen. Keeping the whole thing going without credit or even a name. Like your Ginger Rogers."

"Backwards and in heels."

"Exactly. For many years I was terribly angry about this. Like the eighties businesswoman, I wore men's clothes and thought, only if I become like one of them will I succeed. This is not true. Because I will never be one of them. And they know it, and I know it. So, I throw all that away. I do not know if they take me any more or less seriously, but this is okay. Because I do not care. I am me now."

The lights flickered on the river, the sky a deep indigo now. They were electric lights, though—not the sun, not gas. What would it have been like back then? Scurrying through the tunnels, your family's fortunes in your hands? Night falling and nothing to save you from the dark?

"Would you go back in time if you could?" Del asked. "Is there anything you would change?"

Zoya nodded. Put down her fork. "To begin with, many things for my family. We are Russian Jews. When I was young, we left Saint Petersburg for Israel. A little town called Ashdod. Many like us there. More Russian Jews who wanted a better life, who ended up as refugees . . . But many, as it turned out, who did not want us there at all." She looked out over the water. "And I would want things to be very different for my sister."

"Is she—"

"She was killed."

"I'm so sorry."

"It was a long time ago."

Del set down her own fork. "What happened?"

"We do not need to talk about this now." Zoya stared off into the distance for another second, her jaw tight, then she picked up her wineglass. "I will only say it would be good to change some things. And what about you?"

"Me?"

Zoya gave Del a penetrating look. "For example, you are here with me and not at home with Jacques. What happened back there? Would you change that?"

"A little argument, that's all."

Zoya nodded again. "I know what he is like."

"You know Jacques well?"

"Did you not know? Hasn't he told you? We were together. Until you arrived."

8

Saint-Genis-Pouilly, France

April 28th, 8:03 p.m.

Peter Breedlove stood by the pub's entrance, hanging back in the awkward way he hated. It was as if he retreated to the fetal position every time he was in a social situation. He knew this, but still, it happened every time. On some level, he couldn't outsmart his own behavior, which manifested in ways he couldn't control. As if he needed to prove this, he found himself asking a question that had flitted idly through his thoughts—out loud.

"Is this a party for a woman named Caroline?" he asked.

The four people who had brought him here—Gerry, Erika, Félix, Sahil, all from CERN but not working for him—looked at Peter, then broke into raucous laughter. The song kept going, and the whole room sang along.

Félix clapped him on the back. "Nice one, Breedlove!"

Peter smiled because they did. Particle physics and muons and leptons made sense, but people did not. They thought he'd made some sort of joke. Sweet Caroline? Everyone sang to her, but apparently this was not her party. He made a mental note to remember the song, which wasn't necessary, because he remembered everything even if he didn't want to.

Just smile if they do, and sometimes even if they don't.

He was trying. This was why he had come with these three to this tavern on the other side of the border. While part of him despised the easy way other people laughed and made friends, another part desperately wanted to be part of it—but he wasn't sure what to do now that he was here. The part of him that despised it all whispered to him to get out and escape back to the lab, but Peter remained still. He hadn't come all this way for nothing.

There might be things he didn't understand, but there was something he knew that they didn't. He knew something about the future that nobody else did. He'd proven in the lab that antiparticles could travel backward in time and had demonstrated what he believed was the ability to send information back—even if just by nanoseconds.

Something had happened recently that had proven his theories correct, but in an even more spectacular and unexpected way than he could have even imagined. Problem was, he had to keep *absolutely* secret about it.

Nobody could know. Not even his new girlfriend, Samira.

The four of them were jammed in with a dozen strangers at a long table, and people kept bumping into the back of his chair. And into his elbows. One girl hit him in the back of the head with her purse. Surprisingly heavy. What did women keep in those things?

The room itself was acceptable.

Warm but not hot. Low ceilings. Sweet smell of fermenting hops. Walls painted an off-white that contrasted pleasingly with the brick accents. Brass rails at the bar, which Félix said made the place a real tavern. Actual newspapers hung neatly over dowels in a nook near the entrance with a grandfather clock in brass and dark wood, and a glassed-off room in the back that held large tanks for beer making.

Peter maneuvered into a seat from which he viewed both the grandfather clock and the brew room. He enjoyed the sight of the copper-skinned drums and tubes connecting them. It looked like a lab. And the clock, that was critical. Maybe the only reason he hadn't bolted yet. Seeing the second hand ticking around, steady and unwavering, made him feel secure. Sane.

Once the song ended, the music was turned down to a less deafening level, and the three he had come with began chatting. They asked after each other's partners and children, and then reminisced about a gathering they had all attended.

"You remember Gerry, right, Breedlove?" Félix asked.

The man he pointed to, Gerry, gave Peter a tight smile and nodded. Peter had no idea who the guy was. *Smile if they smile.* He grinned and nodded in return.

Félix leaned into Peter and said, "Gerry sure knows how to throw a going-away party. You should have told us Aringa was going, we could have done another shindig."

Félix winked at Peter, but he hadn't the slightest idea why. Peter didn't like Dr. Ross Aringa. This was public knowledge, wasn't it? But maybe it wasn't. Why would Félix imply that Peter should have helped organize a going-away party? How on Earth was human interaction so complicated when particle physics wasn't?

Seeing Peter didn't respond to his wink, Félix leaned forward on his meaty arms. "So, you're not going to parties. What have you been doing lately? Tell me about your research. Something interesting."

Across the table, the man named Ross seemed to roll his eyes.

Peter ignored him. "I've been expanding on the work of Dr. Sylvain Ringbauer."

"University of Queensland?" Félix squinted. "He did work on Gödel metrics, right?"

"You're familiar with his work?" Peter felt himself relax and realized that Félix was making an effort to connect with him.

"Read through it in grad school. He's the only person that did actual experimental proof of time travel. That's what your research is, right? Fascinating stuff."

Gerry said, "Only on subatomic particles, and no information passed back. Sure, on a theoretical level, the direction of time doesn't matter—but all the king's horses couldn't put Humpty back together again. You can't reverse entropy. Those weren't real experimental proofs."

"I beg to disagree," Peter said. "And I am expanding on his experimental process at CERN. The closed curves described in his research allow time travel in universes described by Gödel's solution. You can send information back in time, as long as the solution doesn't collapse the—"

A buxom matron in a blue dress and white frock dropped four foam-topped liter glasses of beer on the table. They each took one and cheered each other and took sips.

Erika said, "But doesn't this contradict Einstein's relativity? I'm sorry, I just caught the tail end of what you said."

"And the second law of thermodynamics and just about every other macroscopic tenet of physics," Gerry added.

Peter said, "Not if all possible future states remain in limbo until the solution to the Gödel universe model is resolved. The same way wave functions collapse when observed. This is what I was trying to say."

"The many-universes model."

"Not just that. This is the 'can' and 'can't' thought experiment of the basis of physics that will unite general relativity with gravity and quantum physics. It's the element of reversible time and the allowable simultaneous states of reality that are the key. This is a testable, experimentally verifiable—"

"You're sending messages back in time?" Gerry said. "Is that what you're saying? Like 'Hello past world'?"

"In a sense, yes." In a very real sense, Peter didn't add.

"In exactly *what* sense? What is your future self telling you?" Gerry laughed.

Was this man kidding? Or did he know Peter was getting messages from himself in the future?

This was Peter's big secret.

It began with a stupefying revelation six weeks before when Peter had decoded messages from the Allen Telescope Array, a deep space network radio-telescope. The data was scraped from part of the SETI—the Search for Extraterrestrial Intelligence—Institute.

One of the researchers contacted him and said that there was a mysterious signal they had named BLC2. It was like another signal they had detected coming from near Proxima Centauri, signal BLC1, a few years back, which they hadn't fully figured out yet. And yet another new one they called BLC3, which had originated from the same direction as this one.

The odd thing about BLC2, though, was that an AI pattern-matching system had found the noise of the signal seemed to match the non-fungible token of a digital copy of one of Peter's research papers that he had put up on the CERN website. Out of billions of bits of code the AI pattern-matched, it wasn't unusual that a one-in-a-billion close pattern had been found. The researcher was sure this was just a random coincidence, but he wanted to share it with Peter.

Purely out of curiosity, this led Peter to download all the BLC2 signal data from SETI. Samira had suggested it when he told her about the message he got from the researcher, shared a laugh over dinner at the coincidence.

The bolt from the blue came when, on a whim, he programmed his computer to run its own AI pattern matching and to scan through possible matches on his home network. Part of the process was to apply his own 256-bit AES encryption key. Nobody else knew this code, and it was unbreakable, unknowable to anyone except himself. In a sudden flood, the random noise of the BLC2 signal assembled itself into intelligible streams of data. Like a thunderclap, the data assembled into neat ASCII characters. Messages.

And those messages warned him not to tell anyone else about them—because they were from Peter himself in the future.

After the initial shock had worn off, it had all made sense.

His future self had explained everything as if it had come from his own scribbled notebooks strewn around his apartment. With the LHC he was able to send antiparticles back a few nanoseconds, but with a device strong enough, much greater temporal spans were possible. Eight years in the future, they had built an even more powerful supercollider, and the experiment future Peter had devised was emitting radio wave signals that punched backward through time.

He was broadcasting to himself from eight years away, from the spot the Earth would be then, about three hundred billion kilometers toward the constellation Orion. From that distance, it took about twenty days for the signal to reach Earth here, where the data was collected by the Allen Array and stored in the SETI database. Now that Peter had made this connection with his future self, he downloaded the SETI data daily and was receiving messages on a regular basis. His home system decoded the information and sent out text messages to Peter on his mobile.

Peter was blessed with near-perfect memory. His future self was estimating when and where his past self was, and now the connection had been made, he was getting daily missives trying to convince him on the validity of the signal.

The digital messages were one way only—not two-way—he couldn't just text message himself back. At a minimum, there was the twenty-day delay for any signal generated to reach Earth. Some accident or disaster in the near future had disrupted the digital networks. There was a way to communicate with his future self, but that required a more cumbersome process involving physical letters.

The system wasn't perfect, but it worked. The job of a scientist was to eliminate every possibility until only one remained, no matter how outlandish the theory. And Peter had eliminated every other possibility. Only one remained, one he had always known to be true. He knew his calculations were correct. And now it was proven.

He just couldn't tell the world yet.

"Peter, hey, you still there?" Gerry asked.

A few seconds must have passed while Peter stared into space, something he had been doing a lot of lately.

Gerry prodded him and laughed, "Peter, so what's your future self asking?"

Peter smiled to show he was also joking. "That someone must be removed."

Gerry's laugh only came harder. "You mean me?"

"I think he means like Hitler," Erika said. "Am I right?" She turned to Peter.

"Don't even use that name," Gerry replied.

"Are you serious?" Sahil said to Peter.

"Stop." Gerry held out both hands and rolled his eyes. "You can't be serious."

"But," Sahil said, "if there are multiple universes, then what is the point? If we eliminate Hitler here, he will still exist somewhere else, yes?"

It was a well-worn hypothetical path.

Peter said, "It could be possible to stem the tide in many universes at once. We are but one island in a larger cosmos."

"You believe there could be multiple versions of me?" asked Félix.

"There already are." Peter could see them all now. "A thousand. You are a different person to your wife, your lover, your friends. Each person has a different version of you in their mind, and you are different in each reality."

Peter's phone buzzed in his pocket. Another message from himself. *Did you check the games yet?*

Peter engaged in more small talk, ignoring snide remarks from Gerry, before excusing himself to get up and find an English newspaper in the nook by the front door.

"Sports results of the Premiere League and others across Europe." He checked his phone, scrolled back in his texts. Located his string of bets. His hand started shaking. He folded the newspaper and stuck it in his blazer's inside pocket. Found his way back to the table. Lowered himself into an available chair and stared straight ahead.

Félix clapped a big arm around him. "One too many?"

Samira appeared through the door to the pub, and the crowd separated to give her way. The men in the bar all turned to look. Tall and slender and elegant, her hair shining in black waves, her smile warm as she greeted everyone at the table as though they were all old friends.

She leaned down and kissed Peter on the top of his head. "I'll get us more drinks?"

As she turned away, Félix and Sahil followed her with their eyes.

Félix shook his head.

Peter was the only one who didn't watch her go. He was still in shock. The winning games he had messages from his future self the week before matched exactly. The results of three dozen soccer matches. The odds were—he calculated in his head—one in sixty-eight billion. His phone buzzed again. Another text message appeared on his phone, newly decoded from the encryption loop going on his personal machine at CERN.

One more thing. Our wife, your girlfriend, she is pregnant. Congratulations. Ask her to be tested. Today is the day, old friend, the day the world will change.

9

Brooklyn, New York
April 28th, 3:34 p.m.

"Guys, should we really be out here?" Jenny asked no one in particular. The other two teens were ahead of her, almost under the bridge, their laughter tinkling through the air. New York's smog had lifted for one of those afternoons that poured clear sunshine over everything and made most people feel—she imagined—like they were free. Happy. Having fun.

She pulled her shades down and shouted after them, "Okay! I get that mom made you bring me, but can you at least wait up?"

Taylor stopped and looked over at Jenny, one hand on her hip. The riverside out here was empty except for the three of them. The water, even though Jenny knew better, looked like it was inviting her in for a swim, all glittering and blue. "Stop being such a baby. It'll be fun. I'll even let you open it."

"You will?"

Taylor nodded and pointed to Jackson. "He's filming. You'll be a TikTok star! C'mon, it's supposed to be right here!"

Jenny picked her way carefully over on the rocks and caught up with the other two. Taylor pointed. "I think it's that. Go check it out."

A black zip-up bag was just poking out from between some boulders under the bridge. Jenny paused. "What's supposed to be in it, again?"

"We don't know!" Taylor said. "It's an adventure, remember? The app just sends you places, shows you things that are, I dunno, exciting! Weird. Fun!"

Taylor inclined her head and mouthed, "Go." Jenny headed to the bag.

The sand here was cool and squishy, little waves slipping over her toes. Darkness.

The bag in front of her. Jenny knelt, her hands on the zipper of the black bag. Cool. Cold. She pulled it open. The smell hit her, and she gagged as she saw what lay inside.

10

Brooklyn, New York

April 29th, 9:25 a.m.

A scream sliced the spring air, so sharp Del almost dropped her coffee. She scanned the small park. Clumps of parents chatting over strollers. Monkey bars crawling with kids. Slides. Swings. And the scream came again—a squeal, really, now that Del could see where it came from. Of delight. From a little girl, maybe two years old, being pushed on a swing by her mother.

Del let out a breath and sat back on the park bench.

The chill was just coming off the morning air sifting through the soft green of the new leaves. She slipped out of her jacket to enjoy the warmth.

Her nausea had let up the past few mornings, so she'd risked a coffee from the diner on the corner. She'd vowed never to spend six dollars on a coffee if she could help it and was getting used to the slightly acidic taste of the drip stuff again. She lifted it and inhaled deeply, hoping the burnt, earthy smell of it wouldn't set her off. Her stomach stayed calm, so she took a sip. Milky and sweet, exactly right.

Another cup next to her on the bench.

Extra large, extra milk and sugar. She was guessing, but she had a feeling she was right.

The girl squealed again. Her mother pushed her higher and higher. They both smiled like they were posing for an Instagram shot—perfect glowing grins that told the world they were winning.

She'd been thrown by the news the doctor in France had given her, but she hadn't really given herself a chance to process it. Would having a small person around transform her? Make her complete in some way she wasn't by herself? That was the line. The thing everyone was meant to believe. But did she? Could she? She wasn't sure.

What would she have to give up?

Her career?

Jacques had wanted to come to New York with her. Said he should help her track down Dr. Ross Aringa, the physicist who had just quit CERN and returned to the US. She'd said no, since he had added her to the case file at Interpol, she was just as qualified to interview the man. Jacques didn't need to come, as she was already here.

"Ah, now. A heavenly face for this old sinner." A voice familiar, but also new. Gravelly and warm, with more Northern Ireland in it than her dad's. "Keeping out of trouble, are ye?"

Blue eyes, dark hair going gray. Face a little less chiseled than her father's, rounder and cherubic. Beside her, he sat taller than her father, and his presence was more barrel-chested, fairly twanging with restrained energy. Tough. Quick. Ready to fight. Del kept a careful space between them by picking up and holding the coffee cup out at arm's length and shifting on the bench away from him.

"Ta very much. You do this for all your meetings, do you?" He pried off the sippy-cup lid and peered at the liquid within. "How much would they charge for a full one?"

"I asked them to leave a little room."

Del fished a flask from her purse and handed it to him. She'd noticed gin blossoms on Johnny's nose when she'd seen him in Singapore. Broken blood vessels, a sign of overindulgence. She could see them spreading under his skin, too—invisible to everybody else. Like the roots of a cedar, feeding from afar. She wanted to soften him up.

"Clever girl." Even though the phrase sounded like praise you might give to a dog, he said it appreciatively, genuinely. Gave her a twinkly smile while he unscrewed the top of the flask. A sniff, a nod, and he tipped in as much as the cup would hold. Leaving the lid off, he took a sip. Then a larger one. "Brilliant. You'll have some?"

"It's still morning for me."

"As you like." He took another sip, then splashed a little more whiskey in his own cup. "I'll mind the rest for you, shall I?"

Up close, reclining, relaxed, his eyes shaded by the brim of his tweed cap, Johnny didn't look like a terrorist. More like an affable uncle, the kind who always had a sweet or two for his favorite niece. But she'd read his file again this morning.

He let out a contented groan and stretched out his legs. "That's lovely, that."

He was a convicted murderer. "You have to stop what you're doing," Del said.

"Oh, aye. Stop enjoying myself? Sit up straight, listen to the missus?"

"I'm a US Marshal. I have—"

"*Deputy* Marshal."

She ignored his interruption. "—enough on you to put you away. The Lucknow stuff alone, not to mention—"

"Is that right?"

"Teebane. You bombed a van," Del said. "Killed fourteen civilians."

"Paid whatever debt I owed to society. I knew those men who planted that bomb, but I never went in for that sort of thing. I was innocent of that."

Del watched the parents with their kids. Playing. Smiling. Laughing.

"You do know me and your dad are twins? I came into this world twenty minutes ahead, and I'm still the better-looking one."

"Fraternal, not identical," Del said. Close enough, though. In a dim room, he could pass for her father—dressed in the right clothes and with a clean shave.

Johnny poured the rest of the whiskey into his cup and downed it. He rummaged around in the bag he'd set down earlier. Pulled a crumpled piece of lined paper from within it. Set it on his lap, started smoothing it out.

"I have some idea you Americans go in for this sort of thing. Immunity and that."

"I wasn't aware we were negotiating."

"I would never do this in a million if you weren't who you are. And if I wasn't so blessed tired now. Tired of running."

"So, now you're the victim."

"I was forced into this life, from a world you might not understand. And I'm not asking you to. You're the one that asked me, remember? To come here?"

Del let out a long breath. Trying to pick at old wounds was less than useful. Finally, she said, "Do you ever wish you could go back? Change things?"

He looked down at the paper in his hands. Sighed. His shoulders curled inward.

"I'd like to see my brother again, which is why I'm here." He handed Del a crumpled paper. A photo clipped to it. A female Del had seen before—long dark hair, the left side of her face scarred and burned—but where? "I suggest you find out who this is. I'll do some digging myself."

He looked her square in the eye.

"This woman has been following you."

***

Johnny twisted the cap onto Del's small hip flask and handed it back to her. He walked as far as the corner, then doubled back and stood a fair distance from the bench they'd been sitting on.

She was still there. What was she waiting for?

He'd scoped out the park an hour before the meeting—this was her neck of the woods, after all, and he never let anyone get the better of him. Not if he could help it.

The only person who had been there then and was still here now was a dapper little Latino man who carried himself like a coiled spring. Johnny had watched him closely, and he was sure now what it was. The man was deadly—but he wanted to hide that. A cop, or something like it. He'd kept his eyes on Johnny and Delta the whole time they'd been talking.

And the man was still here.

Delta remained sitting on the park bench.

She looked so much like his brother, Sean, even from this distance. Most striking around the jawline. She had the same way of setting it that he did, as though angling her chin to take a punch. Maybe Johnny did that himself, too. Maybe he got that from his brother as well.

Johnny watched as the Latino man across the park gave the carousel a spin, keeping his eyes on Del, not on the lad he spun around. Del got up, retrieved the paper cup Johnny had left behind, and dropped it in a nearby bin, along with the one she had been drinking from. She turned and crossed the park toward the Latino man.

Johnny followed from a distance.

Del and the other man hugged when she reached the merry-go-round. She handed the man a folder, and then they both looked over at Johnny.

He smiled and waved.

Then he turned away and began walking to the other side of the park. Away from prying eyes. A man got up from a park bench and began walking next to him.

"She's lovely," Dermot said. "You sure she's your niece?"

Johnny shoved his hands in his pockets and didn't reply.

After a few steps together in silence, Dermot asked, "Are you sure you want to be doing this? I mean, your brother, he's not well. And a US Marshal? This is playing with fire."

"I am not playing, Dermot. Mind your own business."

"This is my business. Have you contacted your Interpol man yet?"

"I have. Everything is set up."

Dermot looked back over his shoulder. "Do you think she knows you're the one who wanted to meet her in Singapore, not the other way 'round?"

"I'm here to see my brother."

"Sure, you are."

"Mind yourself, Hermit. I'm telling you."

"I'm just saying. This is a dangerous game you're playing. And you're playing it using your own family, Johnboy."

11

Brooklyn, New York

April 29th, 4:12 p.m.

The afternoon turned cloudy as Del walked along Prospect Park, the sunlight flattening to a sheet of gray-white glare as it hit the dirty-sheep's-wool sky. Del squinted against a bit of a headache. Pulled her sunglasses from her purse, put them on. Better. She looked across the street—the brownstones appeared fuzzy, as did the people walking by them. But she could read the hot dog cart's signs on this side of the street, so that was some improvement, wasn't it? The eye drops the doctor had given her in Paris must be working.

She veered to the right around the hot dog cart, but her stomach still knotted from the meaty smell. Headed to the Lafayette Memorial, where she took in a deep breath, let it out. The nausea faded.

She looked up, but not at Lafayette in his breeches and knee-high boots, or at his horse. Del studied the groomsman. A Black man, thought to be James Armistead Lafayette, a slave eventually freed. His first surname from the man who had owned him, his second from the one who had facilitated his freedom. He'd been a military man, a double agent. And had gone on to run a farm in Virginia, owning slaves himself.

Del stared into the bronze eyes of the Black Lafayette. How many layers could be within one person, how many lies to self? Did he think he was a good man? A success? And who was she to say he wasn't? How could she judge someone when she had no idea what it was like to be that person?

Her phone pinged: ten minutes to the meeting.

When she turned onto Eighth, the street where she had grown up, the clouds parted. She took off her shades. Sun glinted off a rearview mirror lying crushed in the gutter, streamed along the facades of the brownstones, flashing from their windows. Brightened the new spring leaves on the oaks and the beech trees, chartreuse and absinthe in her eyes. A sign? Maybe the loa were looking out for her a little bit today. She hoped so. She would need all the help she could get.

As she approached her parents' walkway, a black Porsche SUV with tinted windows pulled up. The passenger-side door opened. And there was Johnny. His tweed cap gone, his rumpled sweater replaced by a tailored dove-gray suit. Hair slicked back. Shoes shined. The SUV pulled away and tucked itself discreetly into a spot down the street. Waiting.

"There she is." He gave her his twinkly smile. A box in his hands, wrapped in black. Bottle sized. Big red bow.

"I hope that's not for me."

"Well, it might be. And it mightn't."

"It better not be for Dad."

He hoisted the bottle in a gesture she'd seen before—the same way he held an AK-47 in her file photos. "Fortifications, like. I haven't spent this much time with coppers in many a year. It's not just you lot who need backup."

"If Mom is here, she'll kill you herself if you let him drink that."

He tucked the box away under his arm in a flash. "I thought your ma'll not be there?"

"She's out shopping. Last I called she was."

"So, just Sean, then? You're sure?"

"As I can be."

"And he's well?"

"He's not."

"I mean is he alright—with the cancer and all."

"The cancer is lymphatic. And it's spread."

"Ah, no. It's terrible, that."

"There are treatments. He'll get through this."

Johnny took a heavy breath, let it out. "He does know I'm coming, yeah?"

"Maybe I should go in first."

He cracked a little grin, a bit sheepish. "I am a bit jumpy, if I'm honest. It's not every day you see your twin brother for the first time in thirty years."

***

It was dim inside the house. Del hung her coat on the coatrack and took her shoes off by the front door. Johnny watched her do this, then did the same. She led him down the hall to the living room, but halfway along, she noticed he'd fallen behind. Found him looking at the family photos on the wall. Her younger self and Missy, dressed up for Halloween as a cop and a witch. Picnics, Christmases, birthdays. Proms. Graduations.

"They're lovely, these." Johnny took a step away from the wall, his hands behind his back, as though admiring great artwork in a museum.

Del hadn't been ready to share pictures of herself in pigtails.

Johnny saw her embarrassment. "They're gas. You should think yourself very lucky."

She turned and continued down the hall, past more framed photos.

The shades were drawn—unusual for her parents, who normally loved to let natural light in. Her father was in his La-Z-Boy. Unshaven, also unusual. The room stifling. Like mold and urine and baby powder had been mixed in a jar and then spritzed through the air. Soccer—or football, as her dad called it—on the TV. Euro Cup qualifiers. Croatia vs Wales, but he watched every game. At least, he did now.

Nobody said anything. Her dad didn't look over or even say hello.

Johnny cleared his throat. "Sure, but it's not the same since Georgie Best."

The TV cut to a commercial, the volume jarringly loud.

And her father still didn't say anything, but the sound cut out. He must have pressed mute on the remote. Long seconds passed.

Finally, her father spoke. His voice low, sounding sore and raw. But hard, too. A barely suppressed rage burned through every word. “What sewer did you crawl out of?” He shook his head. “And you, Delta—didn’t I raise you better than this? Never lead a suspect to your home, didn’t I say?”

“Dad. I thought—”

“Thought, nothing. You don’t know a thing about it. How could you spring this on a sick old man?” Paused to cough. Del took a step toward him, but he waved her off. “I’ll deal with you later.”

“Take it easy on the girl, Sean. She only wanted to give us a hand, like. After all is said and done, we are family.”

“What would you know about it? Those men at Teebane had families. Poor buggers were just trying to go to work. Feed their children.”

“I never killed those men.”

A pause. No one spoke. Her sock feet quiet on the carpet, Del edged over so she stood closer to her father.

Johnny circled around and squatted so he could look Sean in the eye. “I’m tellin’ you the god’s honest here. I didn’t do it.”

Del’s father stared past Johnny at the men on TV. One of them raced around the field smiling, stripped off his shirt. The crowd cheered silently.

“Lookit.” Johnny held out the wrapped box. “I know you’re not supposed to, but I thought we could have a drink. I heard you changed your name.”

A nod from Del’s father.

Johnny said, “Tis a good name, Devlin. Ma would have approved.”

He unwrapped the bottle while Del went to the kitchen. Picked up two dusty rocks glasses from their spots in the cupboard. When she returned, the bottle was already open and missing a few fingers of liquid. Her father and uncle cracked smiles as she walked in. That didn’t take long.

“You couldn’t wait two minutes?”

“You must pick your moments in this life,” said Johnny. Lifted the bottle to his mouth and drank.

Del put the glasses down on the coffee table next to her father. He waved her off again.

Her father said to Johnny, “Will I have to ask?”

"Ask what?"

"What happened to Da?"

"You don't want to hear about that." Johnny paused. Drank. Passed the bottle to Del's dad. "It was the cancer. A couple years past. He did ask for you, y'know. Thought I was you at the end."

"And what did you tell him, while you were me?"

"That I was well and happy. And that I hadn't shopped my brother to the filth, like everybody said."

Another awkward silence. Her dad must have pushed the power button on the remote because the TV went dead. The room darker now. Absolutely silent.

A sip of whiskey from the bottle, and one brother handed it to another.

"He means I ratted him out." Her dad put the bottle down. "Handed him over to the police. Or anyway, that's what everyone thought. Him and our da included."

A clatter of keys at the door, followed by a breezy hello. Del's mother.

"I have chicken!" She bustled into the room, flicking on the lights as she entered. "Lord, Sean, it's dark as a tomb in here!" But her eyebrows rose as soon as she saw what was in the room. Del watched her take it all in—her daughter, her husband, a bottle, and worst of all. Him.

She shook her head and strode away down the hall again.

"Mom!" Del ran after her. Caught up with her in the kitchen, sliding open drawers and slamming cabinet doors. "Mom, it's not—"

"It is not what, Delta? Not your good-for-nothing uncle, back to gloat just when he's sick again? Not your father drinking when I forbade it? When the doctors said it could kill him?"

"No—"

"Not the man who ruined your father's good name? Not the one who broke that family? Kept you from your own grandfather?"

"Well, but—"

"I am a patient woman, but not for this." Del's mom closed the fridge door softly. "Is this why you asked me to go shopping?"

"I just wanted—"

"You *will* go fix this. Or I will. I'm going upstairs to lie down. Ten minutes before I call 911 and scream murder and I don't care what happens. You make sure he is gone before then."

Before Del could say anything else, her mother turned away and left the room, padding up the stairs without another word.

Del was heading back to the living room when there was a knock at the door.

***

Spring sunset rimed the moldings of the neighboring buildings in grapefruit and tangerine, pinks and oranges. Couples walked by with small dogs on leashes, kids clattered over the sidewalk on scooters and skateboards. Her mother's honeysuckle was just starting to flower, making a sweetly scented arbor of the columns by the door. And there was Coleman, her old partner, as lanky and pale as ever.

"Officer Devlin," he said. "I mean, Inspector. What should I call you? Look, I need to talk to you."

Del sat in one of the wicker armchairs to the side of the front door, resisted putting her head in her hands. "Just call me Devlin, as always. What's going on, Coleman?"

"Hey, I'm sorry, I didn't mean to—"

"Don't worry about it."

"Anything to do with that man in there?"

"What can I do for you?"

"Remember the Fire Island killer? Seems like we might have a copycat. Or, well, we don't know, really. Some kids found something . . . Could you come take a look?"

12

Saint-Genis-Pouilly, France
April 29th, 11:45 a.m.

"I'm not even hungry." Peter kept his eyes on his work as Samira bustled around in his tiny kitchen. "I ate. I think. You know I lose track of time."

Samira laughed. "I swear, if I did not feed you, you would disappear into one of your black holes."

She placed a bowl of hummus and plate of pita next to him, then returned to the kitchen. Every element on the stove top was going. Samira hummed as she flitted from one pot to the next, stirring and tasting.

Deep down, Peter thought the processes of cooking and eating were monumental wastes. What was the point beyond rendering the proteins more digestible? Before Samira had come along, he'd been content with canned goods and microwaved meals. But he didn't say so. Her cooking was amazing. Not to mention, she was beautiful. He was helpless and still couldn't believe she loved him.

"I thought I got rid of all these."

He raised his head to see.

She was opening all his cabinets and removing cans and boxes, piling them on the counter. Her nose wrinkled as she read the label on one. "I do not think even a dog would eat this."

Peter looked from Samira to the clock by the front door to the cape on the hook to the floor to the table, then back to his notes. He repeated these motions as he worked, in soothing, perfectly timed motions. Her long hair was tied up tonight, showing her graceful neck and high cheekbones to full effect. Even in the harsh yellow light from the kitchen's track lighting, her brown skin glowed.

The smallest details—the proportions of her facial features, her waist-to-hip ratio, her BMI, her fingernails—were, from a scientific standpoint, perfect. He was aware that there was something almost comical about a woman like her standing in a basement suite with her delicate hand wrapped around a microwavable plastic tub of Chef Boyardee ravioli.

But there it was.

"You should not microwave plastic. Everybody knows this."

"It's faster."

"How much faster can it possibly be? It is one second to put this . . . *food* in a bowl."

"Add all those seconds up."

"I bring you delicious things already in bowls." She bent over him, gave him a kiss on the top of his head. Then stood back to look at him. "This is the same clothing you wore yesterday. Did you work through the night again? I reminded you to go to sleep when I dropped you off, didn't I?"

Peter lost track of what he was thinking about. Tried to repeat the sequence: Samira, clock, cape, floor, table, notes. But Samira was in a different place now, so it didn't help. The thought was broken. Gone.

He shut his laptop and put down his pen.

Folded the paper he'd just been writing on in half and tucked it into his pocket. Scratched his chin, which was bristly. His suit jacket was rumpled, his pants wrinkled. And now that he thought about it, he desperately wanted to brush his teeth and take a shower. "I was busy. I'll clean up in a bit—but I need to get to the clockmaker first."

Samira walked through the apartment. Though it was a semibasement, it had high ceilings and was bright when Peter remembered to open the curtains.

It had come furnished, all those years ago when he had first come to CERN, with items that were made to be temporary. The chair he sat on was white plastic, as were the other chairs in the area that served as his dining room and workspace. The couch against the far wall was white, same as the kitchen cabinets and all the plates and bowls and mugs. The walls were white too, where they showed. All of it had come with the apartment, and all of it was made of plastic or pressed board. Cheap. Disposable. Made to fail. To never see a future.

Peter hadn't brought anything with him from the States except his laptop and a carry-on of clothes. But since then, he'd been buying. Buying time.

The walls of the apartment were covered with clocks. They covered every surface as well, stacked on piles of books and papers. Grandfather clocks, digital alarm clocks, cuckoo clocks, all ticking slightly out of time with each other. Each one procured on day trips to neighboring small towns, where he scoured every shop that looked like it might hold secondhand or antique items. Samira never went with him. She'd accompanied him once, but had become illogically infuriated by his process of inspecting every item in each store. You know you are only going to buy a clock! she'd said. Why do you have to look at every single thing?

He didn't know. He just had to.

The clocks he brought home measured time in a blunt and entropic manner almost completely unrelated to the way he did. They were to his mode of telling time as a medieval barber's hacksaw was to a fiber-optic nano-splicer. Their steadily increasing unreliability soothed him. Reminded him that all things fall apart. His favorites were ones that had to be wound, ever so gently, lest they slow and finally stop altogether.

Samira turned on the TV.

"—New York City, a bag reportedly containing a body or body parts is stumbled on by a group of young people using the geolocation app—"

"Turn that off, please," Peter said, raising his voice to be heard over the newscaster. "I hate the news."

"I would like to hear it," Samira said.

"Please."

She shook her head, but clicked the TV off, then reached up to the rectangular window just behind the couch. Lifted the flimsy white paper blind and opened the little pane of glass behind it. A sliver of daylight struggled into the gloom. Feet and calves walked by. The brightness made his chest constrict.

"Close that," he said louder than he intended.

She didn't. Instead, she walked back through the room and started picking up his papers and notebooks, stacking them neatly on the table. "I will clean this for you. It will be better."

Peter counted to ten in his head, just like his sister had taught him, but his heart still beat like crazy. He counted to ten again. His heartbeat slowed, and he could think again. He knew the words he had to say, although he didn't entirely understand why he had to say them. His sister had taught him these words, too.

"I'm sorry. I didn't mean to raise my voice." He looked at the floor while he said this. *I need it to be a certain way*, he wanted to say. *I don't know why.*

He looked up at Samira. She *was* beautiful. The last three months he had been happier than he had ever been in his life, despite the shock of the messages from his future self. Or perhaps because of them.

But there was no denying Samira was a part of that happiness. It was hard to believe how a woman so giving and so incredible had fallen for him, but she said that in her family, it was brains that were beautiful, and he was the most gorgeous man she had ever met. Who would have ever imagined that he would meet such a woman at the clockmaker?

Speaking of which.

Peter said, "I will clean up when I get back. I need to go and see him. And I need you to go to the pharmacy, could you do that for me?" He handed her a piece of paper on which he had written a couple of words. "Then meet me back here."

"This is what you would like me to do?" She frowned and held up the paper. "Really? Do you know something I do not?"

"Just my OCD, you know what I'm like. Could you humor me?"

The clocks ticked, in syncopation and out of time.

***

Peter walked along the streets of Saint-Genis-Pouilly. He didn't notice the way the sun dappled the nearby mountains through the clouds or the little tables that had popped up outside every bakery and café along the street. Didn't see the budding trees in oversized pink and red pots on the sidewalks or the solid whitewashed buildings, shutters open to catch the afternoon light. Didn't feel the chill as he crossed onto the shady side of the street or hear the laughter coming from a pub down the way. He'd been taking this walk more and more lately, could make it with his eyes closed just by counting the steps. He kept his eyes on the pavement and thought about the future.

Or rather, *a* future. A future in which the digital infrastructure will be obliterated. A future in which he will nevertheless still exist. A future in which he will write messages to himself, this self, this human in this place and time.

He had been instructed to leave physical messages for his future self. He couldn't just beam messages into space, there was no way to send information into the future. Not digitally, anyway, but there was a simpler if cruder way to do it. He simply wrote messages on paper and left them to sit in a box, until they were retrieved by his future self in eight years. Each reply was sent back to him here, from a point three hundred billion kilometers away in space twenty days ago, so a text usually arrived within a few hours of the time the clockmaker stamped onto the envelope.

It was a bizarre process, writing a message on a letter and stuffing it into a box and then getting a text response, but it was the only way they had discovered to make it work. Part of it felt nonsensical, as he was writing messages to himself, and he would obviously remember he wrote these and their content in eight years. His future self said he didn't even need the papers, not really, because just the act of writing them imprinted in his future memory, like Peter was writing into a disk drive in his mind. It was the way these closed time-like curves worked.

After the precise number of steps, Peter arrived. He had been coming here for years, had bought many clocks from the man everyone knew as "the master." Had found out—just when he needed to—that the master also offered a capsule service, a locked box in the back of an old bank vault.

A squat yellow building with a slanted roof, a simple painted sign above the door: *Horlogerie.*

***

Peter closed the door with a soft click, not wanting to disturb a single atom in the shop. The workshop wrapped around him, each wall covered with precise arrangements of hammers, gauges, brushes, and calipers. Glass-fronted cabinets created a barrier between this space and that, each shelf within lined with row on orderly row of gently ticking timepieces cradled in velvet. The sun-warmed air carried hints of wood soap and silver polish, along with the sharp scent of metal on metal Peter couldn't quite find a word for. He stood quietly. There were no bells in the room, aside from the ones in the clocks. He would have to be patient, but the space itself encouraged that.

"Ah!" The master poked his head up from his worktable in the back. Shut off the machine he had been bent over and walked over to greet him. A stately old man with white flyaway hair, tucking a wire-strung loupe up on the middle of his forehead like a third eye. "Peter, my dear boy. You have another message?"

Peter handed it over. And the master had something for Peter. Just delivered today, from the Russian physics institute. Surprised, Peter took the package under his arm and watched the clockmaker stamp the time onto the letter he gave him.

Then walked back home, waiting for his phone to ping.

***

When Peter returned to his apartment, Samira was there, waiting for him. With one shaking hand, she held up the test strip.

"I am pregnant," she said. "How did you know?"

Peter didn't answer. Last week's message from the future had told him to make sure Samira took the test. *Everything was coming true.*

She hugged him. He tried to hug her back.

His phone chimed. He excused himself, went to the washroom, locked the door. Checked his inbox. A message. From himself, from the future.

Do you believe me now?

The text went on, the bubble longer than his screen.

We don't have much time.

He scrolled as he read it, then went back and read it again. Information about the policeman he had asked about, Jacques Galloul. And a warning that someone was following him.

And then.

The clockmaker has been compromised.

Get out of there.

Go use winnings.

Another ping, another message. A picture of Delta Devlin, the marshal from a couple of days ago.

But this wasn't a text from his future self.

It was from Delta Devlin.

What was she doing messaging him?

But as he read the message, another incredible revelation settled in. This was a message from Delta Devlin, but it was coming from his personal server, not from the mobile network. This message from Devlin was coming through the SETI data set. It was a message from Devlin, but in the future.

Delta's next message:

This is a picture of me, eight years in the future.

Another ping. A photo popped up on his screen.

> And this is a photo of your daughter and my son.

Ping.

> They're both dead. You need to stay away from me, Peter. No matter what, stay away from me.

Peter sank to the floor, dropping his phone with a clatter. The child he had only minutes ago found out existed, wiped out. Gone. How could such a thing happen? And what did it have to do with the detective he had just met at CERN?

A light knock at the door, then Samira's voice. "Peter? Are you okay in there? I heard a crash."

"I'm fine," he said, but his voice sounded strangled even to his own ears.

"Peter? What's going on?"

He couldn't—wouldn't—tell Samira any of this. Not a word. He barely believed it himself. He cleared his throat. "I'm fine!"

"I don't believe you. Let me in there, I can help you."

The doorknob twisted, the door bumping in its frame. Peter edged away. And his phone lit up with an incoming text from Devlin:

> You need to leave now. A detective is looking for you. But not me.

Another ping—and the handsome face of Jacques Galloul filled his screen.

13

Saint-Genis-Pouilly, France
April 29th, 12:05 p.m.

On a side street, Jacques smoked a vanilla cigarillo in the requisitioned Mercedes and watched Peter Breedlove walk out of his basement apartment.

The man was tall and almost comically skinny, all elbows and knees. No grace. His sandy blond mop of hair hung over his eyes, which darted about as he walked, flitting their gaze from one side of the street to another. Jacques watched where Peter's gaze was going, as he had when they'd met at CERN.

The man looked unfocused, as though he were miles away, deep inside his thoughts. Jacques took a small black notebook from his jacket's inside pocket and wrote down the details. Then flipped back through it, reviewing his second batch of notes from CERN.

After he and Delta had visited CERN, Jacques had driven back alone. Used his badge to access the facilities. Demanded full access, especially to the security systems and video recordings. Interviewed more staff and collected names and addresses, among other things.

He'd sat in one of the security guard's chairs and watched the footage from each camera. The facility was well covered, with cameras at regular intervals. No corners unmonitored, no stretches of hallway unrecorded—Jacques had seen the cameras himself. But the video from the night in question showed nothing out of the ordinary. Empty staircases, soundless caverns. A young person on the floor near CRONUS picked up bits of wire, cleaning the area. Jacques viewed hours of footage, covered the whole night, and saw nothing unusual. And noted every detail in his book. An absence could be proof, in the right circumstances.

The sun was moving across the sky, casting him deeper into shade. His cigarillo finished, he tossed the butt into the road. Smoke curled from the dark brown paper. Jacques reached into his jacket, took out a moist towelette, wiped his hands clean. And waited.

Kept his eye on the door to Breedlove's apartment building. Eventually, a beautiful woman emerged. Her legs toned. She moved along the street in a pencil skirt and shoulder-baring peasant blouse, the sunlight giving her flawless olive skin a tawny glow.

She headed along the main street, just past the spot where Jacques was parked. He knew she wouldn't be able to see him where he was. He sat back in the deep leather seat, checked his notes again. Nodded to himself, then got out of the car and walked slowly to the corner, arriving as she did.

Smiled as she passed by.

"*Bonjour.*" He smiled the smile he reserved for moments like this.

The woman stopped. Her cheekbones gleamed, her hair pulled back so her slender neck was exposed. She returned his greeting, but not the smile.

"This day was made for a woman as lovely as you."

"I am very busy. Excuse me."

"No, no. You must not rush away. Come, sit with me over there. We will have coffee."

She raised an eyebrow. "No, we will not."

"Ah, I think you will find that I am no liar. We will."

"I really must go."

"I see. You are going to see some other man. Perhaps he is more handsome than me?"

"Not exactly."

"Then come with me. Look, right over there. A little table, two chairs . . ." A pause, then Jacques lifted his hands in the classic gesture of surrender. "Then I will leave you to your day. I am deeply sorry for disturbing you."

He turned away. Slightly. She hesitated, then took a step toward him. "You didn't disturb me. I am running late."

"Well, perhaps some other time, then?"

His eyes met hers, deep brown and warm. And, finally, she smiled. Shook her head. "I am not sure why I am doing this. But here."

She reached for his hand. Wrote a number on it in blue ballpoint. Without saying anything else, she turned and left.

Jacques watched her walk away down the sunny little street. Smiling, he entered her number into his phone, then took another moist towelette from his pocket and scrubbed as much of the ink from his hand as he could. When he looked up again, he saw that the beautiful woman had met with another woman, this one blond. She was slight and well-dressed, seemed very pretty as well, though he could not see her face. They greeted each other with a handshake and then rounded the corner. For a split second, he was curious—why a handshake, and not cheek kisses?—but there was no time to wonder. He hopped back in the Mercedes and drove back.

Just in time.

Peter Breedlove stood outside a small yellow building—housing a clockmaker, of all things, according to the sign—a look on his face like he was in serious thought. A packet of folded papers in his hands. Jacques stayed where he was, across the street and in shadow. Jacques pulled out his notebook again and wrote everything down.

A few minutes after Breedlove went into the shop, Jacques left the car. Walked down the narrow street, being sure to stay out of the line of sight from inside the clockmaker's. Passed the bakery next to the clockmaker's, then turned the corner. And walked around the building to the back.

A small window set into the stone wall at the rear of the clockmaker's shop. A wooden door, painted the same buttercup yellow as the wall out front. Jacques walked to it, pulled the handle. Locked. Jacques nodded, and then returned to the requisitioned Mercedes. Smoked another cigarillo. His eyes on the front door of the little shop.

Breedlove stayed in the clockmaker's for nearly forty minutes.

When he left, he had a small package tucked under his arm. His eyes on the ground, he hurried back the way he had come.

Jacques waited. One minute, two. Got out of the car, stretched slowly. His legs, his arms, his hands. Rolled his shoulders back, let his posture relax. Crossed the street at an easy pace, then walked into the clockmaker's shop.

He let the door slam closed behind him, the resulting *thunk* echoing in the cluttered room. Jacques scanned the space. Very clean, but too many things. And all those clocks ticking away, day in, day out. Enough to drive a man mad.

Jacques leaned down to inspect some of the watches for sale. Silver pocket watches, titanium-backed men's watches, and a row of tiny timepieces meant for ladies, faced with mother-of-pearl and ringed with diamonds. Quite pretty. And off to the back of the cabinet, one in particular caught his eye.

The grinding sound continued, coming from the back of the room, where the shopfront gave way to the workspace. Jacques ambled toward the noise.

The man Jacques supposed was the clockmaker had his head bent over the noisy machine and was working very slowly at a tiny piece of metal. Jacques waited.

Eventually, the man shut off the machine. Pulled a head-mounted loupe over one eye and lifted the piece to inspect it.

Jacques cleared his throat.

The man lifted his head. "I didn't hear you come in."

The clockmaker put the piece down on an immaculate worktable. "And how may I help you?"

"I was just passing by and noticed the lovely gold pocket watch you have in your front cabinet. The one with the little blue flowers."

"*Les jacinthe des bois?*"

"*Exactement.*"

"I would be pleased to show this to you."

Jacques stood back to allow the little man to lead the way. Followed him back to the front of the shop, waited while he opened the locked cabinet.

"This one?" the clockmaker asked, pointing at the little watch.

Jacques nodded.

The man pulled the watch out, placed it on the counter. "The cloisonné is in perfect condition. This is a Victorian piece, retrofitted with a fine Swiss movement."

"She will like this, I think." Jacques plucked the watch from its case, held it to his ear.

"It is for your wife?"

"Only time will tell." Jacques smiled. "I would like to take it, please."

"Wonderful."

"And I would also like to know more about your other services."

"Oh?"

"The locked boxes in the back."

"I'm sorry, I don't know what you're ta—"

"I believe you know precisely what I'm talking about."

"I am doing nothing of the kind. It seems you are doing that, pretending you'd like to buy something. Who are you really, sir?"

"Interpol. But that is not your concern."

The clockmaker's right eye appeared huge behind the loupe. Every wrinkle and spot and twitch of fear magnified. Jacques slipped his right hand into the interior pocket of his jacket. Pulled it out slowly, holding a pair of black leather gloves. He slipped on the left one, adjusting the fingers as he spoke. "What *is* your concern is the welfare of the man who just left your establishment."

"Dr. Breedlove? What are you saying? Is he in some kind of trouble?"

"I will need whatever it is he just left with you."

The clockmaker shook his head. "His letters are locked away."

"This is what I would like to see."

"But it is a time capsule. It has been sealed, locked. Cannot be opened for ten years."

"Or what? Demons will fly out? Be serious."

"I am always serious."

Jacques pulled on his other glove, smoothed the leather over his fingers. "As am I." He looked around the room. "You're quite the workman. Tell me," he continued, lazily withdrawing his gun from its holster. "Do you do any work with guns?"

The clockmaker removed the loupe from his eye. Placed it gently on the counter. Lifted his apron from around his neck. Hung it on a hook on the wall behind the cash register. Turned to face Jacques. "Dr. Breedlove has entrusted those letters to me. I will not fail him."

"Yes, this is very honorable. But you know, there is an easy solution here. You don't have to give me the letters." Jacques looked the other man right in the eye. "Just hand over this time capsule. The whole thing."

14

Brooklyn, New York

April 29th, 6:45 p.m.

Del and Coleman picked their way over the rocky ground near the East River where the kids had made their discovery. The sun was going down, lights coming across the river. Cars zipped by above. The bike path behind them alive with people who skirted the zone cordoned off by police tape with zero interest. These were New Yorkers. They'd seen it all. Del buttoned up her jacket and wished she still had a scarf in her pocket. She'd forgotten how cool it could get by the water, even in spring.

The smell of oil and old fish and a deeper, fleshier stench. The bag.

Del followed Coleman. Under the boardwalk, tucked into the dark. The bag had been left unzipped. A hand trailed out, like a snail curling from its broken shell. Pale and soft.

There was a head, but the face was mangled.

"Do you think this has anything to do with the Fire Island Killer?"

The hands had no fingerprints. Burned off.

"Remember Royce Vandeweghe? Have you talked to him?"

Del shook her head. Stepped back from the bag. Eyed the rocks in the sinking darkness. Flashes of heat, tiny and furious. Scurrying. Probably mice. Or rats. Nothing bigger.

"He's living with Jake's widow."

"Doesn't surprise me."

"Creeps me out."

"What about Dr. Danesti? Does he still have offices here?"

"The Eden Corporation moved their HQ to that floating platform off the coast of California. They're trying to claim sovereignty as their own nation. You must have been following it?"

A sparkling spot caught her attention as they pulled the torso from the bag, a pin on the deceased's jacket. She reached out without thinking or putting a glove on and touched it. A blue enamel square with a silver design and lettering. The same pin Dr. Breedlove had been wearing when she'd met him at CERN.

Her phone buzzed in her pocket. A reminder.

"I've got to go." This was not the reason she'd come back to New York. "I have an appointment."

"Oh, sure." He hesitated.

"Spit it out, Coleman. I have to run."

"You just touched the body. I'm going to have to ask you for a DNA sample. Forensics asks for it now, for anyone around the crime scene. Is that okay?"

***

Del climbed the dozen stairs to the front door of the gray-stone on the Upper West Side, rang the bell, and waited. Pulled her notebook from her pocket and flipped through it until she found her notes from CERN. Dr. Ross Aringa. The physicist Dr. Breedlove had named. She looked up as the door opened.

"Good evening." A spit-and-polished man in a black suit and tie opened the door.

"Dr. Aringa?"

"No, madam. I am his butler. And you are?"

"Deputy Marshal Devlin. He should be expecting me."

"Indeed. Do please come in." He stood to the side and held the door open for her. She walked through, and he closed it behind her. It didn't even make a click.

A maid appeared from somewhere, took Del's coat, and melted away with it.

"Right this way." The butler turned and led her through the tiled foyer. High ceilings, eggshell-white walls, a huge mirror on her left over a narrow marble-topped table. To her right, an ornately carved nineteenth-century newel terminated the matching banister. The stairs themselves were blocked off by a red velvet rope.

They continued through the living room, a massive space dotted with low-slung couches and armchairs. Oddly large spaces between them. A reclaimed farm table stood near the open French doors, mismatched antique chairs tucked beneath its sides. An empty space at either end. Art on every wall. Klee, Haring, Hockney, Matisse, and Warhol, as well as a very small gold frame to the right of the doors that held a sketch of an angel and a bull. Signed by Picasso. No edition number. Out the open French doors and into a walled garden lit by sunken spots and angled landscape lights. Ivy and flowering clematis. A little piece of sky above.

The butler pulled a cushioned iron chair out from under a table. She thanked him and sat. There was no chair across from her. "Would you like a drink? The chef has prepared some hibiscus-rose iced tea. Very refreshing."

"Please."

"Dr. Aringa will be with you momentarily."

Del couldn't imagine that the person who owned a place worth twenty million—with servants—would need to steal anything.

A man in a nurse's uniform walked toward her through the large living room, pushing a sleek wheelchair. Slid it into the space across from Del.

Del stood. Bent to shake his hand. "Dr. Aringa. Deputy Marshal Devlin."

"Pleasure to meet you. You'll excuse me if I don't get up." Aringa's face was tanned, laugh lines coming out as he cracked his joke. Longish sandy hair hung in his eyes, and his handshake was solid. Firm. Restrained strength behind his grip.

The butler returned with a silver tray holding two slender glasses of iced tea. The liquid glowed fuchsia, sprigs of mint bright pops of op art green at their rims.

"Are you aware of the incident that took place at CERN?"

"I'm afraid I'm not."

The man's face was cool—no flushes of stress around his eyes. "Where were you last week?"

"Here, at home. I was working on my book."

"Can anyone attest to this?"

"Davenport, of course. My butler. And possibly the maids. He can tell you who was working that day. Why?"

"A device was stolen."

"This is the first I've heard of it."

Del made a note. "What is your connection to Dr. Breedlove?"

"We worked together. At CERN, as you know. There was a rivalry of sorts between us. On a professional level, of course."

"Did Dr. Breedlove ever make any complaints against you?"

"Not in any official capacity."

"In some other way?"

"Well, no. Not really. We didn't exactly get along, but I respect the man's mind."

"But?"

"We had a feud, if you can call it that. Over something probably only a handful of people care about anyway."

"Please, elaborate."

"Whether closed time-like curves could be resolved at the quantum level or not. Theories regarding quantum gravity and such. We couldn't agree. And eventually, Peter became—agitated."

"Aggressive?"

"I did come to the conclusion that it was time to move back to the US."

Del wrote everything down, then flipped to a new page in her notebook. "Does anyone else have a pin like the one you're wearing?"

"Hundreds. Maybe thousands. Everyone who goes to the LHC gets one."

Del and Jacques hadn't, but then, they hadn't been there as tourists. "Would there be records of who had gotten pins like yours?"

"I wouldn't be the one to ask."

"What about the work you were doing at CERN?"

"I just described it. Would you like a list of my research papers?"

"I would. Send me links?" Del flipped her notebook closed. "So, do you think time travel is possible?"

"Like in films?"

"Dr. Breedlove shared some of his thoughts on it with me. I want to know what you think."

"Peter is one of the smartest people I know. Certainly, his theories may be possible. He has even demonstrated some of them experimentally."

"Dr. Breedlove said I would like his ideas, and he said it as if he knew me."

"He is a strange man."

"He avoids eyes. Anybody's. He's uncomfortable being around people. Is he—"

"He's autistic. He's also Steven Hawking and Einstein rolled into one. Difficult, maybe, but brilliant. He spoke about time travel with you? You should consider that a compliment."

"Because I'm a woman?"

"Because you're an authority figure. Peter is a little overwrought sometimes."

"Overwrought?"

"Paranoid."

"Dangerously so?"

"Peter wouldn't hurt a fly. He's too worried the flies are all out to get him." He laughed.

A waiter appeared and refilled their glasses. Del's phone buzzed in her pocket. More reminders. She had two appointments early tomorrow, both of which made her stomach flutter. Both of which made her more than just professionally interested in getting an answer to her question. "But is it possible? Data time travel? That was what Peter talked to me about."

"Do you really want an explanation? I think the crux of this issue is that Peter was convinced I was sending him messages. And he insisted I was saying things about him. Things I had never said, things I'd never even thought."

"And this was unusual? You did say you were having a feud."

"We were. But the tone changed. He could never produce any of these messages I had supposedly been sending him. His behavior was the reason I had to leave CERN."

She wrote it all down, then another wave of nausea hit. There were other questions she should ask him, but only one she really wanted the answer to right now.

"But what about the time travel?"

"This is a curious question from a US Marshal."

"I need to understand if he's delusional or if this makes sense."

"In theory, we know that black holes could also be wormholes. Openings in the fabric of space. And, perhaps, time."

"So, is it possible?" she asked again.

"Time is an illusion," Dr. Aringa said. "Just like free will. You think it's there, but it isn't. It's a way our minds keep on an even keel, to imagine we are free. But it is all an illusion. Of that, I am certain."

Davenport reappeared. Del said goodbye to Dr. Aringa, then followed the butler through the house and back to the front door. After confirming the date and time in question with both the butler and the maid, Del slipped on her coat, which had reappeared.

As she walked out of the front door, Del noticed a package on the doorstep.

It was from CERN.

15

Brooklyn, New York

April 29th, 11:52 p.m.

The room was exactly as Del had left it—almost. Although her parents had left her karate trophies and books about Renaissance art on her white wicker shelves, her vanity had been shoved into a corner to make room for her mother's paintings. Most of them were ready to ship, cardboard caps on their corners and wrapped in brown kraft paper, but others were in various states of completion. All of them were large. Some were laid against each other in a neat stack that directly blocked the way to the closet. Another group leaned against Del's white dresser, flat against the front of the drawers.

She'd given up and unzipped her suitcase on the floor. She hadn't unpacked in Paris, so why should it be any different here?

She'd gotten back to her parents' place too late to have dinner with them. But her mom had left her a plate in the fridge with a note stuck to it: *Don't eat while you work! Take a break.* Del had pocketed the note, zapped the plate in the microwave, and told herself to eat at the table. But she'd had work to do. She'd made it upstairs, putting the plate down on her old desk and opening her laptop, when she was hit by a wave of jet lag and crawled into bed without eating.

Now it was—she checked her phone—midnight. The house was silent and her parents wouldn't be up for a while, so she'd have time to do what she needed. She got out of bed, opened the Picasso-print curtains she'd made in home economics class, edged her way around her mother's paintings, and sat at her desk.

The pungent smell of last night's uneaten curry hit her as her laptop powered on, her stomach rumbling and coiling at the same time. She picked up the plate, leaned over her mother's canvases, and deposited it on top of her dresser. Caught a glimpse of the framed photos there—her and Missy at the beach, her whole family at one of her mother's gallery openings, her father in uniform. And one of her and Mickey, their arms around each other, smiling. She rolled her eyes and went back to her computer.

First things first. The woman with long hair and burn marks on her face had crept around the edges of Del's mind since Johnny had handed the picture to her. She was positive she'd seen that face before. But where?

She signed into Interpol, then took a picture of the photo using her phone and uploaded it. Search after search returned without a match. Firearms, nominal data, foreign terrorist fighters, forensic data. Nothing showed up in any of the eighteen databases she had access to, including US Department of Justice. So, this woman had no ID and no history.

Either she was clean—or her information had *been* cleaned.

But Johnny had said the woman was following Del. How did he know this? Come to think of it, how did he have a picture of the woman in the first place? It was too convenient, so she needed to be careful of him as well as this woman.

The photo was a standard matte four-by-six, the kind you'd get at any photo counter in any mall. She turned it over. No markings at all, just blank white paper. Flipped it back to the image side. The woman was standing in front of some blurry trees and looked like she was posing for a passport photo. No hint of a smile. Del attached the scanned image to an email and hit send. If she was lucky, she'd get a response before she had to leave.

Next—the other thing that had been on her mind. The app the kids had been using when they stumbled on the body. Coleman hadn't given her the name of it, and when she searched "geocaching app," a few different ones came up. "Cache Me If You Can" was at the top of the list.

Their landing page was bright and cheery, filled with shots of happy geocachers on sunny days. As Del clicked through, looking at their contact page and noting they were based in Singapore, a side banner came up. Amnesty International, looking for donations to help them fight the kind of tactics that Governor Guthrie was advocating. Arrests, tear gas in the streets. Families torn apart. Civilians bombed. Children killed. Del clicked onto another page, and the banner was replaced with an Arby's ad. Her stomach lurched again.

She checked her email—both accounts. One from Zoya in her private email, not the encrypted Interpol one—that was a quick response. It was morning in Lyon, so Zoya was working, but she'd prioritized Del's query. She'd have to remember to thank Zoya for all her help, maybe take her to lunch the next time they were both in the same city, even though she would have to get around her feelings of Zoya having dated Jacques in the past.

The message from Zoya: *This image is Anila Jalili. She's associated with the IRGC.*

Del slumped back in her seat. The Iranian Revolutionary Guard? What was someone associated with them doing here? It would have to wait. She needed to catch a few hours of sleep. She had two big appointments the next day, and she couldn't be late for either.

***

Del woke early the next morning and helped get her dad dressed before driving him into the city to the chemo clinic. The walls of the waiting room were a washed-out gray-green with a sallow undertone. The blinds on the large panel windows were thankfully open, the spring light brightening everything in the space. An apple tree bloomed outside, a slice of blue sky visible above its blossoms, but inside had the antiseptic stink that curdled her stomach.

Del walked her father between the occupied chairs, then tried to help him into an empty one. He shooed her away with a wave of his hand.

"Away with you." He lowered himself using the armrests to support his weight. "I'm grand."

She sat next to him. Her father opened his jacket and took out that morning's newspaper, flicked it open. Del hadn't thought to bring anything other than her phone and wallet. She should have brought one of the US Marshal exam prep manuals, done some studying. But who was she kidding? She wouldn't be able to focus.

She looked around the room.

It was different than the last time. Someone had hand-painted a sign wishing everyone a happy day, drawn with a smiling sun in the background. The people in the room looked younger than the ones in the last place. Almost all of them were with someone.

Del thought back.

Hadn't everyone been alone last time?

But that smell, the one that had been missing from the doctor's office in Paris. Urine and bleach hung heavy in the waiting room air under the halogen tube lighting. Lint and spray freshener. And a pungent wallop of cheap tequila hit her whenever someone used the hand sanitizer at the station by the door. A woman across the room wore an electric-blue wig cut into a bob, which clashed with the backless olive drab robe she'd been put in.

The whole thing felt like a replay of an old movie. One she hated.

Del took a deep breath, let it out. Repeated it enough times that she felt her pulse slowing. *Relax. Remember what you're doing here. You're here for him. We will get through this.*

Again.

Her father turned the page of his newspaper, the crinkling loud in the quiet room. Tutted under his breath. Folded the newspaper carefully over and bent to read. She wanted to hold his hand, tell him it would be okay, but she didn't.

Why didn't she?

He would jump into any fight for her—had literally jumped in front of a bullet to save someone else. But she saw a tiredness in him, around his eyes and in the way he buried himself in the paper.

Del turned to him. "We're going to beat this."

He looked up at her, over the paper. "I know."

"You'll be fine. Just like last time."

"You can see the future now, can you?"

"If I could, I wouldn't let you beat me at gin rummy last night." Del waited for him to smile before asking, "What would you change about the past if you could?"

"I'm like Édith Piaf. No regrets."

Del returned to staring out the wide window. Sparkling fluorescent-green leaves, a finch lifting off a branch in flight, setting the tree's blossoms in motion. Could she say the same as her father? She thought about Mickey, about staying with him even when he hit her those times. She felt the old anger bubbling up, but more that she kept thinking about that asshole after all these years.

Never again.

How old would that child have been now? Ten? She imagined a girl chasing butterflies, boys running after her. Then erased it from her mind. Put a hand on her belly unconsciously. Noticed her father watching. She reached over and squeezed his hand. He looked at her like she was daft, but allowed a little smile. She grinned back.

"I'm glad you're here," he said. "It's good."

She knew he would have preferred to be alone but would never say it.

"I know you have other fish to fry." He folded up his paper and tucked it away. "What with your work and studies and all."

"I wouldn't be anywhere else."

"Live your life, darling. I've lived mine."

She'd been on top of everything just a few weeks ago, had her future all worked out. But like the proverbial best-laid plans, hers were unspooling. Johnny had said this Anila Jalili woman was following her. She needed to find out why, but bringing in official help would require explaining where she got the information from.

"Did you talk to your brother again?" Del asked.

"You cannot trust him," her dad said. "He makes nice, but he's a snake. You keep that in your mind."

A nurse called her father's name. Ushered them into a room down the hall. Smaller, no window, but the same smell. Del stood, insisted her dad sit. She pushed her thoughts away and focused on getting him through whatever the doctor had to say.

The doctor came in, his eyes on her dad's file. He looked up, closed the file, and sat next to her father. "Mr. Devlin. I'm sorry to have to tell you this, but it looks like you have several enlarged lymph nodes now. Adenocarcinoma from the biopsy. The cancer is acting very aggressively."

***

Del dropped her father back home in Brooklyn before taking the subway back into the city. Her father had barely reacted to the doctor's words, had just nodded as if he knew exactly what she was going to say. For Del, it felt like the bottom of the world had opened up beneath her, a black pit at the back of her mind she thought had been filled in.

But she still had her own appointment.

This waiting room had kids' drawings on the walls. Mothers and children. Dogs, cats, walks in leaves. Daddies and cars. Homes. Warm memories. The walls sunshine yellow, the chairs well-worn pine, their 1970s frames reseated with black diamond-hatched Lycra, the original orange vinyl long gone. Del could almost be back in her childhood, except the kids weren't reading magazines, they were playing games on their own iPads. Everyone with wireless headphones. Mothers and fathers miles away, texting, working, talking under their breath, holding meetings while their child waited. This man had been her doctor since she was as little as the girl walking wobbly in front of her, not more than two years old.

He appeared. His bushy mustache had gone white, and he was nearly bald on top. A little rounder than last time. But he gave her the same warm smile he always had.

And she found herself returning his smile. A tightness that had been tangled up inside her came loose, just a little bit, with nothing but the promise of an understanding ear. One she could trust. She was glad she'd come.

"Delta," he said, and ushered her into the examining room. Closed the door quietly behind her.

He asked after her parents. She said they were fine, which was more or less true. She asked about his children and the woman who used to work the reception desk here.

And then there was a lull. The reason she'd called him hung unspoken in the room.

"Okay," he said. "Well, we both know why you're here. We've done the blood work, and yes, you are pregnant. Congratulations."

The tangled thing inside her tightened. Del felt faintly ridiculous. A grown woman, sitting here with her childhood doctor. Discussing what they were discussing. And going back to her childhood home afterward. Why had she come here, instead of going to any number of walk-in clinics? She told herself to get through it, get on with it. Compared to what her dad was going through . . .

Del counted to ten. "I'm not sure that's the right word."

"Why not?" The doctor sat, rolled his chair next to hers.

"It's not the right time."

"It almost never is."

She didn't respond.

"Think about it, Delta. That's all I am saying."

"I just need to figure this out." Her dad always told her to look forward to things, look toward the future.

"Not that you need to, but have you talked to the father?"

After a pause she lied, "Of course."

"Do you want me to schedule an appointment for you? It would be with another doctor, but I can refer you to someone I trust."

"I'm not sure. I need more time."

"We never like to put pressure on anyone in a situation like this, but sooner would be better. Ultimately, it's up to you. You are going to have to make the decision."

16

14th arrondissement, Paris, France

April 30th, 5:02 a.m.

The last time Jacques had looked up from reading Breedlove's letters, the sun had been shining, but it went dark through the night and was now lightening again. He cursed and looked at his watch. There was still time, but he had to hurry. He tapped the edges of the stack of letters he'd been going through one by one, squared the pile, then put them all into a file folder.

Moving quickly, he pulled off his suit and hung it up, smoothing down the lapels on his jacket. As he did so, his hand ran over a small bump. Something in the pocket. He pulled it out. The little gold pocket watch with the cloisonné face cover. *Les jacinthes des bois* perfect and tiny, blue against a pumpkin-colored background. Despite its small size, it had a good heft to it. Its weight in a pocket or a purse would mean it would never be forgotten. That the woman who owned it would always be reminded of the one who had given it to her. Would know that he was watching over her, that she was always in his heart. The gold warm on her dark skin, the blue offsetting her brown eyes. The clockmaker had asked a pretty penny for it, but she was more than worth it. Jacques tucked it away again. He would save it for a special day, a time she would want to remember.

He put on his black tracksuit and sat on the bed to lace up his sneakers. Next to him sat the so-called time capsule from the clockmaker. Really just a steel strongbox, the kind one could find at any hardware store. Good enough for the purpose.

He typed a long message into his cellphone. Grabbed the stack of folders, then picked up his gun and pushed it into the waistband of his track pants.

***

Early morning, still dark with a band of violet in the sky. Jacques drove around the Arc de Triomphe—very little traffic on the circle. Light rain made sparkling puddles, reflecting headlights and taillights as vans and mopeds swished by. Swept along the Champs-Élysées to the roundabout and took the third exit to avenue Foch. Wide green parks lined both sides of the street. A young man walked slowly across the road, popping his hoodie up against the increasing rain. At the next roundabout, Jacques flicked on the windshield wipers and took the second exit to the sunken boulevard Périphérique. Cars hissed by in the rain. He pulled into the fast lane and took the A1 to Saint Denis.

Looked over at the folders on the passenger seat. If what they said was true, he'd have to make this quick. Checked his watch again. *Very* quick. He cursed and hit the accelerator.

This wasn't the requisitioned Mercedes—he'd never take a car like that where he was headed. He was driving a black 1992 Fiat Uno, papers under another name, the car he kept for those times he needed to go unseen. A squat and boxy thing with midrange pep, a car no one would think he would ever even look at. Delta hadn't noticed him in it as she'd gone to that doctor's appointment in Paris the other day.

He exited the highway at porte de Paris.

The beautiful row houses of his neighborhood were gone. Here were only squat apartment blocks, boarded-up shops and broken windows and graffiti. A soiled mattress lolled out of the mouth of an alley, a split plastic bag on it trailing a brown liquid. A sign hung between apartment balconies: Paris Banlieue 93 Contre la Police.

Prayers echoed over speakers strung through the streets and alleys. He drove fast, just missing an elderly woman with a beat-up shopping cart crossing against the light. Street corners jammed, guys in tracksuits and shades lounging on doorsteps, leaning against walls, nonchalantly watching him without watching him. Eyes followed him. Hands shoved into pockets, hoodies flicked up over heads.

He pulled up to an apartment block as crumbling and gray as all the rest. Slammed on his taqiyah, the small knitted cap for prayers. Headed to the front door. Two men peeled themselves from the clutter on the stoop next door, stood in his way. Looked down at him, expressionless.

"*Salaam alaikum*, brothers."

They inspected him closely for a moment. Then one nodded, and the other took a step back.

"*Salaam*."

The men parted, slid back to their spots on the stoop.

The pressed-wood door sagged open, swollen by damp. Jacques pushed it as far as he could, squeezed through. He sprinted up three flights of stairs, jumping over oily yellow puddles in the corners of the bare concrete landings. Smell of piss—from the puddles? Passed more men on guard. Brief nods and more salaams. Turned down a hallway covered in tags. Lightbulbs shattered, glass on the ground. A baby howled further along the hallway, a bass line bumped through the walls.

He opened the last door.

"You are late, brother." A bearded man stood by the window, a gold-and-maroon Quran in his hands.

They greeted each other with salaams, then went straight to their prayers. When they were finished, the other man stood.

His thobe was clean, though fraying at the long tunic's hem. The room bare but for the prayer mats and a ratty mattress on the floor. Bloated spots on the walls showed where the rain trickled down through the building, collecting between the drywall and the industrial gray paint. A small desk in one corner held a closed laptop, a stack of books, and a zipped-up black shaving kit, which Jacques knew didn't contain shaving supplies. There was a reason this man lived in such a place. Certain things were very close by. The man placed the Quran on the desk, then turned to Jacques. Not a finger twitched toward the shaving kit.

Jacques asked, "Are you well, brother?"

"I will be when our mission is done."

"We must keep a low profile, even in the community here," Jacques said. "I am going to have to leave."

"On the mission?"

Jacques nodded.

"Does she know? Your American?"

"She knows nothing more than what I tell her."

"Don't let yourself be fooled."

"And don't let yourself be worried. Everything is under control."

The other man bobbed his head ever so slightly, his long beard sinking to his chest. Raised his hands, palm out. "I meant no offense."

Jacques said, "She thinks she is hiding things from me, as well."

"As you are from her. But that's our life, brother." The man unzipped the shaving kit. Needles and vials gleamed within. "The one we have chosen."

17

World Trade Center, New York

April 31st, 8:45 a.m.

Del stood across from the Koenig Sphere and scanned the crowd. The morning had been overcast, but the clouds were burning off, the sky brightening into a glare. She unzipped her black three-quarter-length coat and pushed back her hood. Fished in her pockets for sunglasses. Better. Not much shade here, and bright light bothered her eyes.

The nausea had tapered off, thank goodness.

It hadn't been easy hiding it from her mother, who'd taken to stress-cooking massive breakfasts just when neither Del nor her father could stomach them.

Liberty Park was packed. Sun glinted off the skyscrapers surrounding it, heightening the effect of the vast open space. Once so full of lives so suddenly lost.

And now it was again full of life.

Tourists and locals stood in clumps in the green spaces overlooking the 9/11 memorial, snapping selfies, talking, laughing. Sat on the angular recycled teak benches sipping coffee. Pushed babies in strollers. Life went on, as her dad always said, even when it didn't.

Del felt exposed on her patch of boardwalk between the bike path and the pedestrian walkway, but then she did want to be found. That was the whole point.

She wondered who would arrive first.

If she had to bet on it, she'd go with Angel—the former SEAL had probably never been late for anything in his life. She asked herself again why she thought any of this was a good idea, pondering the idea of regretting things in the future, but then she saw her uncle. Cutting through the crowd as though the people simply weren't there, his eyes on the sky.

She squinted. Was he whistling?

His hands in his pockets, he stopped beneath the Sphere and read the plaque. Then gazed up at the dented and scuffed sculpture. Del wondered what he would make of it—a prayer for peace recovered from the rubble of the Towers and placed on this spot without a single repair. Each ding and scratch in it the result of terrorist actions right here, in her city. She sometimes had the feeling it would happen again, that New York would always be a target.

Johnny stopped whistling and tipped his cap. To the dead, she hoped, versus to the other side.

In any case, he headed straight for her, though she hadn't seen him spot her. He had a way of seeing without looking, a trick she had as well.

"Lovely day for it." He sauntered up to her. Little wrinkles coming out around his blue eyes as he smiled. "Though I'm not sure what 'it' is, if I'm honest."

Behind him, Del spotted Angel. The private detective had been following Johnny everywhere, keeping an eye on the man.

"Thanks for the company," Johnny flicked his chin in Angel's direction. "Making sure I don't get in trouble?"

"Making sure neither of us do."

Johnny nodded, stuck his hands in his pockets.

Del asked, "Did you see my dad again?"

"You already know the answer to that." Johnny began walking. "He doesn't want to see me."

"Why don't you take him to his next doctor's appointment?"

"That was always our mother's job, taking us here and there. Not sure he'd want me along."

"I'm asking you to ask."

"It's going to be like that now?"

They reached the edge of the park where the towering skyscrapers plunged them into shade. Cool here. Del shoved her hands in her pockets. Get this under control, she heard a voice with an Irish accent telling her in her head. *The man's a snake. Don't let him take the lead.* "We found Anila Jalili, the IRGC operative."

"IRGC?"

"Don't play dumb. What's the angle?"

"Trying to be helpful."

"I'm not stupid."

"I know. I'm angling for forgiveness, if you must know."

"She's entering the country at LaGuardia." Suweil had texted her the flight number and confirmed that the woman was on the plane. "Under another name."

"You didn't think I was a liar, did you?"

Of course I do, Del thought, but didn't reply. And a killer. And a thief. And a thug. "We need to get going if we're going to catch her."

"We?"

"You're coming with me."

"Along with your guardian angel?"

They turned into a side street. Dark and cool, about thirty feet wide. Red brick walls ran the length of it, lined with black metal fire doors to residences and the backs of cafés. None open. Two big metal dumpsters about halfway down, one black, one green, and piles of black garbage bags to the left. A man about twenty feet ahead carried a stack of boxes down a set of sunken stairs to a basement.

Johnny, walking at a clip and pulling ahead of Del, passed the man.

Another slim dark-haired man appeared at the other end of the side street. He walked quickly along the middle of the alley, heading in their direction, then stopped just on the other side of the dumpsters. Popped a cigarette in his mouth. Patted his pockets. Shook his head and swore under his breath.

"Hey," he called as Johnny approached, "you got a light?"

Ten feet ahead of Del, Johnny stopped—looked like he spent a long time thinking about it—but then went through his pockets and came up with a lighter. Del held back, but Johnny walked over to the man, clicked the lighter, and held the flame out.

"Thanks, man," the slim guy said. He took a drag and then looked at Johnny closely. "Hey, don't I know you?"

Johnny shook his head and gave the guy a wink. "All us micks look alike."

"I'm sure I've seen you somewhere. You ever go to Porcellino's?"

While he talked, two more men appeared at the other end of the side street and walked purposefully his way. One blond, one with wavy brown locks, both tall and wide, wearing jeans and T-shirts with the sleeves rolled up to reveal thick arms.

The hairs on Del's neck and arms tingled. She balled her fists and scanned the area, made sure Angel, still behind them, saw what was going on. He nodded at her from the shadows fifty feet back.

"You've got the wrong man," Johnny said.

He gave the slim guy a see-you-later bob of his head, then turned to move on.

"Wait, wait," the man said.

The two goons behind him loomed a head taller than the slim one. They blocked Johnny's path.

"Hang on a second. Let me figure this out." Slim man snapped his fingers. "I got it!" He turned to the two big men. "Doesn't this guy look just like the *coglione* who's been dodging Marcelo?"

The men nodded.

Slim man smiled. "I knew it."

"Boys," Johnny said, giving them his best twinkly grin, "it's what I said before. You've got the wrong man."

"I don't think so," the man said.

The three men moved so Johnny was secured within a triangle. One of the big men swung a beefy arm in a sloppy haymaker. Johnny ducked out of the way, only to get a knee to the head from the other. Johnny wobbled but didn't go down. The men backed up a pace, still encircling him.

"She with you?" the slim man asked. "You might want to ask her to leave."

Fifty feet back, Angel had his hand in his pocket, signaling to Del if he should get his weapon out. She shook her head and urged him to stay back. Del stayed silent but edged a few feet closer to her uncle and sunk into a lower stance.

Johnny said, "She is none of your business, lad. Leave her out."

The men closed on Johnny. He gamely put up his fists.

"Do you have it or don't you?" the slim man asked.

"I don't have the foggiest idea what you're on about," Johnny said.

The slim man shrugged. One of them grabbed Johnny by the shirt collar and thumped him in the stomach with a meaty fist. Her uncle collapsed to his knees and let out a gasp. The other man raised his fist above Johnny's head, but Del darted in, sent a roundhouse into his solar plexus. He stumbled back in surprise.

"Johnny, who are these guys?" Del said.

"Behind you!" called Angel.

Del turned as the slim man came for her. She aimed a low uppercut at his gut, but missed as she was caught in the side of her right thigh by a sharp kick. It knocked her sideways, but she kept her footing and used the momentum to spin into a low sideswipe that knocked the slim man's feet out from under him. He hit the pavement, cursing in surprise as he did. The two other men backed up a few paces like they were wondering what to do.

Del swung around, still in balance, and kept her back to her uncle and scanned up and down the alley. Nobody else appearing. Nobody reaching for a weapon. This seemed to be their version of a talk.

There was just enough time for her to exchange another look with Angel before Johnny rose from his knees and the man with wavy hair headed for him. Swearing, Johnny pounced forward with surprising speed and got his arm around the big guy's neck. Johnny tightened the choke hold and whispered in the man's ear.

Del wasn't close enough to eavesdrop.

She kept her eyes on the blond guy and slim man, who had gotten back to his feet. She took steps backward to increase the distance between them and her.

She fell again into her stance as the blond guy ran toward her. He was big, but half-fat and half-muscle, with a wide, stumpy neck and tree-trunk arms. He swung at her with a lunging right. Del ducked under it. Made a darting jab at the man's ribs, which bent him over, then kneed him with a rising blow to the diaphragm. He coughed and stepped back. Again, he looked unsure of what to do.

"Whatever this is, I don't want to fight," Del said, holding her hands up. "Can we talk? What do you want with him?"

Johnny still had the wavy-haired guy in a choke hold. The slim man cursed, then reached into his coat and pulled out a gun and held it leveled at Johnny's head.

"Stop!" Del hollered. She reached into her jean pocket and fished out her badge. From the corner of her eye, she sensed Angel running toward them. "US Marshal Service. Put your weapon down."

The slim man glanced at her but didn't lower his gun. Johnny released his choke hold. The slim man cursed, then took off at a run. After a split-second pause, the two others followed on his heels. Del considered chasing them, but what would she do? She couldn't arrest them by herself. And if she ran off with Angel, her uncle might disappear.

Johnny leaned down to wipe his knees. "Well, thank you very much, Miss US Marshal Service. Now they know I'm with you. You know how much trouble I am in now?"

Del put her badge back in her pocket.

And unloaded a series of expletives her father would have been proud of.

18

Flushing Meadows, New York
April 31st, 9:32 a.m.

Peter Breedlove kept as still as he could in the line, squashed between a Persian couple having a heated argument and a mother traveling with three children. He watched as the mother wrangled the small humans, always smiling, never losing her temper. No matter how loudly they squealed or how many times they ran off. He had no idea how she managed it. He wanted to run off, too.

His future self had instructed him not to fly direct, but to connect through Toronto, Canada. Peter had no idea why, but he trusted himself. The other more annoying thing was that he instructed himself to pack some of the more critical components in a biohazard container, which required it to go through checked luggage and be picked up at a special counter. His research credentials and security clearance gave him the leeway to check items such as these, with the proper paperwork.

And Peter was good at paperwork.

All airports were the same.

Temperature tepid, lighting terrible, people stressed. The air soaked with an almost palpable anxiety, a feeling that they were all, to a person, running short on time.

Peter shifted his weight from leg to leg as he stood, trying to balance the effort each spent supporting him. Checked his watch and examined the line. Twenty-three people ahead, but he guessed only eight people had a genuine reason to be in the line at all. The rest were hangers-on, family and friends who had no business clogging up the works. If they'd move aside—well, in all honesty, it was likely the line wouldn't move any faster.

But at least it would be a little quieter.

He checked his watch again.

Their flight had arrived thirty-two minutes late, which, added to the three minutes they'd lost on their connector, left them with over two thousand seconds to make up in this day. Peter looked down the line again.

Sixteen people now. Another two groups advanced.

Again, he fought the urge to take off. To walk away and never look back, but he needed the container they had checked into special luggage.

Peter checked his watch again. More seconds gone. Samira stood next to him, reading one of the baby books she had acquired since they'd gotten the news. Overnight, she'd become an expert in changing, feeding, sleep habits, first words, and the importance of talking to the bump.

He had tried to get her to stay behind in France, said that she was pregnant now and maybe shouldn't be traveling. She told him not to be ridiculous, that it didn't even show yet, she was just two months. She loved the idea of coming to New York and seeing his old friends.

Not that Peter planned to see any friends.

He didn't really have any.

Samira raised her eyes from the book and smiled at Peter. "I did not know so much happened in the first few weeks. It is quite amazing."

He leaned out past her to examine the line again. Samira kept her eyes on the book but shook her head.

"Next!"

Peter nearly ran to the desk. A woman with an ash-blond bun smiled with pearly pink lips. The smile looked real enough. Was she immune to the bad lights, cranky people, and everything being late? Maybe she was new.

"I have a package to pick up." He thrust the requisite paperwork forward.

"One sec." She frowned, then hopped down from her raised stool and headed to a back room. Peter craned his neck, but couldn't see past the doorway. Moved to his right and spotted her, conferring with a coworker.

She returned. Smiled awkwardly. "I'm *so* sorry. I can't authorize this for release. You didn't specify what the item in question actually is. Can you specify please?" She pointed a pudgy finger tipped in pink polish at the empty box on the form.

"I'm not required to." He pointed at a different box. "See? Right here."

"I'm going to have to call in a manager. Sit tight, I'll be right back."

***

A woman with long red hair watched Peter and Samira from the end of the line.

"Excuse me," said a handsome young man. "Are you in line?"

She pulled her hair back to reveal her scarred face. His expression changed, and he stepped back a pace. "Ah, so you are in line?"

Up ahead, Peter finally retrieved his package, and the couple moved off.

"No, I'm not," the woman replied, and turned to follow from a discrete distance.

***

Peter loped past the carousels, weaving around slow-moving puddles of tourists and fast-marching businesspeople on cell phones, zigzagging in what he calculated was the most direct route to the taxi stand. He had studied the airport layout before arriving, but then luggage was literally next to the taxi stand at LGA.

Samira hustled behind him, pushing the cart. Peter's hands were full, the biohazard package under one arm, his phone in his right hand. It had taken more precious seconds to clear the package at customs.

A series of dings from his phone—texts coming in one after the other.

Peter's eyes darted from his phone to the people and things around him, back and forth.

> Delta Devlin is in New York. With her uncle.
> You need to stay away from them.

This text followed by another, a long bubble that ran off his phone's screen.

> You can still make it. Get to the stores before
> they close. You need all of this today.

A list of technical equipment.

Peter checked his watch. It would be tight.

As he waited in the taxi line, he checked the account, glancing over his shoulder to keep an eye on Samira. He put in his account number and password—and there it was. With six zeros. He refreshed the screen to make sure it was *really* there.

Not a glitch. Not a joke.

He'd won, and not on a plain old lottery.

The thirty-six soccer teams his future self had predicted to win, he also told himself to place a bet. An online sports combo bet. He'd picked the winning teams that day in just about all the soccer games in the professional leagues around Europe, many of them underdogs. The bet earned him four million Euros, all placed into an offshore account.

Samira puffed behind him, shoving the luggage cart. "In some countries, it would be considered a little rude to make a pregnant woman push this luggage."

"I have a few things to do, work things. I'll meet you back at the apartment. You can use Uber to get there—charge it to my account. You have the address and codes?"

"I am coming with you." Samira moved ahead of him as the next taxi pulled up.

She began unloading the luggage while he was staring at his phone screen again, until he realized he was doing it again and stopped her. Peter told her to go sit down and opened the car door for her. One thing he had to admit, the woman didn't seem to have a trace of morning sickness or other effects of early pregnancy.

But he couldn't have her with him now.

He had to get the things on his list—the ones his future self told him he needed—and he had to get them today. Before the stores closed. Alone. He checked his watch again, then gave the driver the first address on his list. After a second, he also gave the driver ten hundred-dollar bills.

"A down payment. We'll be making a few stops," Peter said. The driver smiled.

The instant the money left his hand, Peter felt better. Lighter. So. He'd get rid of it all, as quickly as he could. He checked his list again. It was a good start.

He got in the taxi. As it pulled away from the curb, his phone buzzed again. It confirmed the worst of his fears. He had downloaded the SETI data for the unknown signals from BLC1 and BLC3 and tried to decrypt them or extract some useful data. If the deep space signal of BLC2 was encrypted data coming from him, what if the other anomalous signals were going to other people?

He held his phone in one shaking hand and reread the new text from his future self:

> We're not the only ones who can send
> messages back in time. There is another team.
> And they are closing in. You need to hurry.

19

Manhattan, New York

April 31st, 10:02 a.m.

Del sent Angel ahead on his matte-black wasp of a Ducati, while she and Johnny followed in the bullet-gray Honda she'd borrowed from Charlie, Angel's husband. She handed Johnny the car's first aid kit from the glove box, so he could patch himself up while she drove. Her leg ached from where she was hit, but she'd rest this evening and ignore the pain till then.

They sped along the highway.

Johnny had found a large Band-Aid and slapped it over a gash on his head, then pulled his cap down over it. Grinned. "Good as new. Tell me again why I'm coming with you?"

Del pulled into the fast lane. Glanced at him. "Who were they?"

"No idea."

"Stop with the lies."

"I owe a few people some money. My business has had some issues lately."

"What kind of issues?"

"What other kinds are there. Money."

"People know you are here? Who did you tell?"

"Word must have gotten out."

"I need names."

Johnny gave her a look, but then began rattling off a series of Irish surnames and nicknames, and telling her stories about when he had met them in the old country. It was an obvious ploy, and she had explicitly told him not to tell anyone he was in the country when she agreed to help him cross customs without raising flags.

She regretted it now, but she needed his help.

As long as they were just regular Irish thugs, she could handle that. She had been forced to reveal she was a US Marshal, however, and she hadn't wanted to pull that card. Too many questions might be raised by people unconnected, and she wasn't quite doing this in an official capacity.

Del had preprogrammed the fastest route to LaGuardia into the GPS and gone through everything with Angel before they left the city. As they neared the airport, she went through the plan again with Johnny.

"Angel will be at the target's gate. You and I watch the exits. Everything relays through me. My contact says the IRGC woman doesn't have any checked baggage, so it's likely she'll leave the terminal soon after arrival. Things could move quickly, so we need to be good to go."

She pulled up to an emergency vehicle spot near the entrance to the terminal and parked. She pulled her dad's NYPD card from a pocket and stuck it in the windshield.

"That's a nice perk, that," Johnny said as they left the car.

"Can we focus, please?"

Del thought about leaving him in the car, but she couldn't trust him alone, and another pair of eyes on the target could only help—if she could believe what he told her. She'd told herself what she'd just told him: that he owed her, and he better start acting like it.

But it seemed her uncle owed a lot of people.

They hustled into position, Johnny limping as he walked. Del felt a twinge—his staggering gait reminded her of her dad.

Suweil hadn't been able to confirm a rental car reservation under the target's assumed name, so Jalili was probably planning on taking a taxi in, or someone was picking her up. Johnny and Del would patrol toward the exits and keep near their car if they needed to follow. There was always a chance the target would rent a car on the spot or have a reservation under another name.

Del scanned the faces coming through the security checkpoint, looked for anyone with scar tissue that would look cool in her vision. There was no telling if this woman, who had almost no presence on any database, would choose to disguise herself. Del tried to focus a few seconds on each person. The place was packed. Families bumping along with multiple carts, people talking and texting as they hurried to their gates, everybody rushing somewhere.

Minutes passed. More minutes than Del had anticipated. Had something gone wrong?

She was just about to text Suweil when Angel's voice came over her earpiece.

"Target in view," he said. "She's at the head of the line, on the way out."

Del turned toward security and almost collided with a woman pushing a baggage cart. A flight must have just come in, as a flood of people spilled through the exit and fanned out.

Angel came on again. "Do you see her?" he said. "She's on your side. Long red hair, gray clothes."

"Right there," Johnny said.

Del paused where she was. She was close to the taxi stand, but couldn't see many faces, as most people were looking toward the road. She gave a long, slow look around the milling throng in the baggage area. And there she was—the woman with the dead zone of scar tissue on the left side of her face. Moving quickly. "Target confirmed—she's heading for the taxi stand."

Del spun on her heel and went after the woman.

Chaos in the lineup, people jostling and calling out and packing taxis full of luggage. Del kept her eyes on the woman, who skipped the line and jumped into a car just pulling up, cutting people off in line. Curses followed the car as it eased away into bumper-to-bumper traffic exiting the terminal.

Del swore under her breath, and into her wrist mic, "I'm getting back to the car."

By the time she ran the hundred feet down the road from the taxi stand to where she had left the Honda, Johnny had reached it and opened the drivers' side door.

"My turn. I can stick with the car if anything happens. Never know what this woman might do, yeah? And you're a good driver, love"—he smiled his twinkly grin—"but I bet I'm better."

It wasn't a bad thought. She might need to jump in and out of the car. That Irish voice in the back of her head kept telling her not to trust Johnny. When was she going to start to listen? Part of her was waiting to catch him out.

The slow traffic worked to their advantage. They pulled out maybe two hundred feet behind the apple-green Jetta boro taxi that Jalili had taken, not one of the iconic yellow medallion taxicabs. Easy to spot. It swerved into the left lane and forged ahead as it hit the highway.

Johnny shot into the left lane and then back to the right, pulling ahead. Not exactly covert driving, if the woman was watching for anyone following—which she probably was. Del had to assume their cover might be broken.

The Jetta was still in sight. Ten cars ahead, then six.

Johnny fought it out with a Hummer that tried to lean into their lane, won, and pulled around closer to the Jetta. Del eased him back, told him to keep a little more distance. They passed Calvary Cemetery. The expressway looked clear across Long Island, cars and semis roaring along under the white sky.

Two cars behind the Jetta, they pulled onto the exit for the Queensboro Bridge.

***

The Jetta pulled up just before the corner of First Avenue and E. Eighty-First Street, and stopped. The woman didn't get out. The Jetta sat there. Johnny drove past and pulled the Honda across the street in front of a Morton Williams grocery store while Del kept her eyes on the other car behind them.

Why wasn't the woman getting out of the cab? Had she spotted them?

She shouldn't have let Johnny drive. He might be trying to blow their cover for some reason.

But the reason the woman was waiting walked almost right past Del on her side of the street. A wiry figure with sandy hair. Behind his glasses, the man's eyes flicked from one spot to another. There was no mistaking who that was.

And there were no coincidences.

Her mind raced.

What was Peter Breedlove doing here?

"You know that fella?" Johnny asked.

She must have been staring a little too hard. "A scientist. Interviewed him once. In Switzerland."

"Seems our target is tracking your man."

The way Johnny said it, he didn't seem surprised, but then he said everything with a grin and a smile as if it all was a joke.

***

Peter waited for the light, then put his head down and walked across the street and into the York Scientific Technology supply store.

Del scribbled the address down on her pad. 1562 First Avenue.

They waited about ten minutes for Peter to reappear with a package under his arm. Across the street and another half block down, in front of the blue awning of the Living Room hair salon, the back-passenger door of a champagne SUV opened.

"Angel," she said into her wrist mic, "you see that off-white SUV up on the right side? In front of the hair salon? Follow them. I'm going to have a closer look where we stopped. Our target seems to be following someone I know."

"Got it."

Del waited for the SUV to take off, and watched the boro taxi Jetta pull out to follow, before she opened the car door and slipped out.

"I'm on it," Angel said in her earpiece.

The Ducati sped past her and pulled into the traffic.

***

The shop was clean and spare and smelled of antiseptic cleaner. Behind a glass counter, aluminum racks stretched from the floor to the ceiling, packed and stacked with packets, bags, and boxes in all sizes.

"US Marshal." Del held up her badge. "The man who was just here. Tall, skinny?"

The man behind the counter nodded.

"I'll need to know everything about what he bought."

The man crossed his arms. "Don't you need a warrant for this kind of thing?"

"Depends on what I think you might be doing."

"Me?" His arms unfolded.

"You really want to do this?"

The man relented after she threatened to call in the NYPD to back her up, explained the man was suspected in a terrorist plot. That had the effect of loosening just about any New Yorker's reticence. Peter had come in to buy a box of neodymium magnets. She asked the man to print out a copy of the receipt. He fiddled with the machine, and eventually handed it to her. She thanked him and left.

"Where to now?" Johnny asked as she got in the car.

She asked Angel, who responded with the coordinates.

***

Angel followed Peter to eleven locations. Del kept track on a piece of paper and sketched his route. He started on the Upper East Side, did a stop at the medical equipment office of Mount Sinai, then hooked around the top of Central Park and back down the west side to meet Eighth Avenue to Aura Industries and ARES Scientific. The cab ducked into side streets and avoided the worst of the crosstown jams.

Well planned.

The shopkeepers in each place put up varying degrees of resistance to her requests, but eventually she had receipts, descriptions, and product numbers from each store. Peter used a different credit or debit card for each transaction, but they were all under his real name.

It didn't add up.

He wasn't being careful. Maybe he didn't need to be. Maybe he was here on a regular business trip. He was a world-renowned scientist, after all.

By the time Peter circled back around from Lower Manhattan, Del was already an hour behind them as she tried to duck into each of the locations and get a list of what he ordered.

She'd have to get Suweil to check these out. She read each product description closely as Johnny drove, but she couldn't see how the items fit together. On second thought, did they? Or did she just want them to? Maybe she was just looking for a pattern where there wasn't one—like seeing a face in a cloud.

Del rejoined Angel as Peter's SUV drove up Sixth Avenue to the intersection at Fifty-Ninth Street, where the trees of Central Park blocked ways north. They turned right and stopped just behind Peter's SUV in front of the Plaza Hotel. Peter, the driver, and a bellboy were already unloading boxes onto one of the hotel's brass-fitted luggage carts.

Del looked back along Fifty-Ninth Street toward the setting sun that was just going down.

The Jetta was a hundred feet behind them, in front of the Park Lane Hotel.

Johnny had positioned them right between their target and Peter. No way they hadn't been spotted by now. Del expected the Jetta to speed off, but the IRGC woman got out. Didn't look at Del but walked straight toward her.

Del looked back to the Plaza's entrance.

Peter paid his cabbie with a fat wad of cash, then handed the bellboy some money. Impossible to say how much, but the bellboy smiled, turned, and carefully wheeled the cart into the hotel. Peter looked around, eyes darting. He followed the bellboy in.

"Target is back on the move," Angel said in her earpiece.

Del looked back, and the Jetta was back on the move.

Had the woman gotten out just to make sure Del saw her? Or to get a better look?

***

After a half-hour slow chase down Fifth Avenue and crossing at Twelfth Street, the IRGC woman finally gave up her taxi and got out on foot heading toward Mott Street. Dusk started to fall, the sky clouding over again, making it seem later than it really was.

The narrow streets ahead were jammed with traffic.

Turning into the street beyond the woman walking down from Grand Street, Del kept her eyes peeled for signs that the target might be doubling back—then caught a glimpse of her, weaving between trucks stopped in the road.

Del got out and began chasing on foot.

The street colors popped around her, red and green and white, four-story brick buildings zippered all the way up with black-iron fire escapes. Chinese lettering along the sides of buildings, storefronts crammed with produce and noodles and glazed meat. Shops spilled onto the sidewalks, impromptu tables made from stacked milk crates selling durians and bok choy and lychees and other things Del couldn't name, their odors combining to a funky vegetable stew that swam through the heavy air.

The target's conservative gray outfit made her stand out here.

People everywhere, talking loudly, walking in every direction, shopping, eating, laughing, carrying babies strapped to their backs. No one running. No signs of disturbance in the crowds.

Which way had she gone?

"Angel—any sign?"

A beat, then the reply in her earpiece: "Negative."

An elderly lady nearly knocked Del over as she shuffled straight ahead, pulling a wire shopping basket. Del stepped aside. Just out of the way of the steady stream of foot traffic. Looked left. Nothing. Right. Nothing. Then—

A clang, loud enough for Del to hear over the clamor. She looked up.

Fire escape. Half a block down. Hanging from the side of a five-story walk-up, a knife-thin space between it and the next, a restaurant on the main floor bridging the gap so its roof formed something of a runway between them. The IRGC woman clambered up the ladder she'd just pulled down.

Del took off after her. "Got her." She gave Angel the location as she ran.

"Roger," his voice crackled in her ear.

Squeezed through a pack of teenagers drinking bubble tea, twisted past a clump of tourists posing for a group selfie, and skirted a dolly stacked with cardboard boxes just outside the restaurant's door. Something slick and alive wriggled in an open Styrofoam box on the top of the pile. Del's nausea kicked back in for just a second, but she held her eyes on the target and kept going.

A tinny double honk sounded from across the street, the driver of a motorbike signaling as he sped through the turn. Angel. Heading left. Right to where the target should end up.

Del dashed across the street.

Up the fire escape, one story, and jumped onto the tar-paper roof of the restaurant. The space between buildings tight, about ten feet wide, walls rising on either side above her, the dark clouds sinking, closing in on her. She shook her head. A gray shimmer in the distance. Anila Jalili, the IRGC woman. Just at the other end of the strip of roof. Del started toward her, the roof giving slightly as she walked. She approached at a gentle pace this time—didn't want to spook the target again.

The woman spun, saw Del, and started toward her.

But then turned away again.

And jumped.

"Holy hell," Johnny shouted, behind Del. He must have climbed up right after her.

Was the IRGC woman running from her? Or from Johnny?

Del sprinted to the edge of the roof, checked to make sure all was clear below, swung herself over, and dropped about ten feet and skidded onto the wet pavement.

Mulberry Street.

More sedate but still busy, the signs here black and brown and white, little lights strung up through the trees and along the outskirts of patios. Crowded, but the people moved slowly, strolling along or sipping wine at outdoor tables, enjoying the warm evening. Cheese and pasta and cannoli stands lined up along the sidewalks. Open trucks unloading even at this time, men standing around smoking.

The IRGC woman snaked through, moving quickly. One of the trucks had blocked the one-way traffic, so Del ran down the street, gaining on the woman. A scaffold to the right. Jalili dipped under it—and a metallic clatter bounded off the walls of the narrow street.

Del slowed. Spotted a gray flash, slipping past the temporary plywood wall surrounding a vacant lot.

Del followed.

She found the spot where the woman had vanished—a space where damp had caused the plywood to sag apart. Slid through. The lot behind was nothing but dirt and discarded bottles and clumps of weeds. Puddles where diggers had done their work, a pile of fresh earth at the other end bordered by a chain-link fence topped with barbed wire.

The woman was at the other end of the yard and looked like she was going to go through a gap fence.

Del called out, "I just want to speak. I know you saw me following you. Anila, right? Your name?"

The woman stopped, turned to Del. She pulled her hair back. The left side of her face scarred and misshapen. She must have been a beautiful woman before whatever accident had befallen her. Maybe it was no accident.

"You're alone?" she said, her accent heavy and Middle Eastern to Del's ear.

"I have friends close by," Del replied. "But I'll keep them back." She raised her wrist and said, "Angel, I'm in the empty lot bordered by the plywood. Don't come in, and keep Johnny out." She said it loud enough that Anila could hear her.

It didn't look like the woman was armed, but she had on a coat that could be concealing a weapon.

"Why are you following Dr. Breedlove?" Del asked, her hands out and palms out. She advanced ten feet toward the woman.

"I could ask you the same."

"Because it's my job."

"As it is mine."

"You must have seen me today," Del said. "Why didn't you try to evade me?"

"Because I needed to speak with you. I've been following you, Deputy Marshal Devlin. We met in Singapore, if you remember. I gave you the good luck satchel. It contained a tracking device, I apologize to say."

"Why?"

"Because you are being targeted," Anila replied. She began walking toward Del. "I have something I need to give you."

The fence behind the woman shook. Someone pushed through the gap in the chain link. A man. Anila had her back to the fence and didn't notice. She was reaching into her jacket. At first, Del thought it was Angel. The man stood up and ran at Anila as the woman pulled something from her coat.

But it wasn't Angel.

20

Manhattan, New York
April 31st, 10:53 a.m.

Del said, "Jacques?"

He held a metal bar in his right hand and walked steadily toward Anila. "Stay where you are, Deputy Marshal Devlin." He didn't take his eyes off Jalili while he said this and took measured steps toward her. "Colonel Anila Jalili, please do not move."

"Jacques, what are you doing here?" Del didn't even know he was in New York. Had he been following her? And how did he know this woman?

He advanced another five steps toward Anila, who spun around. She seemed to recognize Jacques. "Stay back," she said, with one hand still in her coat. She pulled out a metallic object. "Devlin, I need—"

Jacques jumped forward and swung the metal bar, caught her on the back side of her head as she turned to Del. Jalili crumpled like a dropped marionette.

"What are you doing?" Del ran forward, arms and hands out to cover the woman as Jacques hovered over her, still holding the metal bar.

He dropped it.

Del fell to her knees in the mud. Anila lay on the ground, breathing—but slow, shallow gulps. She checked the woman's pulse. Still alive. Del checked the woman's hand. It wasn't a weapon. It was a rectangular metal box.

"Delta, you okay?" called out a voice behind them. It was Angel, squeezing through the plywood gap.

Del said to Jacques, "What did you do that for?"

"I thought she was going to shoot you."

Del pulled her phone from her pocket. When she was a cop, she would've called dispatch. But now? Here? With this mysterious woman bleeding and Jacques here out of the blue? Not to mention Johnny.

She dialed 911.

Jacques grabbed the phone from her hand, ended the call.

"She's badly injured," Del said. "You want this to be a homicide, you idiot?" She held her hand out. Jacques gave her back her phone. "Explain what you're doing here? How did you find me?"

"I was following Dr. Breedlove," Jacques replied. "And found her following him, and then you following the both of them."

"You're the one who took me to meet Breedlove just a week ago. You going to tell me this is all a coincidence?"

"You were the one following him," Jacques said. "Exactly what coincidence do you mean? You told me not to come to New York, but this was because you didn't want me here with your family. I am here for work, not for you."

"I can see that." Del didn't mean that to sound sarcastic, but it did.

"I was trying to protect you."

"I can take care of myself."

Before she could dial 911 again, the phone beeped. 911 had called her back. She answered all the questions, gave the coordinates, explained there'd been an accident and they needed an ambulance immediately.

She stood to give Angel space to attend to Anila. The man was a former SEAL and knew a thing or two about stabilizing someone in the field. Johnny was on his knees next to the woman as well, taking off her coat to make a pillow to prop up her head.

As she spoke to 911, Del paced around the vacant lot.

Jacques remained silent and stood back a few paces. He waited for Del to get off the phone. Angel put Anila in the recovery position.

Johnny took the metal box from her hand, then worked to get her coat free, and as he did, he pulled a thick stack of papers from inside her jacket before he rolled it into a pillow.

Del hung up after the 911 call and walked over to Johnny. "Give me that."

"Delta," said Jacques, pointing at Johnny, "is this your father?"

A siren echoed between the buildings. In the empty lot, lights rebounded red and blue from wall to wall up and down the street.

"That's not an ambulance," said Johnny. "It's the cops." He handed the papers and metal box to Del. "Sorry, love."

He bolted before she could get a hand on him, ran past Jacques to the hole in the chain-link by the back. Angel was attending to Anila, and glanced up at Del. She shook her head, let him go. This wasn't a time for her to be running from a crime scene.

Del rifled through the papers Johnny had handed her. They looked like technical schematics. She folded them back up and slipped them into the inside pocket of her own jacket and put the metal box in there, too.

Jacques watched her pocketing it.

"She wanted to give me something, this might be it," Del said, keeping a steady gaze on him. "Before the police get here, explain to me exactly why you are here."

"I have been following Dr. Breedlove, as I explained."

"And what made you follow him all the way to New York?"

"He has been writing messages to you, Delta. Letters. For weeks."

"Excuse me?" More flashing lights against the brick walls over the fence. Del yelled out, "Officers, this way. We're over here. Get an EMT as fast as you can." She returned her eyes to Jacques. "Did you just say he's been writing me letters? Like what, love letters?"

"In France. He was dropping letters at a clockmaker into what he called a time capsule. Letters that were not to be delivered for another decade."

The words coming from Jacques's mouth made no sense to Del.

Two NYPD forced their way through the plywood gap fifty feet behind Jacques. Del held her hands up and identified herself. Jacques held his hands up as well. The officers came through on their knees and raised their weapons as soon as they saw the woman lying bleeding on the ground. Angel raised his hands as well.

Del leaned in to Jacques and said, "Did you say *time* capsule?"

"Breedlove seems to believe he is communicating with his future self." Jacques began speaking quickly. "I read his letters. He is quite convinced. And he thinks he is talking to you—I mean *you* in the future. But you only met him last week. I think he is insane. I think he may be the one stealing the lab equipment. I followed him, and what do I see? You and this other man already tailing him. I did not know what was happening. And when this woman looked to be pulling a gun on you, I disabled her."

"I'm an officer," said Del to the NYPD advancing toward them. "And my father is Captain Sean Devlin of the first precinct."

They didn't lower their weapons, but their stances softened.

"I work for Interpol. Him, too." Gestured at Jacques with a tilt of her head, her hands still up. "I'm a Deputy US Marshal."

The officers looked at each other. Weapons down. "We're going to need to see some ID."

21

Brooklyn, New York

April 31st, 9:05 p.m.

A drizzly night settled over the city as Del hurried to her parents' place. A clammy breeze blew in from the East River, and she was glad, once again, that she'd dressed for any weather. More rain forecast overnight. A major storm. She strode up the walkway to the house.

Angel and Jacques had both been taken in for questioning at One PP. Del said that Angel, a private detective, had been assisting her with an investigation in her capacity as a US Marshal. She wasn't at liberty to discuss the case, she said. They questioned him but let him go after an hour as he hadn't done anything wrong.

The bigger problem was Jacques. He had assaulted the woman, Anila, and she didn't have a weapon. He didn't have any jurisdiction here and hadn't been invited in any official capacity. They weren't charging him with anything yet, but then he also wasn't talking.

The official line was that Del and Angel had no idea who the woman was, but they also didn't have a good reason for why Jacques had attacked her. Jacques maintained that he wrongly thought she had a weapon, but a policeman attacking a civilian without reason was liable to start a riot these days. They held him, still trying to figure out what to do.

Her mind was swimming as she tried to wrap her head around what Jacques had told her just before the police arrived. That Peter Breedlove thought he was sending messages back in time to himself.

It made a certain sense, after all the talk about time travel Peter had brought up the few times they chatted, but he seemed to have wrapped Del into some part of his psychosis. Jacques said that Peter thought he was getting messages from Del in the future. And she had only just met the guy a week ago. How was it possible he had worked her into some fantasy already?

Another possibility nagged at her.

Was Jacques telling the truth? Why hadn't he told her he was here? Why had he attacked the woman? But with him in a holding cell, she didn't have the opportunity to talk to him more, and she needed to avoid revealing anything about her uncle to the police.

Del's leg ached in the right side of her knee, where she had been caught by that kick. Was it only earlier today? Seemed like much longer ago. The light was on over the front door, but when she turned the key and stepped inside, the hallway was dark.

She needed to sit down and think. Ease off the pressure a bit.

"Hello?" she called.

No laughter from the living room, no lights on in the kitchen. Just about 8:00 p.m., when her parents would usually be watching TV or chatting after dinner. Where were they? She closed and locked the front door, hung up her coat, took off her shoes. Padded down the hallway, flicking lights on as she went.

A note on the kitchen island in her mother's looping handwriting. *At hospital—your dad is not feeling well. Don't worry! Dinner in the fridge.*

Don't worry.

Right.

Del pulled her phone from her pocket and dialed, her heart pounding. Paced around the kitchen while the phone on the other end rang and rang. Finally, her mother picked up.

"Hi, honey."

"Mom, what's happening?"

"Didn't I tell you not to worry?"

"I'm coming down there."

"It'll only upset him, make him think he's worse off than he is. The doctors say he's okay."

"But you're still there."

"He's sleeping now. Delta. You cannot fix everything. Have something to eat, maybe take a bath. There's some nice bubbles in the upstairs bathroom."

"Mom. I'm not going to sit around relaxing in a tub when dad's in the—"

"Please, dear. I know we're all worried about him, but let's take it one step at a time. There is no danger right now. I bet we'll be home before you know it."

"If you're sure."

"It'll be better for him. Keep him calm. Okay?"

"Call me if anything—"

"Goodnight, then. Try to get some rest. Love you."

"Love you, too."

***

Del hung up the phone. Let out a long breath. She checked the time—if she wasn't going to the hospital, she still had to get moving.

Her boss, Marshal Justice, had requested a meeting at the UN building on the Upper East Side at 9:00 p.m. The place still gave her the creeps after her father had been shot there two years before, but she couldn't request to meet the Marshal in a coffee shop. Not after two agents working for Interpol, under his supervision, had been involved in an assault on an officer of the Iranian Revolutionary Guard.

She headed upstairs.

Went straight to her old desk and opened her laptop. From her inside jacket pocket, she pulled the stack of papers Johnny had taken from the Iranian woman Jalili's coat. The small metal box that the woman had pulled out, that Jacques had thought might be a weapon, was nothing more than a solid-state disk drive, similar to the one Del used for backup on her home laptop.

The papers were fresh, like they just been printed out. Maybe twenty pages in all. She scanned through them quickly to get an idea of what she was looking at. They seemed to be mostly case notes, times and dates and places, along with technical schematics. She had been following Peter Breedlove. Perhaps these were related to the equipment he was collecting? If so, how had the woman printed these out so quickly?

One thing was certain, the Iranian woman had wanted to talk to Delta.

She had called Del out by name. And the woman had been following Del, that's what Johnny said, and he wasn't wrong. Del remembered running into her in Singapore, so Johnny wasn't lying, but then he mixed truth and lies to get what he wanted.

And he was the one that handed the papers to Del.

Were they even from the Iranian woman? Or was Johnny up to something? He was the one that put her on to this woman, he had been tracking her as well. Maybe he was trying to pin something on her.

More certain was the disk drive.

Del had seen the Jalili woman pull that from her coat. She had kept her eyes on it the whole time. Whatever was on there, Del was certain it came from the Iranian woman and was what she wanted Del to see.

The disk drive looked like any other. Black and oblong and shiny.

She found a USB cable and plugged it into her laptop. The device's light blinked on, but then she opened the folders contained on the drive, everything was encrypted and locked. Del texted Suweil.

Have something I need you to try to open.
My eyes only.

She would send it in a FedEx envelope to the Lyon office in the morning.

She started with what she had: Anila Jalili.

Her searches came up with unrelated people on social media. Not surprising. Not like a spy working for Iran would be loading up Instagram posts.

Del had heard of the Iranian Revolutionary Guard, the IRGC, and done some research the night before. The term was interchangeable with "Islamic Revolutionary Guard Corps," and was a branch of the Persian Iranian Armed Forces. Where the army defended the borders and maintained internal order, the IRGC was tasked with defending the country's Islamic republic political system—the critical element being preventing foreign interference. At least 250,000 military personnel worked for the Revolutionary Guard, in everything from cyber to navel to intelligence.

Her online searches turned up stories that had come out as recently as earlier that day. Fox News asked and answered: "Is America Funding Terrorists in Iran? Governor Guthrie Says Yes." CNN said: "Black Market Arms: Where They End Up May Surprise You."

Del scanned the articles for mentions of the Revolutionary Guards while leafing through the printed stack from Jalili. She stopped at a page in the middle.

It was a scan of handwritten notes, and referred to a "cell of Muslim extremists, known for terrorist actions." It said the group was involved in a psyops campaign, and that the group had been seeking out and manipulating specific individual targets. Psychologically unstable targets who could be "activated" using their own "psychological weaknesses."

Peter Breedlove's name was written at the bottom of the sheet and circled.

Del shuffled through the rest of the pages, her eyes stopping on the terms "psyops" and "clandestine cell" and "activated targets." The conversation she'd had with Jacques in the vacant lot popped into her head—he had said that Peter believed he could communicate with his future self.

And that Peter also believed Del was in touch with him from the future.

At the time, it had seemed pure nonsense, and she hadn't been able to question Jacques about it as the NYPD had shown up, guns out. They had to take him in for further questioning, and Del hadn't been in a frame of mind to put her own neck out on the line for him—not after he had shown up out of the blue and assaulted that woman. Not just that, but part of her wanted him to be away from her, if she was really being honest with herself.

She sat back.

Hadn't Dr. Aringa mentioned the feud between himself and Peter? She pulled her notebook out, flipping back to her notes from the interview. Ah, here. Dr. Aringa had initially said the feud was professional, but later told her that Peter's behavior had driven him to leave CERN. She should have pushed harder for clarification on that. What exactly had Peter done or said to make Dr. Aringa feel he had to leave?

Did Peter's actions at CERN have anything to do with the communications he was having with his "future self"? And where had those ideas come from in the first place? He was a brilliant physicist. Could he really believe he was in touch with some version of himself in the future?

He wasn't entirely stable, that much Del had been able to sense from her short encounter with the man.

Del continued through the papers. The next page detailed a long list of European football games, dozens of them, with lines and circles going from one to the next. At the bottom was a scan of a betting website connected to a combination win of millions of dollars with Peter Breedlove's name next to it.

From a zippered side pocket on her pants, Del pulled the receipts and product descriptions from Peter's shopping spree. Went through all eleven, entered the descriptions into her browser for powerful magnets and exotic flat-coiled wires and computer processing units—some of the items seemed to match what was on the technical schematics on the papers from the Jalili woman. The total for the purchases ran into the hundreds of thousands of dollars.

The list of items partially matched descriptions of equipment listed on the Iranian's papers. Some, but not all. Del couldn't email the contents of the disk drive to Suweil, but she could at get him to look at what was on these papers. She took pictures with her phone of the papers and sent the schematics and lists of equipment to Suweil. Asked him to look into, in detail, the items that Peter had not yet collected.

Her phone pinged with an incoming text.

Angel, letting her know Johnny hadn't reappeared yet.

What was he up to? Did he have her running a goose chase?

She let out a long breath and checked the time on her laptop—she had to get going. She was still covered in mud from the altercation in the vacant lot. She couldn't show up at the UN building like this.

Del went into the house's single bathroom, the cabinet stuffed with her father's medications, the shelves lined with her mother's makeup and perfume and—bubble bath. Del sighed. No time. Closed the door and turned on the water in the sink, scrubbing her hands and face. Used her mother's apricot peach scrub, then splashed water on her face until it ran clear. Redid her ponytail, smoothed down her hair. It'd have to be good enough.

One thing left to do before she left.

She went back to her old room, squeezed herself past her mother's canvases, then shoved them over as gently as she could. Reached into the closet and up to the top shelf. Fumbled around, pulling down shoeboxes and photo albums. Then felt it, right at the back. Still there. The slightly bumpy surface of the mosaic box she'd made in high school. She wrangled it down, shuffled back to the desk, and set it on the shiny surface.

The box was big enough to hold a stack of records, wide and flat, and covered with broken pottery she'd collected from other students' failed experiments. The glazes ranged from ice-blue to eggplant, some of them glittering with metallic flakes. She ran her hand over it. It was still pretty. Maybe too pretty to be hidden. But she hadn't just taken pottery classes. She'd also taken shop.

Under the shiny skin was a steel strongbox she'd built herself. She still remembered the combination to the store-bought lock—she was no locksmith. Her birthday, together with Mickey's. The lock sprung open.

Birthday cards, report cards, ticket stubs, postcards from friends who'd traveled, photo strips of her and Missy. She tore them all out and pressed down. A magnetic click and the false bottom popped up. The hidden compartment was full of letters. Love letters. From Mickey. She picked one up, scanned it. Shook her head and put it back.

She picked up the whole stack of letters. Why was she keeping them? She tossed them into the recycling bin near the printer, something she should have done a long time ago. There. All kinds of room now.

Del reached for the stack of Jalili's papers, pulling out those with technical schematics. She needed to show these to an expert. Maybe Suweil? The rest went in the box.

Was the Revolutionary Guard controlling a Muslim terrorist group?

Possible, but that didn't make sense. The Persians didn't play well with the Arabs, not in general. Not the Iranians with the Saudis, but then Del didn't know much about the politics in the Middle East. She was out of her element.

One thing was certain—Peter Breedlove was at the center of all this somehow.

She texted Angel: *Is target still at Plaza?*

If what she'd just read was true, the letter, the psyops unit, the receipts for the items Peter had bought, the diagram of whatever it was, all of them could all be tied to what he was doing in New York. He seemed to be building something.

And if the papers she had just read through were real, then why would Jalili have chosen Del as the person to transmit this information? There were literally hundreds of ways the spy could have gotten in touch with someone in the American government.

***

Del opened the door to the conference room on the twentieth floor of the UN Building.

"Deputy Marshal Devlin." Boston Justice turned as she closed the door behind herself. All the lights on in the room. And all thirty chairs empty. "Sorry for dragging you in at night, but I just flew in from Washington. I know you are here for your family, and I heard your father has been taken to the hospital?"

"He's doing well, sir."

"I'll keep this short. As you know, Inspector Galloul is being detained. I heard you were with him."

Del nodded. Boston waved her over to a chair but remained standing. Her phone pinged in her hand. Angel texted back: *No movement on Plaza target.*

"Anything I should be aware of?" Boston indicated her phone.

"Just my family."

"Sit down, Deputy Marshal." No hint of a smile on his face, none of the regular-joe conviviality of their meetings in Lyon.

She sat.

"One PP didn't want to hold you, as you're a US Marshal and the one that called this in. But they do want to talk to you at another time, so be advised, and they will be there with Internal Affairs since your father is NYPD."

"Understood. I will be cooperating completely."

She was already lying, having not reported the papers from an Iranian spy. But she needed to find her uncle first.

Boston continued, "Inspector Galloul is being treated with the respect he is due. However, he did not inform the authorities of his arrival in the US, and he only has jurisdiction as a French police officer. As of right now, he is saying nothing—except he needs to speak with you."

Del sat up as straight as she could. "With me?"

Boston leaned over and spread pictures out on the long conference table. "This is the woman Galloul assaulted. Goes by the name Anila Jalili. She works for a technical wing of the Iranian Revolutionary Guard." He leaned on his knuckles and looked Del in the eye. "How did you come to run into this person?"

"She appeared to be shadowing Doctor Peter Breedlove." Del said. "You'll recall I came to New York to interview Dr. Ross Aringa. I saw Dr. Breedlove on the street here, and I also observed this woman following him."

"By chance? You ran into Dr. Breedlove by coincidence, or were you following him?"

Del hesitated. Lies only forced more lies, but she couldn't say it was by chance. "Jacques informed me of Breedlove arriving in New York. We were working the case together, as you remember, sir."

Boston narrowed his eyes but nodded. "Have you seen this man?" He threw down a picture of Johnny.

"That's the leader of the Lucknow Gang," Del said. "I tracked him down in Singapore."

Boston fanned out more pictures, these ones of Johnny with Jalili. "Did you know that he was an associate of the woman that Inspector Galloul just assaulted?"

"I had no idea."

Del's insides twisted. If Johnny was associated with Anila, could it be possible that his Lucknow Gang was setting up the whole thing? Was Johnny orchestrating everything?

She had been on the verge of revealing the papers she had recovered from the Iranian woman, but now she held her tongue. She needed to find Johnny first. He had lied about the Anila woman, made it seem like she was some unknown person following Del.

Boston said, "It's the worst kept secret at Interpol HQ that you and Galloul have a relationship. You should go and have a talk with him. He's in detention at One PP. He won't say anything more, which isn't helping."

Boston collected the pictures, putting them back in his briefcase. Stopped and looked at Del, shook his head. "Listen, Devlin, we haven't had much of a history together. What happened with Katherine—I can understand you did what you did. But I've held up my part."

"Yes, sir," Del said. She didn't think now was the time to point out she'd done her part too, hadn't told anybody about what the US government was doing in Ukraine.

"Is there *anything* you're not telling me right now?"

Del didn't respond. Sweat prickled her forehead. She kept her eyes on the glossy black tabletop. She was great at spotting lies, but not at telling them. She remained silent.

"I'll ask you again." He flicked through the stack of photos, found the one he was looking for, tossed it onto the table. Johnny again. "Have you seen this man here, in New York? Do you know where he is?"

The truth was, she *didn't* know where he was. "No idea, sir."

The sickness in her gut expanded. She put a hand over her stomach, breathed out. Nearly gagged again, but held it back. It came out as a cough that made her eyes water.

"Devlin. Is something wrong?"

If she told anyone that she'd been communicating with Johnny, they would wonder why she was in touch with him in the first place. But the information she needed to check on might have come from him. If not him, then Jalili. But Del only knew about her because of Johnny. Del's head spun, her legs weak under her, her stomach felt like it was filling with sludge. She curled slightly forward, tried to hold it all in.

That text from Angel, minutes after he'd left to find Johnny.

He's gone.

Delta forced herself to look at the picture of her uncle. "Honestly, sir, I have no idea where that man is right now."

"If that's the way you want to play it, I can give you till lunch tomorrow to figure it out. But that's it. I suggest you get a move on. Governor Guthrie's rally is at Liberty Park tomorrow, so they'll be shutting down the streets overnight. You don't report back to me by noon tomorrow, I'll be coming to take you in myself."

22

Alphabet City, New York

April 31st, 10:45 p.m.

Night in Alphabet City. The rain had gotten heavier after Del left the Interpol offices, so the streets were shining. Sidewalks splashed with emerald greens and electric reds, lights reflected from storefronts and streetlights, outlining the people hurrying by. Most under umbrellas, but some just walking, hoods up, looking for a dry place to land.

This was the part of town Royce Vandeweghe had run to, hiding among the other shattered souls in one of her first cases as a Suffolk County Detective. Her first big case. She'd met him at a bar around here—Eleventh and C, if she remembered right.

Del hustled along the sidewalks, her head bowed against the downpour.

At the corner, waiting for the light to change, Del caught sight of something. Some*one*. A man in a tweed cap, crossing the opposite way. Johnny? The rain in her eyes. She wiped the drops away, but the man had disappeared. If he was ever even there. She couldn't be sure—of that, of anything. Her nerves jangled; her mind raced. She had to find him, but how? Boston had given her until tomorrow. And she had no leads, nowhere to even start.

Think.

Start with what you know, was what her dad always said.

She breathed out, crossed the street again, and walked. No one out tonight on the little patios, all the chairs and tables folded up and stowed under awnings. But the cafés and bars winked with life, flashes of people laughing and talking inside, in cozy, warmly lit spaces, their manner easy and relaxed. Like they had nothing important to think about. Like snapshots of herself, in other places, other times. She'd been that carefree in the past—would she ever be that way in the future? She hoped so. If she could just figure all this out. What did she know?

She was running out of time, so she couldn't afford to get lost. In any sense of the word. She had to get a grip, and she had to do it quickly. Start with the Iranian woman's papers, which she'd pored over before hiding them in her old room.

Four questions needed to be answered.

First, was this a setup? Was her uncle leading her down another rabbit hole? Or was Jacques? The second question was why the Iranian woman wanted to talk specifically to Del. The third item was whether the schematics and papers from the Iranian made any sense. She needed to find an expert, someone who understood Dr. Breedlove's work.

Which brought her back to the physicist. She needed to talk to him.

But Angel had just texted her and said Breedlove had checked out of the Plaza in the middle of the night. He had lost track of him, as well.

She passed a once-vacant lot that had been turned into a community garden, now teeming with vines and vegetable plots, buds and blooms. The colors amplified in the rain, a dizzying profusion of greens and pinks. The scents of earth and chlorophyll pierced the usual grit of the city. She breathed it in. And kept walking.

Del bypassed the cafés with their crowds and performers, headed to a deli up the street, its red-and-white awning lit from below, a beacon of warmth and comfort. The door bleeped an electric chime as she opened it and walked in. Glass-fronted deli counter to the left, aisles of canned and dry goods taking up the center of the store. A meaty tinge to the air, of pastrami and cold cuts. She ordered a coffee, then stood at the counter letting the warmth of the place soak into her tired feet and aching knee. It felt worse than it had earlier—she should probably rest, elevate it, put on an ice pack.

She scanned the bright little room.

Cameras in two corners, a large flat-screen TV behind the deli counter. The sound was off, but the crawl beneath the blond newscaster was clear enough. Tensions between the US and Iran were escalating. The picture then cut to the face of Governor Guthrie. The guy behind the counter caught sight of the senator as he poured her coffee.

He cursed at the screen, then handed her the cup.

"Not a fan?" Del pulled off the lid and added two creams and three sugars. Stirred them in one by one.

"I'm Italian," he said. "I know a fascist when I see one."

She paid, thanked the guy, and swung out of the door, back into the night. The coffee warmed her hands, and even just the smell of it jolted her a bit, woke her up. She took a sip.

She had the receipts and item numbers from Breedlove's shopping spree. The schematics in Anila's papers, but there could be more on the disk drive. She would send that to Lyon in the morning, and like it or not, by the end of the day tomorrow, she would have to reveal what she took from the Iranian woman, and that she was connected to Johnny Murphy.

She had to come clean.

Which might wreck her career.

But there was one thing she could try now. It was a bit of a long shot, but she hoped he would be able to fit some of the pieces together. Did any of this fit to make one thing? And what kind of thing would that be?

She scooted under an awning and dialed. Watched raindrops collect along the scalloped edge, build, and fall. The phone on the other end rang and rang, then went to voicemail. Damn.

"Hello, Dr. Aringa, it's Deputy Marshal Devlin calling. An urgent matter has come to my attention that requires your input. Please call me back soon as possible."

She left her number, then hung up. And walked.

As she turned another corner, she found herself looking at every man she saw, no matter how blurred by the rain. Was that him drinking a beer out of a paper bag? Leaning against the wall of an alley? Smoking a cigarette, shielding it from the rain? Each time she thought she saw him, he disappeared. Johnny. Where had he gone?

She'd told herself that bringing him here, she was doing it for her dad. But she wasn't so sure anymore. She had been doing it for herself.

Her coffee was cool by now but she drank the last sip, almost cold and far too sweet, then propped the cup on top of the pile in an overflowing garbage can.

Checked the clock on her phone. Already past midnight.

She looked up at the off-white concrete waffle of the hospital and let out a breath.

The Iranian woman had wanted to talk to Del. If she couldn't find her uncle Johnny, then she could try and speak to this Anila woman, if she was conscious. If she could get to her. If those papers were real, then Del needed to go straight back to Marshal Justice right now.

Was it possible a terrorist attack was being planned?

The bright lights of the hospital's lobby made her blink as she walked through the automatic door. The smell hit her with a punch, that mix of bleach and bodily functions combined into a scent she both couldn't stand but found comforting. At least it was warm and dry in here. She pulled her hood down and smoothed her hair as best she could. The emergency room waiting area to her right was half full, people sitting or standing in clumps. An orderly cleaned up a puddle of blood on the floor near the bathroom, pink water dripping from the mop as he raised it and plonked it into the waiting bucket.

Del headed to the elevators.

Cameras at each end of the hallway—they were scanning, but she knew there were bound to be blind spots in a setup like that. The nurses at the ER were too busy to watch the door, and she hadn't seen a single security guard yet. How secure was this place? Why had they brought the patient here?

The elevator dinged, and the doors opened. Del punched the sixth-floor button and unzipped her coat as the heat of the building settled in. The doors opened. A security table was set up outside the room, manned by a young officer with short black hair. Del handed over her weapon, cards, phone, earrings, pocket change.

And her ID.

Four FBI agents ranged up and down the hall, along with twice that many NYPD and a few men and women in dark suits who looked like they belonged to other acronym-heavy agencies. Two men at the door, two at security, three more sipping coffee. She stood up a little straighter, set her face to neutral.

Was Jalili under arrest? For what? She had been the one assaulted.

The young officer ran over her arms and legs with a metal detector. Another stared at her ID for longer than was strictly necessary, then waved her through to the room.

Del pushed open the door.

The smell was worse in here. A bloody, metallic fog lingered under the sharp tang of disinfectant. Her eyes adjusted to the dim lighting from the bedside lamp, and she could just make out a person on the bed. The IRGC operative. Jalili. Not moving. Machines beeped softly, tracking her heart rate and slow, shallow breathing.

The woman's face was a jumble of old scars, burned tissue, and newly torn skin, red and ragged and raw. Her head wrapped in white gauze, parts of it gone pink from seeping sores.

She needed more information from Jalili, but she'd seen the shape she was in after Jacques had assaulted her. Was she really hoping the woman would be able to speak?

Assaulted her. Those were the words Boston had used, but it hadn't really sunk in until now.

"Deputy Marshal Devlin." One of the FBI entered the room and turned on the lights, his face flushed in clear and distinct stress blooms.

Del said, "The officer at security let me in."

"That was an uninformed decision."

"I needed to see her. With my own eyes."

He held the door open. "We can continue this outside."

Del walked out, past the man. He let the door fall shut behind them.

The officers up and down the hallway continued drinking coffee and talking about the game that night, but all of their eyes were on Del. Her weapon and her ID sat on the security table. No exit.

The FBI operative approached Del. Squinted at her. "What is the purpose of your visit, Deputy Marshal?"

"I'm here to interview the person in custody."

"This suspect is nonresponsive at this time. What were you doing in there?"

"Didn't have time to do anything."

"This suspect has ties to the IRGC. Were you aware of this when you met her?"

"I wasn't meeting her."

The man didn't express any emotion, but scribbled down notes. "You are aware it's a felony crime to lie to the FBI, even for a US Marshal?"

"Deputy Marshal, and of course I am."

"What exactly are your intentions here?"

"As I said, I wanted to talk to her."

"Just a minute." The man went to speak with the other FBI operatives and police officers in a black-and-blue huddle. They glanced over at Del occasionally, one of them giving her a once-over that would have been almost comical if it wasn't so grotesque.

The man returned, the blooms in his face even brighter now, a fiery shade of hot pink that told Del she better know exactly what she was doing the second she did it. He was itching for a fight. "What is your connection to the suspect?"

"None that I know of." Another lie. Her father would be crossing himself at this point. "I was in pursuit of a person of interest—Dr. Peter Breedlove—when I happened to cross paths with the suspect."

"So, you have never spoken to the suspect?"

A leading question. Del mirrored—she knew all these tricks, too. "Spoken to the suspect?"

"Have you had any interactions with the suspect?"

"Yes. I happened to run into her, as I said."

"Listen," the man leaned forward, his breath acidic. Too much vending machine coffee. "We have security footage. There's no sound, but the suspect is clearly approaching you. Talking to you."

"She wasn't making sense," Del said.

"What did she say?"

"Like I said, nothing I could understand."

"Did you take something from her? The angle of the footage was blocked by your body, but you knelt beside her. She seemed to have something in her hand."

"I was checking her vitals." That was true.

"As a US Marshal, you are aware that anything can be considered evidence in a case like this one. Papers, information? Anything?"

Del shrugged no. She didn't want to open her mouth to lie again.

What the hell was she doing? What was the penalty for lying to the FBI? Jail time at least.

She thought about the people she'd seen earlier in Alphabet City, carefree and happy, drinking, singing. If there was a possible terrorist attack, she had to protect them, but she had to know for sure what she was doing before she made a move, otherwise her career would be over.

The man handed her ID back to her, then nodded at the young officer at the security table. He walked over and returned the rest of her things, avoided looking her in the eye.

"Deputy Marshal Devlin. For the moment, your request has been denied."

"Sir?"

"When you're ready to engage in a more productive way, we can have another conversation."

The other operatives and officers had slowly moved in, casually standing in a horseshoe around her. One caught her eye, then reached over and pressed the elevator's down button.

The only way out—unless she went through them. She took a deep breath.

The elevator doors beeped and slid open.

23

Civic Center, New York

April 31st, 11:15 p.m.

Del hustled through the hospital's ground floor hallway and out onto the street, her heart thumping. She had just lied to the FBI about a possible terrorist plot.

Pulling up her hood against the rain, she crossed the street, turned up an alley, and leaned against the wet brick. Took deep breath after deep breath until her pulse slowed to normal.

Start with what you know.

The FBI agent said they had footage of Del with Jalili. But from where and when? Del didn't know for sure. When had they been in the same area? And when had Jalili tried to talk to her? Del was fairly sure the only time the woman tried to talk directly to her was in the vacant lot, but she hadn't found any cameras in that area. Maybe one of the buildings had cameras—or a neighbor with a phone? And if that was the case, they might have footage of the moment Jacques hit Jalili with the metal bar.

And why was Jalili following Peter Breedlove? What did the Revolutionary Guard have to do with all of this? Were they trying to pin the attack they were planning on the Muslim extremists? Or was all of it being manipulated by Johnny and his Lucknow Gang?

Jacques had shown up precisely when Del and Jalili were going to talk.

What, if anything, did he have to do with it? Had he tried to silence the Iranian on purpose?

The rain fell in fat drops. She thought about taking a cab but knew it would be faster to walk. Even at this hour, the cross-town traffic was at a standstill. She walked as quickly as she could, her mind ricocheting in all directions.

If Johnny had planted the papers on the Iranian, that meant he was orchestrating this whole thing. And if he hadn't, and they were real, Del had no time to spare.

She had to find Peter.

But first, she needed to talk to Jacques.

The inverted concrete pyramid of One Police Plaza rose above her, brutalist corners darkened with damp in the increasing rain and wind. Del walked past the large welcome sign and into the entryway. Took down her hood and unzipped her coat, wiped the raindrops from her burning cheeks. A shift officer with dark hair in a neat bob, who looked to be about the same age Del had been when she'd entered the force, signed her in. Paused when Del gave her Jacques's name.

"George Clooney, huh? He's been asking for you."

"Pardon me? No, I—"

"The detainee in cell four, right?"

Del nodded.

"You two together?"

"I'm here in a professional capacity."

"Uh-huh."

The officer filled out the form on her computer, pressed return. Then got up from her padded chair, walked around the desk. "Deputy Marshal, I'm going to have to escort you. I'm also required to remain outside the room for the duration."

"Understood."

Del and the officer walked down the gray hallway to an interrogation room. One wall taken up with a reciprocal mirror. Inside, a gray table and two gray chairs. Jacques in one of them. The officer unlocked the door, held it open for Del.

"*Bon chance*," the officer said.

Del would take any luck she could get right now, even if delivered sarcastically. The officer shut and locked the door behind her.

Jacques stood. "Delta."

"Deputy Marshal Devlin, Inspector Galloul. I'm here in an official capacity. I need to talk to you about Peter Breedlove."

She'd been kept prisoner in worse conditions than this, and she knew being confined could turn anyone's thoughts dark. Still, Jacques wasn't quite his usual self. His cheeks were flushed, but not in the same pattern they would be in an instantaneous, unconscious reaction.

"Thank you for coming, Deputy Marshal," Jacques replied. He glanced up at the camera in the corner of the room.

Del pulled the other chair out from under the empty table, sat. Set her phone down on the gray enamel tabletop, faceup so she could see any alerts.

First things first. She folded her hands on the table. Steadied her breathing. Just ask him what you need to and get out. "Tell me—why did you take me to CERN that day? Was it because I was pushing you away? In our relationship?"

Now it was Del's turn to glance self-consciously up at the camera. Then again, this wasn't much of a secret.

And Del needed to know.

Because that was what it had felt like. That morning, Jacques had wanted to come in to work with her, but she had refused. She felt like he wanted to pull her closer, and she was pushing him away. He had requested to have her come onto his case so that he could get her into his car that day, get her closer. That's what she remembered feeling.

"I'm not a teenager, Delta. There was a request from your superior, Mr. Justice, for me to add you to the case. You had just been to the Interpol cybercrime HQ, and there was an angle for this in the proceeding."

"Marshal Justice requested that you take me?"

“That’s right. He asked me to take you to CERN.”

“Why?”

“I did not ask your boss why.”

Del rocked back in her chair. She was trying to ignore her habit of watching people’s face for lies, but Jacques’s face was cool and calm. He was telling the truth. Or looked like he was.

The information was like a bomb going off inside her brain. Could she even trust Marshal Justice? Maybe that’s why she hadn’t revealed anything at her meeting with her boss. Maybe she didn’t trust him, her instincts guiding her. Was she getting played again, like what had happened with Katherine?

Jacques eyed her as she took this in.

She tried to remain calm, but she felt pinpricks of sweat along her forehead, her cheeks flushing hot. She’d have to try something else, or he’d know he was getting to her. “Why didn’t you tell me you were coming to New York?”

“You did not want me here. I did not want to bother you. I knew you were with your family, but I needed to come for work. I was following Breedlove, nothing to do with you.”

“Why didn’t you want me to talk to the Iranian woman?”

“I had no idea the two of you were supposed to be talking. To me, it looked very much like she was intending to shoot you.”

“You used unnecessary force.”

“I did not mean to hurt her like this. I just needed to stop her from hurting *you*.”

Jacques’s cheeks had cooled a bit by now, and he sat there calm and, to all appearances, mellow. Something about what he’d just said prickled Del’s mind, like the first signs of an allergic reaction. What did he think he knew? Was she missing something?

Jacques leaned back in his chair and regarded her calmly for a minute. His eyes thoughtful, his mouth far from smiling. Then he sat up, reached out for her hand. Del hesitated, then shook her head. He nodded. “Professional capacity, yes?”

“Yes.”

He sighed. "Delta. I heard about your father. Back at the hospital. I am sincerely sorry."

His sudden empathy had the feeling of him trying to align with her. An attempt to elicit a shared empathy. Like he was trying to manipulate her. She hadn't brought up the papers and disk drive she found on the Iranian because the cameras were still on in the room.

But there were other questions she needed answering. "Why didn't you tell me about Zoya?"

"What about her?"

"That you two were together. Until I came along."

"She told you this, I suppose?" Jacques leaned back in his chair. "Please go tell them to turn off their listening devices. I must tell you something. Something very personal."

She said nothing, but after a pause rose and went to the door.

When the shift officer came to open it, Del told her that she and Jacques were a couple, but it wasn't known around the office, and she was a bit embarrassed. She knew the rules, but they needed some privacy, just for a few minutes.

He didn't look surprised. He would have to file a report detailing her request, he said, but sure. He could give them a minute to themselves.

The small red light on the camera in the corner of the room blinked off after a few seconds.

Jacques waited for her to sit back down before he leaned over the table and whispered urgently, "I told you before about the letters Peter has been sending to himself—to a person he believes is himself in the future."

"So, you were being serious?"

"He also thinks he is getting messages from you."

"I know. You told me this earlier. That's not—"

"I have been trying to piece it together, but the timeline makes no sense. I introduced you and Breedlove only last week—yet it seems he has been getting messages from you from before that. Before either of you even knew the other existed. I don't know the explanation." He looked at Del. "These messages say you have a son."

Del's cheeks burned but she said, "Why would he say that?"

Her phone buzzed. An incoming text popped up on her screen. It was from Coleman, her old partner. Del's throat constricted as she read it.

> DNA from body kids found in bag. Under fingernails. Partial match with DNA sample.
>
> Your DNA.
>
> Need explanation.
>
> Quickly.

"I need to go," Del said.

***

As she rode the elevator down to the technical services floor of One PP, Del queued up the photos she'd need. Days, weeks, and months slid by as she scrolled backward in time, searching. Her stomach lurched as she went through everything again. She needed to stop, sit down, and look at everything carefully. But she didn't have time. She had to keep going.

The doors opened on concrete walls, gray fabric cubicle dividers, neon lighting. The officer at the main desk directed her down a narrow hallway to a very unglamorous room—wide worktables piled high with papers and file folders, stacked high with cardboard boxes. Big screens though, and lots of them. At this time of the night, all of it was run by one officer.

Del showed the tech officer at the table her ID. And the first photo she'd pulled up on her phone, one of Jacques smiling at one of their dinners together, their last night out in Paris.

"I need a detailed log of this man's activities since he arrived in the US. His port of entry and everywhere he's been."

Jacques and Del had agreed not to take pictures of each other on their phones—too personal, and they were supposed to be keeping their affair discreet. But one time she'd been waiting for him as he paid their bill at the restaurant, and as he stepped outside, he looked so content and handsome and—something had moved her to preserve that moment. He didn't know she'd taken the photo, now she was using that private second against him.

"Send that image to me?" The officer slid a card over, the technical services email and phone number printed on it. "Whenever you're ready."

"Can you pull facial recognition from traffic and security cameras for me as well?"

"Same target?"

Del shook her head and sent over two more photos.

Johnny in one of the pictures from her file, the one Angel had given her so long ago, holding an AK-47. He was younger then, but still wore the same kind of cap and had the same defiant look in his eye. It would be enough.

The next photo was of Peter Breedlove, looking every bit the mad professor in his profile picture from CERN. Lab coat, goggles, electronics in the background.

"Any connections we should be looking out for?"

"Undetermined at this time."

The man made a note. Took down the dates and times she wanted searched, Del's ID number, name, and phone number. "We'll get in touch if we find anything."

"Could you prioritize the last one?"

"Lab coat guy?"

She nodded. She knew where Jacques was, and he wasn't going anywhere. Johnny was—well, for the moment, all she could do was hope Angel would be able to track him down. She needed to find Peter. As soon as she could. One way or another, he was involved with something he shouldn't be. The IRGC, or Johnny and the Lucknow gang. Either that, or the professor was out of his mind, or all of the above at the same time, somehow.

Her phone buzzed in her hand.

She checked it automatically, only remembering as she did so that she really didn't want to know if it was Coleman again. But it was someone else. Someone who might be able to help her figure out where Peter was—and maybe even what on Earth he was up to.

"No problem." The officer cleared his throat. "Anything else?"

"Sorry, I have to get this."

The man nodded and bent to his work.

She walked back down the carpeted hallway, her footsteps muffled. Restrained herself from answering within earshot, finally picking up on the fifth ring. "Hello, Dr. Aringa. Thanks for getting back to me."

"You're a US Marshal. Is one allowed to say no to you?"

Del paused. "Well—"

"I'm joking. Though I suppose I shouldn't be. I've had some wine. I'm sorry. Let's start again. How can I help?"

"I need to speak to you in person. Can I come by your home?"

"Again, I suppose I am not allowed to decline?"

Del's phone buzzed. Someone else was calling. "I'll be there in an hour."

The other call was from her mother. "Del, honey? You need to come to the hospital. It's your dad."

24

Presbyterian Hospital, New York

May 1st, 3:05 p.m.

An officer put a hand on Del's arm. A man with a graying beard, not as old as her father, but older than her. He'd been at one of her birthday parties. She couldn't remember his name. The guys from his precinct were doing a rotation at the hospital, making sure Del's mom would never be alone. Just in case.

"Your dad's one tough nut," the officer said. "He'll pull through."

True or not, it was what she needed to hear, and she hung onto the words like a life preserver as she pushed open the door.

Del had arrived in the tiny hours of the morning, stayed past lunch and called Boston to say they needed to delay their meeting. From her perch on the attending room couches out front of the ICU, she made calls and checked messages.

A hacking cough, crinkly sounds of shifting under blankets. A groan. The overhead lights off, two little islands of weak light from the incandescent lamps beside the bed. She looked across the room. Her mother sat with her head held high at her dad's bedside.

Her dad wasn't moving.

He lay on his back under a thin blue sheet, his eyes closed. Tubes in his arms. His skin pale, just the barest hint of color showing around his cheeks and sinuses. A steady beeping from the machines attached to him.

Alive, but not well.

Del crossed the room with soft footsteps, her sneakers squeaking lightly. Her mom looked up, smiled when she saw her.

They hugged. Tight. Her mom's smell blocking out the hospital stink. Del relaxed and held back tears. She kept her arms wrapped around her mom until the squeezing in her throat subsided. The ache behind her eyes died down. Wished she could tell her mom everything. Ask for some help. Now wasn't the time.

She pulled away.

Her mother gave her an appraising look, one eyebrow going up. She leaned close to Del, kept her voice down. "You look terrible, honey. And are these the same clothes you left the house in yesterday morning?"

"Mom, I'm fine. I've been working."

"If you say so."

"How is he?"

"Missy's on her way."

"It's that serious?"

Amede looked down at Del's father, then rearranged herself in her chair. Patted the one beside her. Del sat.

"They're telling me he had a small stroke."

A *small* stroke? It sounded like being a little bit pregnant. As soon as she thought the word, Del remembered the appointment later this week. Couldn't think of that now.

She reached over and took her mother's hand. They sat in a silence broken only by bleeps from the machine. Her knee was throbbing, so she stretched out her leg.

Her mother's eyes went straight to the injury. "You hurt?"

"Part of the job, Mom."

She looked at her dad, so pale under the sheet. And it hit her. *This* was family. Whatever Johnny was to her, it wasn't this. He'd used her. For some reason she didn't understand, he'd wanted her to find Anila.

He was manipulating her, just as her dad said he would. But why?

A stirring from Del's dad. His eyes opened slowly, and he smiled as he saw them sitting there. "My girls. You don't have to be here. I'm fine."

"You are not fine, Sean." Her mother rose, smoothed the sheet over his chest, tucked him in. "Now lie still."

He turned his head slightly, trying to see Del. She got up from her chair too, moved closer to him, leaned down so he could see her. He gave a weak laugh. "It's just one thing after another with your old man, isn't it?"

"Dad?"

"It does keep me on my toes." His voice crackled like dry leaves. "Not literally, of course."

"You need to rest." Del's mother turned to her. "I'm going to get him some ice chips. You stay here."

Her dad watched her mother leave, then reached for Del's hand. "I'm going to be fine. Go do what you need to do."

"This is what I need to do." She squeezed his hand.

He squeezed back. "I've been watching the news. The rally for that hideous Governor Guthrie, angling for that senate seat."

She'd almost forgotten about it. Her phone buzzed in her pocket. She ignored it. Her phone buzzed again. It could be Angel saying he'd found Johnny, or maybe Suweil with news about the equipment list or images of the schematics she'd sent him. Or it could be Coleman, or One PP.

She nodded. Waited until her mom came back and hugged her goodbye. Leaned over and kissed her dad on the forehead. Told him she would be back soon.

She could only hope she was telling the truth.

***

Del hurried to the hospital's taxi stand mercifully shielded from the rain by an overhang. Six people ahead of her. Should give her time to check her phone. The first group of texts were from Suweil.

We researched the list of lab equipment you

sent earlier. The technical schematics are for some kind of magnetic containment device? Details are beyond our level of expertise. Perhaps talk to a research scientist at CERN? We did get a hit on the lab equipment. Zoya located a clandestine auction on a darkweb server, the meeting in New York tomorrow morning. She set herself up as a buyer. Will send you details.

A second group of messages came in from the technical group at One PP—a list of locations that Jacques had been spotted at since he had arrived in New York. A few of Peter Breedlove. There were cameras all over the city running facial recognition, more than there used to be even the year before.

Del was sure someone was running the same sort of search on her.

No way to hide these days.

A polite honk from the taxi stand. She looked up and saw she was the next in line—a space in front of her highlighting how long she had been staring at the text from One PP.

"Sorry." She got in the taxi and closed the door behind her. "It's been one of those days."

"No problem," the cabbie said. "Seen people in worse shape than you, that's for sure. Don't you worry about nothing. You're gonna be alright."

She gave the driver directions and sank into the springy leather of the back seat. Let out a long breath. The rain pelted the car as they wound their way to the Upper West Side.

***

The technical team at One PP had found two locations Jacques had stopped at for more than an hour. She texted the addresses to Angel. She would stake out one location, while Angel sat outside the other.

And they would see what popped out.

It was the best she could do for now. The information on Breedlove had him at the Plaza Hotel, but nothing since he had disappeared last night. As soon as Suweil sent the information for the lab equipment auction, she would chase that down.

Outside the taxi window, the rain was increasing, a rough wind lashing the trees. She checked her phone anxiously, but it had only been a few minutes. No updates. She needed answers more than anything. She needed to know how dangerous Dr. Peter Breedlove might really be, and who was manipulating him.

***

At Doctor Aringa's building, Davenport once again answered her knock, and a maid took her coat and whisked it away somewhere. Aside from this, almost everything else was different.

A wheeled coatrack sat in the hallway, and the red velvet rope barring the stairs had been removed. She followed Davenport to the living room, where the couches and tables and rugs had disappeared. The floor was covered with red, white, and blue balloons and a hefty dose of confetti in the same colors. A microphone stand was being dismantled at the far end of the space. A few people lingered over drinks, sitting on a group of folding chairs while the rest were packed up around them by silent staff dressed all in black. Slung across the far wall was a banner with the words "Scientists Against Guthrie's Existence" written on it in bold blue letters.

"We're not subtle," Dr. Aringa said behind her. "But then he isn't either. At least we're SAGE." He laughed and wheeled around her, waved a server over. "A drink for the Deputy Marshal?"

"No, thanks. If we could just—"

"One minute." Dr. Aringa ordered two whiskeys anyway. "Drinking for two," he said with a grin.

"I don't have much time, Dr. Aringa," she said. "I didn't know you were entertaining."

The guy was visibly inebriated, and it was the middle of the afternoon.

"Not entertaining—nothing entertaining about any of this." His whiskeys arrived on a silver tray held by a server. He slammed back the first in one gulp. "Do you know what kind of threat that man poses to science?"

"If we could stick to the matter I mentioned on the phone. It's urgent."

Dr. Aringa took a slug out of the second whiskey. Lowered his voice. It still carried through the room, staff members and guests turning around to see what was happening. "There's nothing we can do. This kind of thing?" He waved his other hand around, indicating the room, the microphone, the banner, the confetti. "What happens when you spill ink on a page? *The page never wins.*"

The people scattered around the room had stopped talking. All attention now focused on what their host was up to.

Del leaned down. "Dr. Aringa, I really must insist. Is there another room we could use?"

Dr. Aringa blinked once, twice. Looked around the room. Then stared up into her eyes, his own bloodshot. "I can really be an ass when I want to. My apologies." He handed his unfinished second whiskey to the server, then spun in his chair. "Right this way."

***

His study was in a sunroom off the kitchen, a tiny place that might once have served as a year-round herb garden. Its square footprint included three glass walls, the fourth being a thruway to the rest of the house. One of the glass walls had been plastered with layers of handwritten notes and diagrams. The rain pounded outside.

Dr. Aringa rolled over to his workstation, which ran the length of the covered wall. Three large flat-screens, plus two laptops and a projector—Del followed the line of sight to a brick wall painted white across the little walled yard.

A knock.

"Just come in." He shook his head, his eyes on his screens. "I keep telling them I don't have time for mindless formalities."

A young man dressed all in black entered, carrying an ornately carved chair with an oxblood leather seat that he placed next to Del. Another came in behind him and set to lighting pillar candles in tall holders all around the room. A maid followed with a silver tray holding a carafe and two coffee cups on saucers. Sugar, cream. She set the tray down on a low table, far away from anything electronic.

"Mr. Davenport thought this might be just the thing, Dr. Aringa. Please let me know if you need anything else."

Dr. Aringa kept his eyes on his screens and waved his hand in the maid's general direction.

"Thanks," Del said to the staff as they left.

"None for me," Dr. Aringa said, not turning around. He reached under his desk, opened the door of a little fridge, pulled out a can of Red Bull. Cracked it open. "Help yourself. Davenport sincerely hopes one day I'll start drinking coffee like a normal person—but I run on taurine."

Del poured a coffee, added sugar and cream, stirred. The silver spoon clinked against the porcelain. The candles flickered. She took a sip. Set her cup down.

"Dr. Aringa. Please listen. I can't reveal where I got this information." She pulled up the images on her phone of the list of equipment and schematics from the papers she had recovered from the Iranian.

Dr. Aringa took the phone from her and scrolled through the list. "What would you like me to do? Can I email these to myself?"

"I would prefer if you didn't. What could the device described in those schematics be used for?"

His eyebrows going up as he read. He turned to his screens, one of them projected on a wall behind him, and started typing in web searches. And prices, which he entered into a spreadsheet. The total ran into the millions.

"Sit back," Dr. Aringa said. "This might take a while."

***

"From the looks of this, someone seems to be building a kind of magnetic containment device."

The same thing Suweil had said.

Aringa continued, "I'm not sure that all of the equipment listed here actually exists. For instance, these here are described as high-temperature superconductors, which isn't possible using known materials. Not using technology we have available today. Perhaps in the future, but not yet. But much of this is, while very expensive, quite possible."

"You said containment—exactly what would it be containing?"

"Antimatter." He reached under his desk and pulled out another Red Bull.

"Antimatter?" Del repeated the word without really understanding.

Dr. Aringa popped the top of the energy drink and took a sip. The drunken cavalier attitude he had when Del first arrived had evaporated and been replaced by something that resembled fear. "I'm going to make a leap here—does this have something to do with Peter Breedlove?"

"I'm not at liberty to say at the moment, sir. It's an ongoing investigation."

"Did Peter take anything from the LHC, in this investigation that I'm not at liberty to be involved in?"

"Like what?"

"Could be something small. Even the size of a coffee thermos. Did he come to New York? Is that why you're here?"

"When you said antimatter, what did you mean?"

"Exactly what I said. Anti. Matter."

"Which is what?"

"The technical description is rather boring. It is matter composed of antiparticles. Minuscule numbers of antiparticles are generated daily at particle accelerators like the LHC. In fact, this has been a focus of Dr. Breedlove's work, generating vast new quantities of antiparticles which he believes enables him to send information back in time. The generation of negative energy solutions behaves as if the particles are propagating in reverse temporal sequence. He might be right. Despite our differences, he's one of the most brilliant minds I have ever encountered."

"You really believe time travel is possible?"

"Either not at all, or information is flowing as freely backward as it is flowing forward. The illusion might be our own frame of consciousness, or simply that we are only observing one universe."

"And what did antimatter have to do with his work?"

"More of a byproduct of his work with the super collider, but a rather dangerous one, it seems. Whoever designed this machine described in the schematic was aiming to collect antimatter, contain it within a magnetic field."

"And why is it dangerous?"

He took another nervous sip of the energy drink. "To date, in all the particle colliders around the world, the total production of antimatter had been only a few billionths of a gram. But with the upgrades at the LHC? The experiments Peter was running for his time travel experiments. I fear he may have been producing the stuff on far vaster scales."

"Again, why would it be dangerous?"

"An antimatter weapon."

Del felt the hair on the back of her neck prickle. "Like a bomb?"

"An immensely powerful one. Antimatter weapons cannot yet be produced due to the current cost at maybe"—he looked up at the ceiling—"sixty trillion dollars a gram? But the theoretical advantage of such a weapon is that antimatter and matter collisions result in the entire sum of their mass energy equivalent being released as energy, which is at least two or three orders of magnitude more powerful than the most efficient fusion weapons."

"Two or three orders of magnitudes?" Del reached back into her science class memory.

"A thousand times more powerful than the most devastating thermonuclear devices, Marshal Devlin. A thousand times more powerful than a hydrogen bomb."

"And you think Peter Breedlove could have made this weapon?"

"Not with current technology. It would take innovations that are decades away to build the device described in these schematics."

"But if he had, how big would it be?"

"The actual antimatter itself?" Dr. Aringa did a mental calculation. "A megaton device would require ten or twenty grams. About the size of a marble. But the containment device? I have no idea."

Del felt the blood draining from her face. The size of a *marble?*

Dr. Aringa reached behind him and pulled a whiskey bottle from a shelf. He poured himself two fingers into a crystal glass. "If Peter is here, in New York, Marshal Devlin, you need to find him. And you need to do it as quickly as possible."

25

Civic Center, New York
May 1st, 4:15 p.m.

A hooded figure glided through the automatic doors of the hospital, the slight swish of the doors closing against the rain the only sound accompanying it. Past the emergency room waiting area, sparsely populated with people sleeping or reading or talking quietly. Down the hall. It disappeared into the waiting elevator, and the doors closed. The timed cameras on the main floor whirred silently after it, recording images of the empty hallway.

The elevator doors opened, and the hooded figure slid out. Unseen by the officers and operatives napping in chairs along the hallway. The security desk empty. The officer who had been in charge of it busy showing the two guards at the door something on his phone. The hooded figure swept past them and through the door on the other side of the hallway.

Machines beeped in the near dark. The hooded figure closed the door behind it. Turned toward the bed, the only one in this private room.

A woman lay there, her eyes closed, her face a mishmash of old scar tissue and new bruises. Her head was wrapped in gauze, her arms trailed tubing hooked to hanging drip bags.

The machines beeped.

Step after silent step, the figure approached the woman on the bed.

***

Del left Dr. Aringa's and started walking. She needed to clear her head.

He'd offered her his car and driver, but she'd declined. This was more anonymous, even if it might take precious minutes longer. The rain had died down to a light spatter, the drops refreshing her as they hit her cheeks. She kept her eyes peeled for signs of disturbance. Johnny could be anywhere. But the sidewalks were empty, the alleys quiet.

The ball at the entrance to the subway glowed green in the gloomy afternoon light. She hurried down the stairs. Almost subconsciously, her eyes flitted up and around to pick out the locations of all the cameras on the platform as she walked onto it. She stood in a tiny slice she gauged would not be covered by their sweeps. And waited.

The platform shook as a train hurtled by in the other direction, then slowed to a stop. Newspapers blew by her feet. She pulled her phone out. Read the texts again. Tried to put the pieces together. How did they all fit?

That last text from Coleman. What did it mean? She remembered the CERN pin on the body the kids had stumbled on. Closed her eyes and pictured the scene. Had she really reached out and touched a piece of evidence? Coleman said she did, that's why he asked her for a DNA sample. She'd given it to him without question.

Had she misjudged there too?

That made her think of Johnny. How could she have let herself be used? Her dad had told her flat out that the man was no good. She should have listened. She'd always listened to him before all this. Why had she stopped?

A rumbling as her train approached. It stopped with a screech, and the doors squealed open. She stepped in. No one in the car except a teenage couple making out. Del headed to a window seat, sat. Leaned against the cool wall and stretched her right leg out as far as she could. The pain in her knee pounding now.

As the train sped along, she tried to make sense of what Dr. Aringa had just told her.

The information she'd found on the Iranian woman, Anila Jalili, seemed to be real. The parts Peter had collected made some sense to Dr. Aringa. But he wasn't doing it on his own. Was the Iranian spy trying to warn Del, or were they playing a game?

She had no proof of anything coherent, just some receipts and a list of parts, but there was one thing she did know now—Breedlove could be building something. The man had just about rebuilt the entire LHC.

Her stop was next. She stood, the car jolting under her feet as it slowed and stopped. The doors slid open, and she took off. Not a second to lose.

When she reached her parents' house, she opened the door and headed to the kitchen. Her dad kept the spare in a drawer under the microwave. She slid it open, found the key, put it in her pocket.

The kitchen clock ticked in the otherwise silent room. Del walked down the hallway, turning to go, when she caught sight of the rows of family photos lining the walls. Remembered the way Johnny had looked at them, how he'd told her she was lucky. Part of his charm act.

She hustled out the door.

Her dad had a spot down the street he'd been renting for years. Del rounded the corner, and there she was. A teal 1979 Lincoln Continental her dad always referred to as "Sharon." Not her mother's name. Not his mother's name either. Del had never been able to get the story out of him, but she did know her own mother would rather walk than hop in the car. And now that Del looked at her again, Sharon was a very Johnny car for her dad to have.

Did the twin brothers have anything else in common?

The car felt like it always had, like a low-riding barge, sailing down the streets, the engine smooth as glass. Smelled like leather polish and her dad's aftershave and—cigarettes. Del shook her head. He was still smoking in secret. She rolled down the window, let the cool spring air curl in. Warm and clean, washed by the rain. Her dad kept Sharon tuned and running like new, though he rarely drove her anywhere these days.

The rain was easing off even more, her wipers on intermittent. Swish-clack. Beat. Swish-clack. Beat. The pitter-patter of the drops on the windshield dazzling, carrying all the colors of the city. Smeared into rainbows as they were wiped away.

Something soothing about it, hypnotic. The combination of the motion and the lights loosened the tightness from her, made her feel wide awake, even though she hadn't slept in who knows how many hours.

At the corner of Avenue A and Fourteenth, she pulled into a spot up the street and parked. A cyclist sped by, her tires swishing through the puddles. Del kept her eyes on the windows of the address, watched for lights, movement. There was nothing. She tilted her seat back, stretched out her leg.

A buzz on the passenger seat. Her phone lit up with a text.

Coleman. Without really meaning to, she had glanced over, seen his name. She sat up. Picked up her phone and read the text.

Her heart felt like it stopped. Had she read that right?

> Female Iranian national in hospital died two hours ago. Footage of you in her room near TOD, officers on duty will testify you were there. FBI too. Cause of death under investigation.
>
> We need you to come in.

No rush of adrenaline, no tensing of stomach. Del took a long, slow breath in. Then let it out. Her dad had always told her to accept the things she could not change.

But her mother had taught her Angela Davis's revision of that saying. "I'm changing the things I cannot accept." A calm settled over her. Everything slowed down—the angled sunlight breaking through the clouds and hitting the bright green leaves on the oak trees, the wind sweeping trash by on the street. She could see everything now. She knew what she had to do.

Very calmly, she picked up her phone again. And, just as calmly, she blocked Coleman's number.

The phone pinged.

Her heart rate sped up again. She raised the phone. It pinged again. She couldn't look.

She looked.

Suweil.

Thank god.

Read the text again. It was an address—where the meeting was supposed to happen. The darknet buy. There still hadn't been any action here in an hour, not a flicker of a curtain or a second of sound.

Del texted Angel, who was at the other address. Asked him to meet her at the new spot Suweil had just sent her. She dropped the phone on the passenger seat and started up the car.

***

The sun hit the windows of the buildings, the puddles, the tarp tents in the alleys, scattering the light in shades of honey and goldenrod.

Her dad popped into her head. So pale, so small in the hospital bed. But still with that same glint in his eye, still cracking jokes. He'd done what she was doing now, and he always kept it together. Always figured out a way through the mess. She could do that, too. She knew she could.

But if what Coleman said was true and the Iranian woman was dead, what did that mean for Jacques? And for her? Jalili was the piece Del needed, but as soon as she found her, now she was gone. It felt too planned to be an accident.

Coleman had said something else, too. That Del's DNA was tied to the body those kids had found. She didn't have the faintest idea what that meant. But she knew it fit in somewhere.

She'd started with what she knew. What would her dad do next?

Del turned the corner onto the street Suweil had texted her, and there, right in front of her, was a black Porsche SUV. She checked the plate. Johnny. The bastard.

Wide awake now, she put in her earpiece. "Angel? You there?"

"Affirmative."

"Eyes on the Porsche."

"Already on it."

"Keep six. Don't let him know we're on him."

"Roger."

Del tailed him, with Angel close behind her.

A man Del had never seen before leaned through the window of the SUV. Then waved over a young guy carrying a package. The kid handed the box through the open window. Then the door opened, and Johnny got out. Shook the man's hand, said something to the young guy. The three of them laughed. Then Johnny got back in the SUV.

"Angel?"

"On it."

The SUV rolled away. Del waited a beat, then two, then started Sharon to follow. The buildings and storefronts looked familiar, and Del realized where they were going. Back to where she'd just been.

The Porsche stopped. Johnny got out, leaving his door open. The driver's-side door swung wide. It was Dermot, the man with the eye patch. He got out, closed the door, then walked around to the open door. Leaned in and pulled out a box. The thing Johnny had just bought. Carried it close to his body, like he was afraid to drop it.

Johnny sauntered down the alley as though he was just out for a stroll. His shoulders relaxed, hands in his pockets. Dermot carried the box to the back door of the building, set it down gently. Tapped on the metal fire door and stepped back.

The door opened.

A lanky form unfolded from it. Eyes darting this way and that, scanning the alley, Johnny, Dermot, and everything in between.

"Is that—?" Angel asked in her ear.

"Peter Breedlove," Del confirmed.

"I'm coming around."

Del picked up her phone and had one hand on the door handle, about to open it, when Peter's darting eyes met hers.

He looked right at her. Behind him, the sun hit a white wall, shining almost painfully bright through a sudden break in the cloud cover. Del blinked. But the wall wasn't white—there was a message written on it.

"Del, what are you staring at?" Angel asked in her ear. "What do you see?"

"It's not possible." She got out of the car. "I'm the only one who knows how to make that color."

"What color? That wall is white."

A color only she could see. The same white-on-white effect she used in her own paintings, with paint she mixed herself. She was the only person who knew how to make it.

Peter's head was steady, his eyes on her, not darting anywhere.

Low in the sky, but just at the right angle, the sun shone bright on a mural, massive letters standing out in white-on-white. But the colors. Nobody else could see that color. The ten-foot-high letters had to be painted with the spinach-strained white paint that Delta mixed herself, that only she knew about, that fluoresced in bright *ishma*-white in sunshine: DELTA—I KNOW YOU'RE FOLLOWING ME.

Peter stood in front of the words and looked back at them, and then straight at Del.

Her skin prickled, just as it had at CERN. Nobody else walking on the street would even be able to see those letters painted white-on-white on that wall. How could Peter have known she would be here? How could he have had the time to prepare—how did he even know about her special paint that she used only in her own studio?

"Del, you okay?" Angel's voice in her ear.

She shook her head and scanned the alley and there he was. Johnny. Looking right at her and heading her way. Angel turned the corner, Johnny in his sights. Dermot turned and headed her way too—and she saw Peter grab the package and dart inside the building.

"Deputy Marshal Devlin."

Del was about to spring forward, but rocked back on her heels.

Her old partner Coleman was twenty feet behind her, his weapon drawn and aimed at her. "I'm very sorry to have to do this. But you are under arrest."

26

One Police Plaza, New York
May 1st, 6:48 p.m.

Del sat with her hands folded on the gray enamel tabletop, just as she had less than twenty-four hours ago in a room like this one, in this very building. Except this time, she had no belt, no shoes, no ID, no wallet. They had let her keep her phone, and she was being held in an interrogation room—but these were the only professional courtesies she'd been granted. Otherwise, she'd been booked in like any other joe off the street. She held her back very straight, her feet flat on the floor. Legs not crossed. Ready.

The welcome sign outside One PP had been turned off when they brought her in, the foot-high letters gunmetal and drab against the concrete as the police car turned the corner.

Coleman hadn't taken her in through the front door, of course, but she'd seen the sign as they went around the back. Would she ever get to go in the front door again?

She kept her breathing steady and focused on a scrape on the wall. The gray paint peeled away in a gouge about six inches long and an inch wide. What had happened there? Maybe someone had put up a fight, been pushed against the cinder blocks, clawed and bitten and struck out, tried to get away?

She hadn't. She hadn't resisted at all.

And so here she was, in an interrogation room, just like Jacques. Except for one tiny difference. He was considered a detainee.

She was under arrest, but she appreciated the mercy of letting her keep her phone. At least for now, and under the assumption she was being monitored. They knew her father was ill. Still, part of her was furious that a man who had assaulted a woman got better treatment than a woman of higher rank, no matter the differences in evidence or charge. And that part made her sit up a little straighter, open her eyes a little wider, listen a little more closely. Never let your guard down, her father always said.

Her phone buzzed on the tabletop—incoming texts. From Missy.

> Just arrived. Dad not good. You need to be here.

She didn't have time to respond—voices at the door, jingling of keys. But what would she have said? How could she explain any of this to her family?

The clatter continued, then the door finally swung open. She didn't turn her head, didn't twitch.

"Deputy Marshal Devlin," Coleman said. "I'm really sorry."

She didn't say anything. Sorry? He'd just arrested her and he was *sorry*?

"You're in my spot."

Of course. She was the perp. He needed her to be facing the reciprocal mirror. She stood, walked around the table to the other gray chair, and sat in the same position. Back straight. Hands clasped. Head held high. If Coleman needed her to be facing the mirror, who was on the other side? Del's stomach contracted.

"There are some details relating to the case I need to discuss with you. I'm obligated to inform you that this conversation will be recorded." He gestured to the camera in the corner, its eye directed at her, dark and unblinking. "May I proceed?"

She nodded. She'd been read her rights, and anyway knew them by heart. Better to say nothing until she knew more.

"Your phone is still available to you. Is there anyone you'd like to call?"

"Not right now."

Coleman sat across from her, looking younger than ever. Not a wrinkle on his pale skin, not a worry line in sight. No stress, no blood rushing to his face. Even so, his blue eyes held—not sadness, exactly. Sympathy? Maybe. But it was possible there was nothing there at all, that she was just seeing what she wanted to see.

Coleman took his cap off, placed it on the table. "DNA with a very close relationship to yours was found under the fingernails of the body discovered by three juveniles using a geolocation app. At this time, it is not confirmed to be a complete match. But the odds are very good that it is, in fact, your DNA—or that of a very close relative. Do you understand?"

Del nodded.

"Do you have an explanation for how your DNA, or that of a very close relative, came to be under the fingernails of the deceased?"

She shook her head.

"The body was discovered two days ago. Can you provide details of your whereabouts?"

It was right after she'd arrived in New York, the same day Johnny had arrived in the city.

She sat still, her back straight, stomach churning. Coleman watched her carefully but didn't repeat his question. For whatever reason—some sense of loyalty, maybe, since they used to be partners—he gave her a minute to think.

If what they had was a partial match, her DNA would be included in the familial batch.

If she didn't give them a name, she was implicating herself. Since Coleman had mentioned a family relationship twice, it was plausible to think they suspected Johnny—if they had talked to her boss, and someone started adding things up—and hoped she would give him up herself.

But could she really believe that Johnny had accepted her help, landed in New York, then immediately killed someone and framed her for it? So blatantly? So obviously?

She'd wanted so badly to connect with him, maybe she'd ignored the signs. She'd done it before, with Mickey. But she was supposed to be different now—all her training, all her hours of service. All to protect others. But what was any of it worth if it didn't protect her? Correction. What was it all worth if she didn't use it to protect herself?

She needed to get everything clear in her head, to calm down the whirlwind. Figure out whose web she was stuck in, and how to get out of it. And for the moment, that meant she had to stay silent on the subject of Johnny—and everything else.

She sat with her hands folded on the table. More seconds passed.

"I need something, Del," Coleman said. "Can you provide any explanation of how a partial match to your DNA came to be under the fingernails of the body? We're going to need to get samples from your mother and father—"

"They had nothing to do with this."

"We're going to need to talk to them."

"My father is in hospital."

"We know. You can't help me?"

"Look, I have no idea."

Coleman nodded, let out a sigh. "Okay, then. I'll be back in a bit."

After the door was closed and locked behind him, the interrogation room was silent. The concrete walls and floor threw off cold instead of warmth, the chill creeping through her plastic standard-issue slippers and up her legs. Her right knee throbbing. Her back aching. Her mind racing with a crazed energy, the other side of which was total exhaustion. But there was no time for sleep.

After he'd called her paranoid, Jacques had told her about Peter. His messages, the time capsule. And then he'd told her to leave New York, though he couldn't tell her why.

Her phone buzzed with incoming texts. Of course, any of her messages would be reviewed by the police, but not the encrypted ones, not unless she gave them passwords. Heart thumping, she angled her head at the phone to read them.

Would it be her mother or sister? Was there news?

It was Suweil. But instead of calming her down, his messages made her break out in a panicky sweat.

> Jonathan Murphy sent messages to somebody inside of Interpol. The messages were encrypted and put onto a general server. We do not know who had access to them.
>
> I know this Mr. Murphy is your uncle. It was not difficult to come to this conclusion using basic image searches. Miss Delta, it will not take long for this information to get out.
>
> I will try to buy you a few more hours.

She remained still, not wanting to flinch. Anyone could be watching her right now, looking carefully for any signs of stress. Just as she would. But her pulse was racing, her mouth had gone dry, and a spider-hole of pain dug itself in behind her eyes.

Her phone buzzed again. More texts. She forced herself to read them as they arrived.

> I have also discovered that your friend Inspector G has a hidden background of domestic violence charges against him.
>
> Came across sealed hospital records from three years ago. Battery against at least one woman.
>
> Also, Insp. G has been changing Interpol records, hiding and degrading reports of extremists. Police have unearthed these and are going to arrest a cell in Paris. They have issued an arrest warrant in France.
>
> And I am sorry to say I can see you have been modifying records as well.

Miss Delta, it does not look good that the two
of you are together.

Another series of clangs at the door and Coleman reappeared, a cup of coffee in each hand. "They let me bring you one."

She could smell it from here, slightly burnt, sweet and warm. She started to shake her head, but then put out her hand to accept it. Coleman set the coffee on the table and sat in the chair opposite her.

Del wrapped her hands around the cup, pulled it close to her. The heat brought her fingers back to life, traveled up to her wrists and arms and relaxed her. But just for a second.

"Your boyfriend, Inspector Galloul—" Del cut him off with a shake of her head. "Well, whatever he is to you. He was released last night. After you spoke with him."

Her hands clenched around the coffee cup. He was *what*? She held her face in neutral—or at least tried to.

"Nice guy. I guess. Except that we got intel from Interpol just after his release. Seems he's been erasing data related to terrorists from Interpol's records. And has connections to a long list of Paris extremists. Might be for his job. Might not. Know anything about any of this?"

Del shook her head. She took her hands from the cup, folded them together instead.

Coleman continued, mostly addressing the bottom of his coffee instead of her. "We also have new information on the IRGC operative. Name was Anila Jalili. She was poisoned. She died right after you left her room." He paused here to give Del an inquiring look. She didn't move. He went on. "We're not accusing you of anything, but you know how this looks."

"Like a setup," Del said quietly.

The trip from Dr. Aringa's house to the subway to her parents' house came back to Del in flashes. She'd avoided every camera, and hadn't spoken to a soul. No alibi.

"We also reviewed the video clip of you and Ms. Jalili together. We're working on a lipreader and software to find out what she said, but do you want to enlighten us? What did she say?"

"Not much. She just said we had the wrong person."

Coleman didn't believe her. "Now is the time to let us know."

Del wrapped her hands around the coffee, but her stomach gave another heave. She took them away again.

"We have video of this man who took something from her. Do you know this person?"

Coleman opened a file folder and pulled out a photo. It was Johnny. But she shook her head.

"What did Anila Jalili give to you?"

Del stayed silent.

Coleman put the photo back in the file folder and closed it. Sighed. "I'm sorry to have to tell you this, Deputy Marshal Devlin. But since you're refusing to cooperate, I've been told we're going to have to try a different tack. They let me try again—but now we both have to do it their way."

Coleman stood and left the room.

A young officer with slick dark hair entered. "Your phone, please, Deputy Marshal."

She handed it over.

"Please stand. Hands behind you."

She rose, put her hands behind her back. The young officer snapped on handcuffs, held her lightly by the arm.

"This way, please."

And she let him lead her down the hall. Past Coleman, his face burning with stress flares. Past the room Jacques had been in just hours ago. Down a long hallway. The lights cheap flickering fluorescents, the walls gray-green. The air refrigerator cold, the scent of pine cleaner doing its best to cut the odor of vomit. Past the holding cell, jammed with last night's perps and suspects. Along another hall, this one pale yellow, lit with yellow bulbs that triggered a pulsing in her head. Empty cells on either side as they walked and walked in silence, their footsteps echoing.

At the end of the hall, one cell stood open, its wall of bars slid back. Inside, three walls of cement blocks, a tiny window, a toilet, and a bare cot.

The young officer escorted her into the cell. He exited, pushed the bars closed, and locked her in.

"Back up, please."

She walked to the bars and turned around. He unlocked and removed the handcuffs.

Checked the lock on the bars.

And then, without another word, the young officer turned and walked away.

***

Free and clear. Johnny leaned back in the leather seats and closed his eyes. Just another couple of hours and he'd be airborne and flying back to safety.

"Watch out, you git!" Dermot lurched the Porsche around a jaywalker and pulled to a sharp stop in the drop-off zone. The place was a zoo—people and cars going every which way, taxis honking, a lollipop man wearing ear defenders trying desperately to control the flow of the crowds. Chaos. Just how Johnny liked it.

"Have a pint for me when you get there," Dermot said.

"Right you are." Johnny opened his door, got out, took his carry-on from the back seat. Caught a glimpse of Dermot and shook his head. "It's only a few days. We can't travel together, like. Heat score."

Dermot nodded.

"And I need you to stay put. Things might need tidying up."

"Aye. Away with you, then."

Johnny patted Dermot on the shoulder. One more pat and he closed the door, and the SUV pulled away.

Alone at last.

First things first. A pint would be lovely, now that he thought of it. No need to wait until he landed.

Johnny headed into the terminal—even more of a melee in here, if that was possible. Pint first, then look in at the bank. He was already checked in, so it was just security, walk on, and Bob's your uncle.

Except for the bit about his niece. He didn't love that. Pint first, for sure. He headed to the nearest bar—massive TVs everywhere, tables scattered about, brass railings and a coffin box. Good sign. But only Bud on tap.

"Sorry," the lass behind the bar said, "we're out of everything else. It's been crazy today!"

Ah, well. The universe was forcing his hand. "Whiskey, neat."

He sat on a stool and surveyed the crowd. People zipped this way and that, no one paying him any mind. He pulled his phone from his pocket, logged into one of his accounts. The one he'd told that skinny scientist to deposit the money into.

And it was there. A million American dollars.

He should've ordered a double.

The lass dropped a cocktail napkin on the bar, then set his whiskey down. "Anything else?"

"No, I'm grand."

His phone buzzed as a text came in. From one of his lads keeping eyes on the brother.

Sean in hospital. Not looking good.

Well, he couldn't do much about that. But he could do a little something for Del. He brought up her contact on his phone, started entering the coordinates of the package. Might help her out if she was in hot water. She was a sweet thing. He was about to hit send when he felt a tap on his arm.

He turned around.

"Can I join you?" The dapper Latino man—Angel. Shite. Never paid to lose focus.

"Suit yourself." Johnny put his phone face down on the table.

"Going back home?" Angel pulled a stool out from behind the bar, sat. Ordered a whiskey and another for Johnny.

"Something like that."

"Listen, you have no reason to trust me, but I think you should know—you're running out of options here."

Johnny took a sip. Put his glass down. The sun shone gold through the whiskey. He was so close. In a matter of hours, he could be away with millions of dollars, free and clear.

"You should stay here and help."

"And why should I?" Another sip. Lovely.

"Del trusted you."

"Ah, now. She never."

"She did. Now she's locked up. You used your family connection, used your own brother, and now he's about to—"

"I didn't cry at my own dad's funeral. What do you want from me?"

Angel looked at him, his face serene. "I know you're going to Budapest. You stay here any longer, FBI will round you up. But if you get on that plane, I get on it, too. And Interpol greets us at the gate on the other side. Either way, you're inside a jail cell end of day."

"I'll take my chances."

"You'll never see your brother again. And I guarantee Del will never see you again. At best, her career will be over because of you. At worst, she's going to jail, too."

"What the hell do you want me to do about it?"

27

Presbyterian Hospital, New York

May 1st, 8:55 p.m.

These places made Johnny's skin crawl. He knew there were all kinds of reasons a person might go to a hospital, but he'd only ever been in one to say goodbye. Look at those poor buggers in the waiting room. How many of them would come out of it okay? Never mind the sad stories on the floor he was heading to. He pressed the up button on the elevator. When it arrived, he stood out of the way to let a shriveled old woman shuffle on ahead of him, pulling a wheely contraption of tubes and bags after her.

"Where're you headed?" he asked the old lady. She cupped a hand behind her ear. "Which floor?" he asked, more loudly this time. It was as he feared—she was heading where he was. He pressed the button for the ICU, ignoring the one on the bottom of the panel. Morgue.

It wasn't the suffering and death that bothered him so much. It was the downright tidiness of it all. Everything organized and managed and tagged with a dollar sign, right down to the last breath. It was inhumane. The end should be as random as life—at least that way, a man stood a chance against it.

When the elevator stopped, he held the door open for the old dear, though he knew he didn't have to. Sensors and that. Still, it felt better to do so. How they'd been raised. She smiled a wrinkly smile at him and tottered off down the hall, pulling her bags of god knows what along with her. Johnny walked straight ahead to the brightly lit reception desk just across from the elevator.

The lass there looked up from her computer screen when he said hello, a faint hint of surprise crossing her face. "Hello there. Can I help you?"

Johnny said who he was here to see and gave his name. "We're brothers, like. Twins."

"I was about to ask what you were doing out of bed, Mr. Devlin." She smiled.

"Murphy," he corrected her.

"Ah, sorry."

He must be looking like absolute bollocks to be mistaken for a cancer patient on his last legs. He'd have to go for a shave when all this was over.

The lass gave him the room number and explained what he'd have to do before going into Sean's room. Put on special gear and that. Offered to come with him, but he smiled and said he was grand.

He was not so. But he wasn't about to tell her that.

It took him no time at all to find the room, but he stood in the hallway for nearly ten minutes, screwing up the nerve to actually go in. For one thing, what he'd said to Angel at the airport was true. He hadn't cried at his own da's funeral. And for another, *she* was in there already, curled into an armchair near the end of Sean's bed. Johnny could just see her where the curtain went around, hiding Sean from view.

"Get it together, man," he said to himself. Then shook his head. Talking to yourself now?

He found the mask and gown and gloves and the goo to clean his hands, got it all on as best he could. Then tapped at the door. Amede lifted her head. He raised a hand, gave a little wave. Her mouth set into a flat line, but she rose and came to the door.

She opened the door only a crack, hissed at him through it. "What in heaven's name do you think you're doing here?"

Going to a fancy dress party as a man from space, he wanted to say—

but he held his tongue for once. Now wasn't the time for his mouth to get him punched in the face. "I'd like to see him, if you'll allow it. I am his brother, after all."

"Is that supposed to be a joke?"

"Not a funny one. Surely you can find it in your heart. It may be the only chance I have before—"

Amede held up a hand. "Please. Let us all think positive thoughts now." She gave him a quick scan from head to toe, then opened the door and let him in.

The room was cold as a fridge. The lass had explained about that, said it lowered the chances of bacteria and such growing and making Sean sick. But still. No wonder Amede had been all huddled up in her chair. Poor woman. He'd send a couple of blankets up from the gift shop on his way out.

"Missy's taking a walk, getting coffee. I think I'll join her. Let you two have some time together." Amede looked him in the eye. "Don't go thinking I trust you. I just don't suppose he has anything left at this point that you could steal or ruin." She edged around him, then the sliding door vacuumed shut behind her.

Johnny walked around the curtain, and there he was. His little brother. Never looked so little in his life.

He wanted to hold his hand, but he didn't want to hurt him. He wanted to wake him, but he didn't want to scare him. Or make him angry. So, he just stood at the side of his dying brother's bed.

And he cried, the big man. Lucky these places were always well stocked with Kleenex.

One of Sean's eyes peeped open. Then both. And he looked surprised, if that could be said of a man with tubes coming out of him every which way.

"I don't think you should talk, and anyway, I doubt that you can with all that in you," Johnny said. "You look grand, by the way."

Sean rolled his eyes and cracked a grin. It was a little weak, but he looked more like his old self. Like the Sean he'd known when they were kids and that, before everything went—

"I want you to know I'm sorry, Sean. For everything that ever went crackers between us. For the family and missing all that time, and you missing da—"

Sean waved a hand like he should stop, shook his head slowly back and forth on the pillow.

"No, now, let me finish. I'm sorry I buggered everything up. And I think there's something I can do now. Maybe it won't fix what happened, but it could go some way to fixing something that needs it right now. But I need your help."

***

No one to call, and anyway, no phone. Del had heard people who'd ended up in jail hollering through the bars, howling about their innocence. And she was starting to understand why. Even though she knew perfectly well there was no one around, that all the other cells were empty, something rose within her, stronger with every minute that went by. A scream. It pulsed through her, building and building the longer she kept it in. She stood where she'd been when the young officer had left, clenching and unclenching her fists. Holding the scream in check.

It had to be late morning by now. She had been in here most of a day already. The night shift had left a little while ago, and Del had tried to get some sleep on the hard bench. She had to get out, somehow—didn't have a second to waste, and yet the seconds and minutes and hours slid by with her trapped in here. But screaming would just make things worse.

Del let out a long breath, took one in. Did it again. Then kicked off the slippers they gave her and started pacing. Getting rid of the slippers was a useless act of defiance. The concrete floor cold on her socked feet, the air around her chilled and musty. She kept going. Around the cell, around and around, her right knee aching, but feeling better the more she moved it.

Her parents had their gods, things they couldn't even see but could call on when they needed them. What did she have? What did she believe in? Things that were equally unseen and just as unattainable. She'd hung her hopes on nationhood, on ideas like liberty and justice, and it was all starting to smell a little sour. Like everything she'd ever trusted had turned out to be make-believe. So, what could she believe in?

She'd been trained to protect people, to save lives. To help. She could still get behind that, couldn't she? Wasn't that what she was doing right now? No. This mess was because she had decided to bend the rules to try and do something for herself.

She stopped. Worked the kinks from her shoulders and hips, stretched out her knee. Then started walking around the cell, again and again. Her footsteps keeping time with her thoughts.

Her dad. She had to get out of here, go see him. But how? What could she tell Coleman that would be true, and not just something he wanted to hear? Soon she would have to come clean, no matter what, and maybe it was even too late already.

Johnny had been sending messages to someone inside Interpol.

Someone who wasn't her.

Jacques? Suweil? Had he asked someone else for help, for a favor, the way he'd asked her? Or was he selling her up the river to save his own skin? She had no way of knowing what Johnny had put in those messages—but Suweil's text had said he knew Johnny was her uncle. And that it was only a matter of time until other people caught on. No one else had a reason to be looking, so maybe that would buy her some time—unless Johnny was sending someone a message right now. All he'd have to do was start the process of getting the information to the right person—he didn't have to know beforehand who the right person was. She knew how quickly things could get where they should be going, even in a massive operation like Interpol. But she didn't have Johnny's messages, and she had no way to get ahold of them.

But if Johnny had been in touch with Suweil, why would Suweil tell her that? Maybe he'd been in touch with Boston Justice. Could that be? Could Johnny possibly be working for Boston? Or was Boston a mole for Johnny, informing him about Del's actions? Were any of these possibilities true?

Coleman hadn't seemed too pleased that Jacques was on the loose.

Maybe there was something to that? Could Jacques have been

communicating with Johnny? Jacques had been into the Interpol databases, had erased information. He could have done other things, too. Coleman said Jacques had ties to extremists in Paris, and whatever he'd been deleting had to do with that. They had never really talked about his religion—or hers, come to think of it—but she didn't think he was an extremist. Observant, yes. She'd always seen his faith as a good thing. But had she just been seeing what she wanted to see, the whole time they'd been together? Had she been rendered helpless by a handsome face again? Why did she keep falling for the same kind of guy?

She stopped mid-stride as her stomach heaved. Eyed the toilet and breathed long and slow, in and out. The queasiness subsided, but the strangled feeling in her chest didn't go anywhere. So she threw a punch . . . and felt better. She threw another one.

What did love even mean? Her dad always said there was a word in Irish that meant crime as well as love. That sounded about right.

It was kind of the same in English, it just took more words. Crime of passion, he stole my heart, thief of love . . . As though it was just a matter of one person getting close enough to the other to take whatever they wanted. Shouldn't she know how to protect herself against that by now?

She took another swipe at the air. Not quite as satisfying as punching Mickey, but it did seem to be helping. Mickey. She hit a one-two at his gut. What had she ever see in him? Or really—what had he seen in her?

Something about her had told him she could be exploited. Something about her at the time had told him she was weak and needy and didn't think too much of herself. She thought she'd gotten over that. But here she was, going through it all again with Jacques. And Johnny. In different ways and for very different reasons. How could she have been so wrong about both of them?

She really had thought she was in love with Jacques. She punched the air. Idiot. Love. What a fool. Two more punches, then a kick.

She'd been here before. Had this sick feeling in her, felt her skin crawl every time she thought of him. Mickey then, Jacques now. *A history of domestic violence.* She dropped her hands. This whole time she'd been asking herself and everyone around her what they would do differently if they could go back in time—but she *was* back in time, right now. Stuck. Doing the same things the same way.

If Jacques really was connected to extremists, did that make him a murderer? Just like Johnny? And if he was a murderer, what was growing inside her? And wasn't it better to just end whatever it was here? But was it the child's fault, any of this?

Then Peter's words came back to her. He'd said their children would know each other in the future. What kind of a sick person would make such statements?

The kind that was building a bomb—she answered her own question.

And what did it mean that Jacques had shown up in New York just as all this was going on? Did it mean anything? Or was she doing it again? Making connections between things that had nothing to do with each other?

She walked in circles, around and around the cell. Her footsteps nearly soundless, her toes cooling now that she'd slowed down.

What would she *really* do if she could go back?

She picked up her hands again, took her stance. Aimed one punch at Mickey's face, then another and another.

What would she do?

It was a pointless question. Even if time travel was possible, the outcome would be the same as long as she was the same. It wasn't time travel that could change anything for her.

She had to change things herself.

Get Jacques out of her life for good.

She still had the appointment tomorrow. Whatever the baby turned out to be, it would tie her to Jacques. Forever.

She had to go through with it.

It wasn't the kid's fault. She'd never even wanted children. And to bring someone like Jacques into the world—what would that make her?

Of course, she could make all the decisions she wanted, but she was still stuck here in prison. What was she supposed to do about the appointment now?

She reset her stance, threw one punch, then another. Then lobbed a series of jabs at her invisible opponent's gut. A roundhouse to the head. And then another battery of punches. Quick breaths, her feet light on the cold floor. But she was warming herself. So warm she was starting to sweat. Kept her arms moving, one swipe after another.

How would she ever find out who Johnny had been communicating with at Interpol? Did it make a difference? Whoever it was, Johnny had done it. Used her. Even though she was family.

Anyway, what had family ever done for her father? Look at the mess Johnny had made of that. Brought nothing but pain and suffering to those he supposedly loved most. And his DNA was her DNA. Why would she ever want to bring more of that into the world?

"Take it easy on the poor devil," a familiar gravelly voice said. "There's nothing to him."

Del dropped her hands and turned around. And there was Johnny.

"Looks like you're getting out, lass." He smiled.

An officer she hadn't seen before—the morning rotation—unlocked the bars, slid them open. Del couldn't think of a thing to say that wouldn't compromise somebody, so she kept her mouth shut as the officer turned away and walked down the hall. Johnny winked at her and pulled something from his jacket pocket.

In his hands, he held her father's ID and badge.

28

Financial District, New York
May 2nd, 11:05 a.m.

So much for making her own choices.

Del was a block away from One PP before it hit her. The bright sun and white sky made her blink, but the reality of what she'd just done woke her up. Her initial elation twisted inside out, and now she was furious with herself for going along with Johnny's plan. But it was too late—she was a fugitive.

Johnny whistled a happy tune as he walked along, the sun glinting off the brass buttons on her dad's uniform. Del kept pace as they wove through the throngs of people on their way to work. The streets were jammed, cars and buses and scooters and cyclists bunching as traffic heaved slowly along, horns honking. The sidewalks were busier than normal too, even for this time of day, buzzing with people hurrying every which way.

A group of people in "Americans For Guthrie" T-shirts walked by, passing a group of people in rainbow unicorn onesies who were blowing bubbles and handing out pamphlets. Of course—the rally. It had slipped her mind again. The area around Liberty Park would be blocked off by now for the event itself, whole neighborhoods packed with the accompanying masses of protesters and counter-protesters, clogging the city with gridlock from end to end.

She had to have a serious talk with Johnny, but where? Scanned the street for an out-of-the-way corner, a spot that would be unlikely to have cameras.

Catching sight of Johnny out of the corner of her eye, Del could swear she was walking along with her dad. The uniform and clean shave suited Johnny's swagger, and he caught everyone's eye as they passed by, giving each a cheery nod of the head, like an old-timey cop in a newsreel. Meanwhile, she felt about as presentable as a wad of chewed gum.

The officer who had booked her out had given her back all her belongings, so at least she was wearing sneakers instead of slippers. But her hair was a disaster, her skin grimy, her clothes rumpled and muddy. She was sure that if they stopped to ask people, even without the uniform, they would peg Johnny as the law-abiding citizen and her as the ex-con.

She sidestepped a puddle, skipped over a steaming manhole cover, then almost ran into a guy on a longboard as he swerved around a bike courier, both on the sidewalk. She shook her head and moved on.

Where was Johnny?

Couldn't see him anywhere. Her arms and back prickled with a sudden nervous sweat before she spotted him ten paces away in a crowded spot near a corner. Kiosks and food carts swamped with customers, the air thick with the mingling smells of coffee and warm pastries. Del's stomach contracted—not with nausea, but hunger. When had she last eaten? It didn't matter. She didn't have time to stop.

She hustled over to stand beside him. Spoke quietly. "You know, I'm still a US Marshal."

"I think you'll find the usual pronunciation is 'thank you.' What most people say when someone helps them. Here, you might be needing this." He glanced up and down the street, then slipped a black metal object into her hand.

A Glock.

She shoved it back at him. "Put that away." No telling who used to own any weapon he had, or what it had been used for. The man had already seemingly implicated her in one murder, was he trying for another?

"Suit yourself." He slipped it back in the pocket of her father's uniform.

"You know what the penalty is for breaking out of jail?" She wasn't even sure.

He shrugged. "You know the way back to your cell."

Del glanced around at the word "cell," but no pedestrian within earshot reacted. Either didn't hear or didn't care. Or didn't care to hear. New York had a way of letting people hide in the open.

She let the crowd swirl by her for a moment, and the weight of time sank down on her again, silently ticking away within her. How long did she have to get this all worked out and sound the alert? She had no idea. But judging by the hectic normality of the people on the street, she wasn't too late. Yet.

"No more joking around," she said, keeping her voice flat. "I need to ask you some questions." Gestured to a quiet spot, a tiny green space with tables and stools bolted to the pavement.

Johnny turned and caught the look on her face. Nodded. And—almost surprisingly—followed.

She sat, even though every second she stayed still stretched the limits of whatever time she had left. She needed him to really listen.

He sat across from her.

Where to begin? There were a million questions bulleting through her as she looked at her terrorist uncle, his expression infuriatingly peaceful. As much as she still had her doubts about Johnny, he *had* given her the chance to figure this out. If she stopped—or was made to stop—it could all be over. For god knew how many people.

She asked, "Why were you selling parts to Dr. Breedlove?"

"Who?"

"The skinny scientist you met with. You had a package for him."

He flushed around the cheeks, the gin blossoms around his nose lighting up. Stress. Which didn't necessarily mean he was lying—but did tell her he didn't like the question much. "Well, it's all part of the racket, isn't it? Not my usual thing, playing delivery boy. But—remember those lads in the alley?"

"The ones who were going to kill you?"

"You can probably guess what they were after."

"Money is typically the primary motivating factor."

"Too right. So, I had to come up with a bundle. I had to sell that part."

"What was in the package you delivered to Breedlove?"

"Does a postman know what's in the letters he drops off?"

"You must have some idea."

"Aye, barely. Some kind of scientific equipment."

"What could it be used for? Could it be part of a weapon?"

He looked at her with a little frown, the first she'd ever seen on his face. No stress blooms. "I have no idea. But why do you ask? I'm the one sticking my neck out now. You tell me, what's going on?"

"I'm asking the questions."

"I did you a good turn just now, wouldn't you say? Time to drop the shield a bit, maybe."

"Tell me what you know about the papers we found on Jalili. The Iranian woman."

"I told you everything when we found them on her. Did you find something else after I left?"

"No." She wasn't about to share any of those details with him. Not yet.

"Then what are you asking me for?"

"How do you know Jalili?"

"Like I said before, she thinks I'm a competitor."

"Anything else?"

He shrugged. "The world is a big place."

"What do you know about the IRGC?"

"As little as possible, to be honest."

This wasn't getting anywhere. "The police found my DNA on a dead body."

"What are you on about?"

She told him about the bag the kids found.

"The poor wee buggers. They'll have nightmares."

"I'm sure they will. Can you focus, please?"

"Oh, I'm sorry. We're only allowed to talk about how things affect you, is that it?"

She looked him in the eye. “Coleman told me that a sample from under the fingernails of that body matches my DNA—or that of a very close relative. Be straight with me. Did you have anything to do with it?”

“Are you being serious?”

Del raised an eyebrow.

“Anyone ever tell you you’re the spit of your ma when you do that?”

Flattened her lips.

“I had nothing to do with it.” When she didn’t reply he added, “I didn’t kill that poor soul those kids found.”

She wanted to believe him. DNA could end up on a person for all kinds of reasons, and finding forensic evidence under the fingernails of a corpse didn’t always mean that whoever the evidence pointed to was the murderer. But if it wasn’t Johnny’s DNA and it wasn’t hers, then whose was it?

“I didn’t do it,” he said again. His cheeks and sinuses calm and cool.

As far as she could tell, he wasn’t lying. Which meant somebody had planted the body—and the DNA. But who would want to implicate Johnny? Maybe the people who tried to kill him because he owed them money. But what if whoever it was wasn’t trying to implicate Johnny? The only other person they would be trying to implicate was—

“You alright there?” Johnny asked. “Looks like someone just walked over your grave.”

“I’m fine,” she lied. The hairs on her arms stood up, just like they had at CERN.

“When did you last eat? Or sleep?”

She waved his questions away. “I told you, I’m fine. Let’s get going.”

It’d been hours since she’d spoken with Dr. Aringa, and if everything he said was true, she needed to find Peter. *Now.* Who knows what he could be doing in every minute that ticked by?

Del put her hand to her eyes and forced back the tears that threatened to fall. That Irish voice again in her head, her dad’s voice—you have things to do. Go do them. Do not mind me.

Johnny eyed her. Started looking through the pockets of her dad’s uniform, pulled something out. Not a gun this time.

He handed her a paper napkin from a deli. “Not quite a hankie.”

Del took it, but put it in her pocket. "How did you get my dad's uniform and badge?" Something occurred to her, and she looked over at Johnny. Still couldn't quite trust him, but his face was cool and calm. "You didn't—"

"Break into your parents' house and steal them? I did no such thing. Your dad gave them to me. Gave me his keys and said where to find it all."

"Excuse me?"

"I went to see your dad. Told him you needed help."

"How is he?"

"Grand."

"Tell me. Honestly."

"Ah, sure you don't want to hear anything like that. You'll go yourself."

Del nodded.

"I'm sure you know your dad has a terrific memory. Always did. Spotted things no one else saw, too. Not unlike yourself."

They started walking again, through the little green space and out the other side. The crowds were thinner here, and the leaves of the trees above them shone jade and lime, lit from behind by the sun.

"I suppose that's what made him a great copper, right enough."

"What do you mean?"

"Would've been a great thief."

Del shook her head, let out a laugh in spite of herself. A little of the tightness unwound, for just a second. But then the pressure came back, and she picked up her pace.

Johnny easily kept stride with her. "Where are we going, anyway?"

"I need to see if dad's car is okay. And there's something I want to check."

"Your dad's car?"

"It should still be at the scene. I don't think Coleman had it towed—"

"When he arrested you?" Johnny grinned.

"Thank you for pointing that out. No one at One PP told me it had been impounded."

They turned another corner. Trees taller here, the greens deeper, the shade cooler.

"You know, I might be able to help."

She had to find Peter, so she'd start where she'd last seen him. He could still be there. If not—

"Alright. Is there an address where I can send Dermot? He might not ever make it in that traffic, but—"

"Just let me think."

They walked in silence for a while. Johnny whistled—a song she was sure she'd heard before. Something her dad used to sing?

"Are you thinking about that frog?"

"What are you talking about?"

"That French fella. Your boyfriend."

"He's not my boyfriend."

"Whatever you say. He works with you at Interpol, isn't that right?"

"I know you've been sending messages to someone in the organization."

"Now why would you go and say a thing like that?"

"Because I am a detective."

Johnny sighed. "I suppose it was only a matter of time."

"Were you sending messages to Jacques?"

"I don't know. I've no idea who I've been communicating with. The messages were encrypted. Whoever it was gave me all the information I needed."

"Can I read them?"

"I deleted them as they came in. Incriminating evidence."

She didn't have to read them to know who Johnny had been in contact with. There was only one person it could possibly have been, only one person who had access to all the information Johnny or anybody else would need.

Bile rose in her throat, and she stopped walking. A cold sweat broke out along her arms.

"Are you sure you're alright? You've gone a bit green."

Shook her head. The sweat dissipated as she breathed deeply, in and out. "Can I borrow your phone? Mine's out of commission." She'd taken out the SIM card and powered down her phone when she'd gotten it back at One PP. No telling who might want to track her through it.

Johnny dug around in the pockets of her dad's uniform, came up with something in glittery red. "A burner. You can lose the case, of course. Though it does jazz it up a bit, if you ask me. Consider it a gift." He handed it over. "Always good to have more than one about you. Never hurts to be a little under the radar, so to speak."

From memory, she texted Angel's number, asked him to go to one of the addresses the technical services officer at One PP had sent her.

They rounded a corner and headed up the street. Sharon, the teal Lincoln Continental was still there.

Johnny let out a low whistle. "She's a beauty. I always wanted one like this. Had a picture up in our room when your da and me were kids. This is his car?"

Del nodded.

"Lucky beggar."

"We should move it."

"Why?"

"To stop police coming here to get it."

"True. Listen, I'll move her while you get your ducks in a row. Give me an excuse to drive her for a bit, too."

She started to hold out the keys, then paused.

"I'm not going to steal it. A promise from one copper to another. If I was going to run off, why would I be back here?"

She let out a breath. Put the keys in his hand. He winked, got into the car, and sped off.

The car wasn't the only thing still in place.

The message was still there, written on the white wall in paint only she could see.

DELTA

I KNOW YOU'RE FOLLOWING ME

Keeping one eye on the building, checking for any movement, Del walked over to the wall. Got close to it, looked up. Put her hand out, touched it. How had Peter done it? The paint was a blend she'd made up herself—the number of people she had told about it she could count on the fingers of one hand. Not even Jacques. How could Peter have known about it?

A sound behind her—Johnny clearing his throat. "Are you dead sure you're alright, love? Maybe you need a bit of a rest. You must have been staring at that wall for ten minutes now."

There hadn't been any movement in the building, nothing at all. Peter probably wasn't there. They needed to check inside—no sense or possibility of bothering with warrants at this point—but she had a feeling it was a dead end.

There was only one person knew her well enough to have set all this in motion.

29

Chinatown, New York
May 2nd, 11:25 a.m.

"What's your plan?" Johnny asked.

Doyers Street chattered around them, a pedestrian-only zone packed with restaurants and shops and people sitting outside on folding chairs. Many of the awnings torn and ragged, but the sidewalks clean. Chinese lettering on signs running the lengths of the buildings. Shoppers hustling about dragging wire baskets behind them, little ladies shuffling along, old men sunning themselves, packs of young people drinking tea and smoking. Everybody talking loudly—some yelling from one sidewalk to another, carrying on conversations across the road, music blasting from storefronts on all sides.

Before they'd left the last address and the white wall, Del texted Angel, asked him to cover it. The technical services officer at One PP had sent her two addresses, and she wanted to make sure both had eyes on them. Just in case. There was still a chance she was wrong about who she'd find here, at the other address she'd gotten from One PP.

Del looked up at the thin red-brick building, rising stories taller than any other around here. Black fire escapes. Checked her notebook.

"That's it."

They headed over. Johnny carried on with his Officer O'Hara routine, giving everyone he passed a chipper grin and a bob of the head. Most of them ignored him, and some outright scowled.

"Not fans of the filth around here, I take it."

"You could say that."

"Interesting." He toned his act down as they reached the front door of the building. Locked, a row of buzzers next to it. "What did you say was your plan here?"

"We're going to ring the buzzer."

"That's what they teach you in detective school, is it?"

She shot him a look but had to admit that he was right—if only to herself. Why had her first inclination been to treat this as a visit? The man she was pretty sure was in this building was a suspect. But she wasn't a US Marshal or detective or Interpol officer right now. She was a fugitive.

Johnny sized up the door, inspecting the lock while appearing to just walk to and fro. "Shouldn't be a problem. Take me two shakes. You need to get in there, talk to whoever you're looking for, yes?"

Del nodded.

"What happens if you don't find who you need to find?"

"Very bad things."

"Give us a hint."

"I'm not ready to do that yet."

"Well then, there's nothing to decide. Just pretend you don't know me. Listen, it's not like you're doing it. And I'm the copper here, after all. At least that's what these folks will see."

If anyone had told her a week ago—a day ago—she'd be breaking into a suspect's possible location with her terrorist uncle, and that *she* would be the one on the run, she'd have told them to pull the other one.

Del stepped back to give Johnny room, then took slow steps back and forth around the front of the building, watching for anyone coming or going, and keeping eyes on the people on the street.

No one went in or came out, and not a single person seemed at all interested in anything they were doing.

And Johnny was right—it took him no time at all to get the lock open. They walked into the entrance hall. Stained red carpet, peeling wood paneling, a smell of boiled cabbage and mold. The lights some strange orange bulbs made to look like flames in sconces holding fake candles at either side of every door.

"Spared no expense in here."

Del held a finger to her lips, shushed Johnny. He put his hands up in a jokey surrender but kept quiet.

No elevator, so they crossed the lobby and headed up the stairs. No fake candles here, just naked fluorescent tubes at every landing. Del blinked in the yellow-white light as they went up. Walked as quietly as she could, but the mildewed boards sank and whined under her weight, complaining even more at Johnny's. The smell of cabbage worsened at the second floor, only to be replaced by a mysterious meaty odor on the higher floors.

As they reached the fourth floor, Del's burner dinged—she'd forgotten to switch it to vibrate. She pulled the sparkly red phone from her pocket as it dinged again and again. Put it on silent, her heart pounding. Then stood on alert for a minute or two. Took low breaths and waited, making sure nobody had heard her phone go off. All was quiet. She checked the phone.

A text from Angel:

Someone emerged from the location

The text was followed by a photo of a woman wearing sunglasses, a scarf wrapped around her head and hair, like a lady going for a drive in a convertible in the 1950s. Del couldn't make out much else.

Sorry about the photo—best I could do

She was moving fast

Del texted back:

Stay on her. Don't let her out of your sight, no matter what.

She examined the picture again, but still couldn't get any real sense of what the woman looked like. Definitely didn't recognize her. Maybe she was Peter's girlfriend?

As she closed the texts, she caught sight of the time at the top of the screen. Was this phone right? It couldn't be that late already, could it? Her own phone would be buzzing like crazy with incoming texts by now, if it had power. Almost noon—Boston's deadline for meeting him. He and Suweil and god knows who else would be trying to contact her.

Like her mother and her sister. Her hand tightened around the burner in her pocket. They must be worried about her, and they had enough to think about right now. She wanted to text them, call, see how her dad was doing—but she had to focus. This was bigger than her and her family. It could be everyone. She let go of the phone and kept going.

They reached the fifth floor. Gestured to Johnny to stay where he was, just out of sight around the bend of the landing. She put her ear to the door, her heart beating too quickly again. Nothing. Cracked the door open and scanned the hallway. Same decor as the lobby, but most of the orange lights had burned out. And it was silent and empty.

She gave the all clear to Johnny. Then walked to the end of the hall, the sounds from her footsteps muffled by the soiled red carpet.

Listened at the door. Voices.

She leaned her head closer to the door. Breathed shallow breaths, her heart racing. Two voices. A male and a female.

Johnny was right behind her. Leaning forward and listening, too.

They eyed each other. That Glock Johnny had offered her earlier would've come in handy right about now. At least he was carrying.

Del closed her eyes and listened. The people suddenly stopped talking—and a jingle for a fast-food place came on at top volume. Just a TV.

She let out a breath. Johnny smiled.

"Got another one in you?" she asked, keeping her voice down.

"Whatever it takes."

But instead of jimmying the lock, he knocked. The hollow sound of the pressed wood door echoed up and down the hall. Del shot him a look and held her breath. No sound from the other side.

"Always pays to check first." Johnny bent to the lock.

And they were in.

She closed the door behind them and slid the chain lock into place, then turned around.

"Now *this* is living," Johnny said.

A single room with a hot plate by the door, bathroom at the other end of the square space. Tattered sheet tacked over the window, probably once white, but now a gray the same shade as damp caulk. Ashtrays overflowing with the dark brown remains of some kind of fancy cigarette, a smell in the air of smoke—but something else too, something sweet.

Vanilla?

TV blasting CNN. A chipped chest of drawers. Bare foam mattress on the floor. No bedding anywhere—maybe he hadn't been sleeping? Or maybe he just hadn't been sleeping here. No food anywhere, either. Not even a can of something. She glanced into the bathroom—a ratty towel hung off the doorknob, a roll of toilet paper sat on the floor. No toiletries.

The Jacques she knew would never stay in a place like this.

Then again, she didn't know the *real* Jacques.

"We should think about changing our gear. They'll be looking for people who match our descriptions by now."

Johnny opened the drawers—and pulled out sweat suits. The closet door was ajar, not a thing hanging in it. No suits, no uniforms. Not like him—if the person she thought was staying here really was. He was a Mercedes-and-pressed-suit man. She couldn't imagine him choosing to stay in a dingy hole like this. Could it be someone else? Had she gone down the wrong path?

As Del walked over to the corner furthest from the door, she saw papers. Everywhere. Some neatly stacked and in folders, others strewn all over the floor.

Johnny left the drawers open and joined Del. They looked at the scatter of sheets. He said, "Just start anywhere, I guess, right?"

Del nodded and bent to a pile.

Information about Jacques and Interpol, about games to bet on, about herself. Some pages were fairly lucid, with "future Peter" just hinting at the nature of data time travel, explaining how it worked. Others looked like rapid-fire thoughts with barely any sense to them, at least not that Del could see. And many pages were thick with notation—scribblings about physics that Del couldn't make head or tail of.

What had Jacques said? That she needed to leave New York, that he had information he couldn't tell anyone, not even her. Was that information somewhere in these pages?

She took a closer look at one of the pages filled with equations. The handwriting at the top of the page was clear and evenly spaced, becoming more cramped and spidery and frantic as it moved down. She turned the page over.

The whole of the other side was nearly illegible—Peter had written equations horizontally on the page, then turned the page and continued writing across those lines. Cross-writing, something people used to do when paper was a scarce and expensive commodity. But by the looks of things, he had access to plenty of paper. Why had he done this? And if the information she needed was on a page like this one, they'd be at this for days.

Del turned to another pile, read page after page, her head spinning. Tried to put the letters into order, tried to figure out when Peter's communications with his "future self" had started. Thankfully, each page was dated. Peter included the time as well, down to the second. She started new piles, sorting, and sifting by date.

After many minutes of this, she stopped. There were whole days missing. So, this might not be everything Peter had written to his future self. There could be more letters. But where?

Del put down the papers in her hands. Shook her head and went over the piles she'd put together one more time. She couldn't make sense of it. Just when she thought she was getting somewhere. She let out a long breath.

Even the bare foam mattress looked appealing.

Johnny's gravelly voice came from across the room, where he'd been looking through other scattered papers. "You should come take a look at this."

She walked over. "What is it?"

"Not good." He handed over a stack.

Page after page filled with the same words.

A great evil
One that must be erased from history
No matter how many lives it takes

Del flipped through the stack—more pages, all the same. A great evil. What was Peter talking about?

A rattle at the door. The chain held, pushed taut. Then a voice. One Del knew too well.

"Hello? Who is in there?"

Johnny sprang to the door. Del stuffed the papers she was holding into her jacket pocket and thought about getting out her weapon but took her stance instead.

"Excuse me? Whoever is in there, you should know who you are dealing with here. Those papers are Interpol property—do not touch them!"

A kick at the door, then another. The chain held, but the cheap doorframe splintered, pulled away from the wall.

And the door opened.

Del cocked her fists.

Jacques.

Johnny caught him in a headlock. Jacques struck out with his elbows, getting Johnny in the gut. In return, Johnny flung Jacques onto the floor and put his whole weight on him. "What are you doing here, lad? These are all yours, you say?"

Jacques strained against Johnny, then caught sight of Del. She stood frozen—she hadn't been able to make a move when she could have helped, and she wasn't making one now. Why? After all this, she didn't want to hurt him? She hated herself for standing still, but she couldn't make herself do anything. "Delta. Why did you bring the police with you? We can settle this, just us two. I can explain."

"Don't you talk to her, boy-o. You're dealing with me now." Johnny held Jacques down.

"Who is this man? He looks like your father, but isn't he—"

"Never you mind who I am." Johnny looked over at Del. "What do you want to do with him?"

What *did* she want to do with him? Her father's cap had been knocked from Johnny's head, his cheeks and sinuses flushed, his gin blossoms zinging to life with blood and stress. He looked more like his old self now. The body under the boardwalk flashed into her mind, the hand curling from the unzipped bag.

Only one person knew enough about her to have set all this up. But even if she managed to take Jacques in peacefully, what would happen to him? Would he just be set free the next day? They'd already let him out once. It had to have been Jacques all along, planting information for her to find. He had silenced the IRGC operative when she'd tried to talk to Delta. She should just drag him to One PP and tell them there was a terrorist cell being run by Jacques Galloul, but part of her resisted it. But was she only doing that because she was his lover?

Johnny grunted, "Del, my girl. What do you—"

Jacques twisted free and rolled over and over, out of Johnny's reach, then ran for it. Banged out the battered door and thudded down the hallway. Johnny went after him. Del shook her head, suddenly clear, like she was waking up. Tore after them. Out the door at the end of the hall and onto the fire escape.

Just in time to see Jacques take off down the ladder.

When she got to the edge and peered over, she could just make him out, stories below. How had he gotten down there so fast? Johnny was clambering down after him at a good clip, but then Jacques leapt—and landed on the roof of a passing truck.

30

Chinatown, New York

May 2nd, 11:45 a.m.

Del tore down the fire escape stairs, Johnny just ahead of her.

"Keep your eyes on him!"

"What d'you think I'm doing?"

Del winced as she reached the first floor—her right knee felt like it disjointed. Jacques had jumped from here, but there was a ladder. Johnny let it down as Del rubbed her knee and kept watch on Jacques.

The Frenchman swayed into a crouch on the roof of the cube van, then splayed himself flat. The van bumped along the alley for a block before stopping. Del saw Jacques's lips moving, likely swearing a blue streak in French and English. He ran down the front of the van and disappeared behind it.

Johnny had the ladder down.

She hopped onto it and took the rungs as fast as she could, jumping the last few feet into the alley. A metallic clanking came from above as Johnny followed.

By the time Del reached the van, the driver had gotten out and hauled open the rolling rear door. A man in a stained white apron opened the back door of the restaurant they were behind and propped it open with a brick. The driver and the man in the apron stood behind the open van, smoking cigarettes and chatting, laughing with each other, their backs to the open door.

Jacques peered out from behind the van, spotted Del, then ran in through the door into the restaurant. Del gave a hand signal to Johnny and headed in, gravel clicking under her feet.

She stepped into a dark, cool room piled high with open boxes of produce, green and earthy smells rising from them. No Jacques that she could see. Sounded like the next room had people in it—lots of them. She glanced over her shoulder and saw Johnny was right behind her, then moved through the darkness to a doorway, bright lights beyond it. She stuck her head through the door and surveyed the space.

Great clouds of steam rose from massive stoves along one wall of the kitchen, with cooks moving from pot to pot and calling orders to each other. A waterfall ran behind the wok station, where more cooks tossed vegetables into sizzling pans. Waiters flitted in and out of the chaos picking up plates and bowls, while bussers dropped off brown plastic bins of dirty dishes near the sinks at the other end of the kitchen. Live fish swam in a huge aquarium built into the wall so their glittering scales would be visible to the guests in the dining room. The mix of smells—ginger, garlic, fish, and meat—made Del's stomach growl. She ignored her hunger and stood in the doorway, scanning the room from end to end. A commotion erupted. Jacques was tangled up in the incoming stream of bussers across the room.

Del darted through the gauntlet of cooks, with potlids and dropped woks clattering in her wake. The cooks yelled after her. She kept her eyes on Jacques, who was getting hollered at by the dishwashers. He bulldozed his way through and sped through the swinging doors. Del followed, close on his heels now.

She pushed open the red-vinyl padded doors and swung into the restaurant. The place was crammed wall to wall, every seat at every table filled with the lunch crowd, what little space remained between tables taken up by waiters and men in white aprons pushing trolleys of stacked bamboo steamers. The air filled with the brittle clinking of chopsticks on porcelain and plastic over the rise and fall of endless table chatter, all of it cut through with the noise of an ill-fitting Top 40 radio station. Del zigzagged around tables and waiters, Jacques doing the same just feet in front of her. Angry voices behind her indicated Johnny was bringing up the rear.

A tiny woman wearing a black sweat suit with a white Bic pen behind her ear moved from the station by the door right into Del's path. Held up a hand.

"What are you doing here?" the woman yelled. "Very busy right now. Too busy for games!"

"I'm a detective—"

"Oh, no. You show me warrant or you go now."

Jacques had almost made it to the front door, but his way was blocked by the line of people waiting to be seated. He squeezed through them slowly, slipping by one person at a time.

The tiny woman stood her ground, right in Del's way, her hand still held up.

"Please." Del leaned around her. "I really have to—"

"You go now!"

"Could I please just get past you?" Del spotted a small opening to one side of the woman and swooped around her, just catching Jacques's eye as he plowed through a knot of people at the door. Curses rose after him.

Why was he running if he wasn't guilty? And what had he read in Peter's letters? When she'd talked with Jacques in the interrogation room in One PP, he'd said he had information that he couldn't tell her. Something he said Peter wrote. What was it? Only one way to find out. Del ran after him.

"Look sharp!" Johnny pulled up behind her. Pointed, then paused with his hands on his knees, breathing hard. Jacques was pulling open the door of a place across the street. Del took off.

Just as she reached the other side of the street, a group of teenagers drifted out of one of the restaurants, laughing at something on one of their phones. They walked slowly, eyes down, talking loudly to each other, their group spanning the width of the sidewalk. Del darted one way and then the other but couldn't get through or around them.

"Excuse me!" she called out at a higher volume than she'd intended. The kids shot her dirty looks but slunk out of her way. She nodded her thanks, then wedged between them and opened the door to the place Jacques had gone into.

Darkness. She stood still while her eyes adjusted.

The shop was long and skinny and packed floor to ceiling with shelving, each level stuffed with boxes. The windows stacked high too, bright sun peeping in through gaps. Porcelain bowls and rice cookers stood in neat piles next to open boxes holding everything from chopsticks, key chains, and nail clippers to embroidered slippers, children's pajamas, and folding scissors. Kites and red lanterns and strings of little white lights in colored paper globes strung along the ceiling. Wafts of incense folded over her.

A crash erupted from the back of the room, followed by Jacques's voice, shouting in French.

Del sprinted forward.

Jacques pulled himself out from under a toppled stack of bamboo furniture, tossing pieces every which way. Del scooted out of the way of a launched bamboo stool and stumbled into a row of huge white porcelain pots painted with cranes and dragons and butterflies. Jacques heaved a heavy-looking carved wooden table over, blocking the way, before running behind a folding screen open for display.

The shopkeeper approached Del, his cheeks red with stress.

From behind the screen, Jacques cursed. Crashing sounds followed. Del ran to the table Jacques had put in her way—it was taller than her, lying on its side, and it was as heavy as it looked. She put her weight against it and slid it over, boxes teetering over and falling all around as she did so. Cleared a slim path. She ran along it and ducked behind the screen.

Some kind of storage area. Massive cardboard boxes had been stacked to the ceiling here all along the back wall, and the little space smelled strongly of sandalwood. Jacques was pushing boxes aside, throwing things out of his way, moving box after box after box. But behind them nothing but wall. No back door.

She yelled, "Why are you running? I need to know—"

He reversed course and raced past her. She reached for him, but he was too fast.

Jacques bulleted down the path she had just cleared and ran to the front door. Del took off after him. The shopkeeper yelled at her as she flew past, and she got to the door just as it closed behind Jacques.

Back out onto the street, people everywhere. No sign of Jacques. Or Johnny, for that matter. Del paused to catch her breath, her heart thumping loudly in her chest. Sweat trickled down her back, and her right knee throbbed now that she'd stopped.

She looked up the street one way. Nothing. Back down along the other side, harder to see into the nooks on the shadowy side of the road. She squinted. Then caught sight of Jacques, sticking to the shade across the road, his sand-colored coat flapping behind him. She ran.

Through another door. Into a pink room crowded with mirrors, the walls lined with hairdressing stations and manicure booths, a group of little sinks at the back. Light classical music played at a low volume. The space was clouded with the overpowering fumes of nail polish and hair products, and sprinkled with women who all seemed to start talking at once as the door closed behind Del.

A receptionist sat at a table near the door, her eyes wide open as she looked toward the back of the salon.

"Did a man just run that way?" Del asked. The woman nodded.

As Del sped away to the back of the salon, she avoided looking in any of the mirrors. Didn't care to see how disheveled she was right now, and didn't have time to stop and fix anything anyway. The women's eyes followed her, some of them turning in their seats to watch.

Del just saw the back door closing as she reached the entrance to the back room. So close! She picked up the pace and slammed out of the door.

And there was Jacques, standing still in the parking spots behind the salon, pinned in place by Johnny, who approached from the other side.

In a pincer movement, she and Johnny closed in on him. His eyes darted from one to the other, then away.

And he hopped on the back of a scooter, pushed the driver off, and gunned it.

***

Del shook her head, let out a long breath, and sat down on the back step of the salon.

"Well, that buggered it." Johnny joined her, both huffing and puffing.

When she'd caught her breath, Del looked at Johnny. "I could've used some help back there."

"How was I to know that shop didn't have a back door? Now what?"

Now what, indeed. Del stretched out her sore knee and let out another long breath. "We need to find Peter Breedlove."

"Who?"

"The skinny scientist."

"As I was trying to tell you earlier—I can help."

"We're already both going to jail. *Back* to jail. I'm not sure how much more assistance I can handle from you."

"I put a tracking device in the box. When I sold him that part. Insurance, like."

Del took a second to let her brain wrap around this new information. "Why didn't you tell me?"

"I was telling you. I was trying to send you the coordinates of the package when your man there stopped me at the airport. I swear I was. I'm not a complete arsehole. I wasn't going to leave you hanging. Not entirely, anyway."

His face told her he was both lying and not at the same time. Flares of hot pink up his cheeks, but they could be from running as much as stress. "You're saying you know where that part is?"

"As long as someone didn't find my tracker. It's a wee thing."

Which Peter, if he looked inside the device, would probably discover in a split second. The guy had helped design one of the most complex devices on the planet, but then again, was he more of a designer or a technician? It didn't matter, and Del didn't have anything more to go on.

She raised her eyebrows at Johnny. "Well?"

He dug his phone out from the pocket of her dad's uniform, opened the app for the tracker. "There it is."

A gray dot appeared on a map of the city. Johnny tapped at the screen. "We might have a bit of luck yet." He showed her the list of locations. "It's been in the same place all day."

"And where is that?"

31

Tribeca, New York
May 2nd, 12:12 p.m.

They took a cab down Canal into Tribeca, but with the rally today in Liberty Park, the police had blockaded half of lower Manhattan. Del and Johnny had sat side by side in the back of the yellow cab, not speaking, as they inched through the traffic. After ten minutes, Del decided it would be better—and faster—to go on foot.

At least, for her it was.

She paused under the shade of an oak tree at the corner of Centre and Worth to stretch out her aching knee and let her uncle catch up. The sky bright and cloudless, the sun shining down warm. Thomas Paine Park was dotted with people picnicking, lounging in the grass, enjoying a stroll hand in hand. The neo-Gothic columns of the US Federal Courthouse loomed to her left, and a block further west was One Police Plaza, where she had just escaped from.

There were street and traffic cameras everywhere here, but she had no time for worrying or hiding. This wasn't a covert operation anymore. This wasn't even a mission or a case. She was on the run now, a fugitive in her own city. She considered calling Coleman, but she needed some answers first. Someone was pulling her strings and wanted her out of the way, and now she had unexpectedly gotten unstuck from the web.

She needed to use that to her advantage.

Unless it was Johnny who was spinning this web, in which case she had to keep him close. Soon she would find out.

Blue sky above. So much for the forecasted storm.

Johnny stopped beside her. Hands on his knees. Sucking wind in heaving gulps.

"Need a break, do you?" he gasped.

"Less than you need a ventilator."

When he'd recovered a bit, she pulled out his phone and checked the tracking app again. "Should be over there."

She pointed. Looked up.

Two blocks over, past the thirty-story monolith of the Javits Federal Building, a newly hatched skyscraper stretched into the pale sky. The first twenty stories of the concrete skeleton were complete but not yet sheathed, the building capped by a red structure encircling the top.

The map app listed it as the Tribeca Luxury Apartments.

It was right at the end of Duane Street, which was cordoned off with cement blocks intended to stop trucks or even tanks from accessing the road. The IRS building was just across from the Javits, the two of them prime targets for any attacks. Not to mention the Federal Courthouse, the New York Supreme Court, and more.

This area was packed with possible objectives for an attack. Lower Manhattan was a target-rich environment, especially if Dr. Aringa was right. Was there a weapon of mass destruction hidden in lower Manhattan? In a suitcase? Or something larger? Built into the building? Or something so small it would be impossible to find, unless you knew exactly where it was.

She looked again at the gray dot on the tracking app.

She still wasn't sure if this made any sense. Part of her was screaming to call in the cavalry, but another part of her shouted caution, that this might be another diversion by Johnny.

"Should we split up?" he asked. "You do one floor, I do another?"

"We do this together. You get out of my sight for a second, and—"

"What? You going to scold me to death?"

"Don't test me. Stay close." She should have taken that gun from him.

They walked the last block side by side, weaving through pedestrians while they kept their gaze up, searching for any movement on the upper floors.

The entire construction site was surrounded by temporary fencing laced over with orange nylon. As they approached it, Del inspected the top of the tower, trying to figure out what the red casement was for. And didn't skyscrapers usually have some scaffolding around them from the ground up? Something else was off. She checked the time on her phone. Just after noon on a Tuesday.

There was no movement anywhere on the building, inside or out.

No workers, no security she could see.

She said. "Why isn't anybody working?"

"Union dispute," Johnny said. "I looked it up this morning when I saw where the package had stopped moving around. Work stoppage."

Seemed a little too convenient. An abandoned skyscraper in this neighborhood? There had to be security of some kind, more than just cameras. "What else did you find out?"

"Something to do with the funds—it's being built by a company out of Hong Kong. How they got that contraption there." Pointed up to the red cap at the top of the unfinished building, a kind of sheath that covered the entire perimeter. "That's a skyscraper machine. The lads build the concrete structure inside it, and the platform raises itself as the building grows."

"Unless everyone walks off the job."

"Can't build itself, quite. Not yet, anyway."

They reached the boarded plywood wall surrounding the building. Del checked between gaps, but tried to look like she wasn't. She looked up at a CCTV camera on a lamppost. Smile for One PP, she thought to herself.

All was quiet within the construction site. Not a person in sight, but that didn't mean there wasn't security personnel. She didn't have time to scout. This was going to have to be messy and from the hip. They had stopped halfway down the block.

"This has the feeling of a trap, I don't mind telling you," Johnny said.

"Every time I'm with you, it feels like that."

"Hey, be nice."

"This is me being nice." She forced a smile.

Johnny going to see her father had softened her up, she had to admit, even if it was to plan something illegal. Her father might be on his deathbed, and his brother had finally convinced him into a life of crime—using Delta as the reason. A surge of guilt competed with the rising terror of getting closer to the gray tracking dot.

Del waited for a couple pushing a baby stroller to pass before standing on her toes to look through a square cut-out section in the plywood wall. She assumed it was made so that curious onlookers could check out the inside, without needing to prop themselves up on a fence.

Nobody was within sight left or right. Two of the boards next to them had been pried apart.

"Okay, give it to me," Del said, and held out her hand.

"What?"

"The gun."

She checked the weapon. Made sure a round was loaded and checked the clip. She slipped it into her jean pocket, then grabbed around her uncle's waist.

"Hey, hey, what's this?"

She produced another weapon from under the uniform. Another Glock. "I'm sure you understand."

"I'm sure I do not," he replied, but he didn't try and take it back from her.

She made sure this second one wasn't loaded and separated the clip, then handed him back the gun. He grumbled but put it inside the uniform.

Del knelt and slipped first through the loose section of fencing, waited for Johnny to come through, then they walked together across the gravel yard surrounding the concrete foundation, their footsteps throwing up clouds of dust that hovered around them as a slight breeze carried it. Looked like the work stoppage had happened in the middle of a shift. Machines stood scattered about, some of them with their doors open. Tools on the ground, not put away.

They entered the building on the ground floor.

A hushed darkness, suddenly isolated from the city noise, cut across by shafts of sunlight, the entryway soaring above them. A pigeon whirred, raising a cloud of cement powder. Del raised her eyes to a square of pale sky embraced by the ribs of the tower. It felt familiar, the enclosed vastness.

"Like a church," Johnny said, keeping his voice low.

That was it. The same feeling she had when she was at CERN.

"Stay quiet," Del whispered, and crouched, urging him to do the same.

She scanned the semidarkness of the ground level for any stabbing beams of flashlights, any sign that a security team was in here with them. That someone might have seen them. Nothing. No sounds above the distant honking of cars.

Twenty-two floors. Del had counted as they approached. Checking each one together would take twice as long. She had his phone and had checked his pockets. No other communication devices she could find.

"We split up," she said. "I take the east side, you the west. If you see anything, stay hidden, meet back at this staircase before doing anything, you understand?"

"What exactly are we looking for?"

If he was leading her on, he was being awfully good at it. "Anything unusual."

They split up to check out the ground floor and discovered there were two central staircases and six elevator shafts. More equipment left everywhere, like this was the Pompeii of New York construction. Del was more than slightly relieved when Johnny returned to meet her, skulking gracelessly through the shadows. He wouldn't make much of a cat burglar.

"Nothing but tools and equipment," he said.

"Let's get to the top and work our way down in more detail," Del said. "Do a quick scan at each floor."

"You sure? All the way up?"

"Can you make it twenty flights?"

He cursed but nodded.

Del said, "You do the west staircase, I'll go up here."

Johnny headed fifty feet to the other concrete column that supported the center of the building.

Stair climbing was her least favorite gym activity. Del's knee ached at every step. Each floor she came out and surveyed the open concrete and waited for Johnny to appear at the other staircase, his face more crimson at each stop.

Very little stealth in this.

The sound of her footsteps echoed.

Each step she had to resist the urge to phone someone, to call this in. If there was an attack coming, if there was a bomb, she needed to warn the authorities—but she still wasn't sure if this was yet another misdirection by her uncle. He sprung her out and literally led her by the nose here. If anyone was heading into a trap, it was her.

But she had no choice, and she hated the feeling.

Even more than that, she needed to warn her family. What was the blast radius of a weapon like Dr. Ross Aringa had described? Aringa wasn't sure, but said that pound for pound it could be a thousand times more powerful than a thermonuclear device. Presbyterian Hospital was two, maybe three miles? Would there be fallout? Radiation? She had no idea.

Just a few more floors and she would find out if this was real, or if her uncle was leading her on another goose chase.

She waited longer about twelve stories up. Had to go to the other staircase—wondering if Johnny had lit out and run—but found him huffing and puffing halfway up. She told him to take a break and took the opportunity to look around. The city spread out below, the river sparkling, the sun shining. A steady stream of people made their way down Church Street toward Liberty Park. She could just hear muffled chants. The rally. It was supposed to start in the early afternoon, not more than ten blocks away.

The stairs up to the last half-completed floor were blocked off, but ladders led through gaps in the blocks of cement already formed in a grid along the two-hundred-foot square platform. She climbed. Heard someone talking. Balanced on the fifteen-foot high aluminum ladder, Del glanced at the cement below, then pulled her weapon. Wind buffeted the red nylon webbing that enclosed the open edges of concrete.

She reached the top.

Blue sky overhead crisscrossed by the red metal girders of the skyscraper machine. A metal corridor led outward toward the edge, with twenty-foot gaping holes in this half-finished platform. Forty feet to her left was the opening where the other staircase came up. She waited a beat, expecting to see Johnny's face appear at the opposite staircase, but she couldn't wait. Weapon forward, she swung around and out of the corridor and into open space, nothing but sky blue above her.

And there he was.

Thirty feet away at the extreme southwest corner of the platform, not ten feet from the yawning edge, with no protective barrier between him and three-hundred feet of open space.

Peter Breedlove sat at a makeshift desk of plywood set atop a sawhorse.

Two black satchels by his feet. Papers spread all around him, his head bent, writing at a manic pace. A driving wind picked up some of the sheets, blowing them over the edge and sending them spinning onto Manhattan below. Del snagged one up that scattered toward her. It was the same as some of the pages they found at Jacques's place in Chinatown, the same handwriting. She picked up another one—it was the same, too.

A great evil must be erased from history. It is time.

Over and over, the same words repeated on each line.

"I've been waiting for you." Peter stopped writing and looked up. Unsurprised. His face cool and calm, no stress blooms.

Del held her weapon steady. "Hands up, Dr. Breedlove. Please don't move."

"You told me I would meet you here."

"Why did I tell you that?"

"Because you needed me to tell you in person. That my daughter and your son are going to grow up together. That today we are saving their lives."

"I don't have a son."

"Yes, you do." He looked at her midsection.

She hadn't told anyone except her own personal doctor here. It didn't matter. Maybe he had been tailing her, or had someone follow her.

"Whatever you think this is, Peter, it needs to end now."

"This will never end. Not unless I stop it. Our children's lives are at stake, Delta."

"Then let's save them."

"That's what I am doing. I am saving the whole future of humanity."

He smiled as he said it, calm. Resigned.

Utterly deluded.

Del said, "I never met you before I arrived at CERN. I am not the one telling you to do these things."

"You have been messaging me for months."

"That's not me."

"It is you, but from eight years away along this timeline. In what you would call the future."

"It's not the future to you?"

"Depends how you look at it."

"And how do you?"

"You told me all about your special vision, how you paint with it."

Del kept her weapon up and quick-checked behind her. She edged two feet closer. An opening in the cement floor ten feet long between her and the edge of the platform. Wind sucked and spiraled dust through the opening and blew back her hair.

"I told you about my paint?"

"I know everything about you." Peter pulled out another sheet of paper, started writing again. "You told me that when you finally do know I'm right, tears will come to your eyes and blue bells will be ringing."

"Someone is manipulating you, Peter. It's not me."

"Then who? Answer me that."

That was the question Del had been struggling with. Suweil said messages had been logged in at Interpol. Johnny had contacted someone there. Only one person knew enough about all these lab thefts. Only one person was so close to Del that they knew everything about her. Only one person she knew that had ties to Muslim extremists, if she could believe that, but then what choice did she have?

Jacques had already lied to her. He had beaten his previous girlfriend, Zoya, unless Suweil was lying to her as well, which didn't make any sense.

Jacques wasn't the man she thought he was.

That much did make sense now.

Her heart split open a little before reforming. Hardened. She had to admit the only truth that was possible. "Do you remember Inspector Galloul of Interpol?"

Peter nodded and kept writing.

"I think he's been doing this. Inspector Galloul is the one making you think you're in communication with people in the future. It's not real. None of it is."

"You told me you would say that."

Peter finished what he was writing and let the paper go. It was caught by the wind and soared over the edge of the platform. "You're the one who is being manipulated."

"We can stop this. Right now."

Labored wheezing behind her. Del caught sight of Johnny clambering up the ladder a hundred feet back. He saw her and stopped.

Peter's eyes darted from Del to Johnny and back again. "Deputy Marshal Devlin, I see you brought your uncle with you."

Johnny said, "Think of me as her partner. Keep talking." He topped the ladder, then walked a few paces toward Del, but further out toward the edge of the concrete platform. He crouched to steady himself against the wind.

"That's close enough," Peter said to Johnny, and then to Del, "Do you really think my future self is the only person who can send messages back in time?"

"What are you writing?"

"The truth."

Del edged closer. "Are you building a bomb, Peter?"

"More of a containment device"—he glanced at the two black satchels—"but yes, if I turn off the power, it would release an enormous amount of energy. One could think of it as a bomb, but I prefer to think of it as a timeline correction device."

"Is it in one of those bags?" She indicated the satchels. Were there two bombs?

"Small enough to fit in a suitcase, yet powerful enough to change the world."

"You'll kill millions of innocent people."

"Nobody is innocent in this, and this is not the only world they live in. Do you see them flocking to Guthrie's rally?" He kept writing. "There's another group—an organization trying to control the future. But it's not just one. The universes spawn into a multiverse, and we're trying to control the timelines, let them converge."

Del said, "Gödel metrics. Closed time-like curves, right?"

"You do understand."

"Dr. Aringa explained it to me."

A scowl crossed his face. "He is one of *them.* They're the ones that are sending back messages to other teams. He is one of them. They're the ones that are trying to stop me. Using you."

"He told me you were sending threatening messages to him."

"That's not true. He was the one. And you see? He's controlling you right now."

"I'm not being controlled by anyone," Del said, but even she didn't believe it. Someone was pulling her strings like she was a drunk marionette, careening from one position to the next.

"It doesn't matter what you believe anymore. I needed to tell you this in person. I know you're going to be alright, even if I die, because I know that my daughter and your son will unite in the future and continue the fight."

"Samira? That's your girlfriend, right? Where is she? She's pregnant?"

"I sent her away on a flight this morning."

"Who is this other group? Dr. Aringa? You think he's involved?" Del edged closer. "Peter, who is the great evil? What are you writing about?"

He stood. Raised his eyes. "You must know by now."

She followed his gaze. Through a gap in the cement floor and construction equipment, she saw a sliver of the street twenty stories down. Streams of people on Church Street, ant-like swarms waving flags, singing, chanting, on their way to the rally.

Guthrie.

Governor Guthrie. The event today. Of course. It wasn't a building he was targeting, it was people. It was the politician. This was political. She hadn't thought of looking up his political affiliations. Still staring down, she sensed movement in her peripheral vision.

"Keep back," she told Johnny.

He had advanced toward Peter along the windswept concrete deck.

"Did he say you were pregnant?" Johnny said to her.

"I don't have time to explain," Del replied.

"And there's a bomb? What kind of bomb?"

Peter stood up from the desk. Dropped the pen, but now had the two black satchels in hand. He took a step to the open edge of the platform.

Del said, "Don't move, Dr. Breedlove. Stay right where you are." She had her weapon up, but what was the use of shooting him? That close and he might fall from the edge, and what if the fall damaged the containment device? Didn't the antimatter just need to contact any regular matter? What would happen if it fell from this hei—

He stepped back.

And disappeared.

32

Tribeca, New York

May 2nd, 12:45 p.m.

Del jumped down three stairs at a time after fireman-sliding down the ladder. She sliced up her hands doing that and smeared the blood onto her blouse as she tried to wipe away the stinging pain. She hit the landing of the nineteenth floor awkwardly and skidded in the dust, her slipping feet sending her crashing to the ground on her bad knee. The impact knocked the wind from her.

The Glock clattered across the cement.

Cursing and yelping in pain, she scrambled to her knees.

"Calm down, lass," Johnny said, following quickly down the stairs behind her.

"He's about to kill hundreds of thousands of people. Including us."

"Panic never helps."

"I'm not panicking."

"I am. Tell me more about this bomb."

"You used me."

Johnny sat on the last step, hands out, palms toward her in surrender. "I was trying to save my own skin. I've always been a bit selfish that way."

"You used my father. Your own brother. And he's, he . . . "

"I owe some very nasty people an awful lot of money. They would kill me for it. Those goons in the alley, they were for me, if that wasn't obvious enough."

"*You* killed someone when you arrived here. I should never have trusted you. They found your DNA under the fingernails. A man stuffed into a suitcase."

"Again, I swear to everything holy, that was not me that did that. I never killed nobody, not even those poor souls in Teebane all those years back. Someone was trying to frame me, or maybe—"

"What?"

"Frame you. Or me. I don't know, but I had nothing to do with it. And I didn't mean no harm, as I said. You wanted to find me, after all. I helped you."

"No harm?" She shook her head.

"No *great* harm. I thought you were in on it, anyway."

Del rocked back on her knees. "In on *what*?"

"I heard you, upstairs there. You said your boyfriend is the one that's been manipulating Breedlove. Inspector Galloul, isn't it?"

"And?"

"I've been messaging with someone at Interpol. I always figured it was him. He's the one in charge of the lab equipment investigations, no? He was making a bit on the side from all this. It's what I would do. Making a percentage from deals selling the equipment, while providing cover from the top. He must have been the one that put me in touch with you."

"Where?"

"In Singapore."

"I tracked *you* down."

"I'm afraid that little birdy singing songs in your ear was me. Figured you and Frenchy were together—"

"How would you know that?"

Del hadn't even let people at work know she and Jacques were a couple. She hadn't even told her mom and dad. How would her uncle—a man she had never met who lived half a world away—know this secret?

"It's not exactly your best kept secret, lass. I got all my info on where and when to buy this lab equipment from this Interpol contact, though. I figured maybe you might be in on it, too. Lovebirds looking to guild the cage?"

Del had put out feelers to try and track down her uncle—and all of a sudden, a few months back, just when her and Jacques were getting serious, reports began filtering in. It had been easy to find Johnny, in the end. Too easy, apparently. "So, you let me find you?"

"Breadcrumbs. I heard you wanted to meet me."

"Because you wanted to use me."

He shrugged. "I thought it was just for money, but a bomb? What were you talking about up there? What kind of a bomb are we talking about?"

She got back to her feet and passed him, began jogging down the stairs again. Slower this time. Eighteen floors to go, and then a mile to Liberty Park. She needed to pace herself. And she needed to make some calls.

Calls she should have already made.

What just happened up there? She took out Johnny's phone and checked the tracking app. The gray dot was still moving steadily toward Liberty Park, but she had no idea how. When Peter disappeared over the edge, her and Johnny had scrambled to the edge and looked over, but there was nothing. No distant body fallen onto the construction site below. No escape onto the lower platform down, not that they could see.

Like Peter had vanished into thin air. Like magic.

Except when she checked the tracking app, the gray dot was now on the move. It was moving down along Broadway, one street east, as if he had dropped into a cab. Except the streets were blocked off. It made no sense.

But it didn't need to anymore.

One way or the other, this had been staged. A carefully choreographed magic trick. She had been led up here on purpose, this performance for an audience of only one.

She dialed a number from memory into the phone.

"Hello?" answered a thready voice.

"Missy? Is that you?"

"Delta, where are you? We've been trying to call—"

"I had to turn my phone off."

"You—"

"I'm sorry."

Her sister burst into tears on the other end.

Del said, "What happened?"

"Dad, he's not doing well, you need to come here, right now."

"What's happening?"

"Septic shock. Something is leaking from his lungs into his bloodstream. They can't control the infection. Delta, he's asking for you."

"How bad is it?"

"Bad."

Just that one word, spoken quietly, ripped into Del like a twelve-gauge at point-blank. She stopped on the stairs and forced herself to hold back tears. She gritted her teeth. "Tell him I love him. I'll be there soon as I can."

Sobs on the other end. "Come soon, Del, we need you."

"Missy."

"Yes?"

"I know this is going to be hard to hear—"

"I've had about all I can take today, Delta. What is it?"

"You need to leave there—"

"What? Are you insane?"

"Right now. Take the kids. Take mom. Get as far out of New York as you can. Do you have a car?"

"We took the subway."

"Get outside right now, and get in a cab. Go upstate, do you still have your friend in Plattsburgh?"

Her sister's voice rose in pitch. "Delta what are you talking about? We can't leave dad now."

"Take him with you."

"Are you kidding me? You haven't seen him, we ca—"

"There's a bomb." Del began jogging down the stairs again. "In a couple of minutes, they're going to start evacuating the city. You need to be ahead of crowds. Do you understand? Get the kids out of here."

A moaning wail on the other end of the phone. "Delta, we can't—"

"Go now!" Del screamed. Tears streamed down her face. "Take Mom. Tell Dad, he'll understand."

"He's dying. I think he's dying."

Del's tears now erupted like geysers. She gasped out, "You need to go, Missy. Just go. Now. Please. I'm begging you to trust me."

She hung up and jumped down two stairs at a time, trying to focus through the watery sheen, wiping her face with the back of her hand holding the phone.

"I assume the news isn't good?" Johnny said from behind her.

She ignored him and tried to dial another number from memory. Her old partner. She had to stop running down the stairs to make the call.

"Detective Coleman," he answered. "Who is this?"

"It's me." She began walking.

"My God, Delta, what the hell are you doing? Did your dad break you out of detention? We just looked at the camera roll. I thought he was in hospital? Did y—"

"It was my uncle. My dad's twin."

A pause on the other end. "I didn't know he had a brother. You never—" Voices said for them to pass the phone. Coleman told them to be quiet. "You need to come back. Maybe I can smooth this over. We say someone took you out for questioning. We just got an Interpol Red Notice about your boyfriend, Jacques. This looks bad, Del. You need to come in."

She took a deep breath. Rounded the landing on the tenth floor and stopped.

Coleman said, "Did you hear me? We can still fix this. I know you didn't—"

"You need to evacuate." Del headed down the next staircase.

Another pause. "Evacuate? The building? Is something going on in One PP?"

"Manhattan. You need to evacuate all of lower Manhattan. Right now.

33

Financial District, New York

May 2nd, 1:02 p.m.

At this point, the police tracking them made no difference. She took out her phone, clipped the SIM card back in, and powered it up. She kept Johnny's phone with the tracker on it, and gave hers to him. That way she could contact him, but she could also log in and find him if she needed to, using a find-my-phone app on the web. Assuming he didn't ditch it, but they were past all that now. All the subterfuge, all the lies. She told Johnny to go one block further and take West Broadway down to the 9/11 Memorial, and to get his buddy Dermot to go down Broadway itself. Everyone on the lookout for Peter.

Or Jacques.

She would take Church Street, straight down the middle.

The gray dot on the tracking app had sickeningly settled at the Freedom Tower. At One World Trade Center. Thousands and thousands of people had gathered for a self-described Patriot's Day celebration at Governor Guthrie's rally today, right in the 9/11 Memorial park and Liberty Park next to it, to the south.

Thousands more were inside the building itself, and how many millions in the city?

Del had been eight years old when 9/11 happened, and that terrified, empty feeling was always on the other side of an invisible door within her, always waiting to be opened again. Her father had been working at First Precinct, just blocks from the World Trade Center, and had been part of the emergency response. They lost four members of their precinct that day and might have lost her father if he hadn't been helping people to safety two blocks away.

He had come home that night, covered in the pinkish-gray dust of the Towers' collapse, and they had cried together all through the night until she fell asleep in his arms.

To be a New Yorker meant always feeling like a target.

And now they were doing it again.

A searing mix of fear and anger tore through her gut as she bounded down the stairs, taking five and six steps at a time, feeling like she was barely touching the cement. She didn't feel her knee. Didn't feel anything at all.

She had just told her sister to abandon their dying father. But he couldn't be dying. That wasn't possible in her universe, there was no version of her world that didn't include him. He would recover. She had to go to him.

But she couldn't.

Her father would understand, but then he might not even exist to understand soon. Her brain fought for control of the uncontrollable.

She found herself dodging between the jackhammers and diggers on the ground floor of the site, unaware of even the last five floors of stairs she must have come down. Del sprinted to the plywood wall to the west of the site. Sunlight streamed down, the glare reflecting in her own tears welling in her eyes. She wiped her face with the back of her hand, snot coming away, and she screamed.

No time to find the loose boards.

Still bellowing, she launched into the plywood wall with a straight kick. The wall bent inward, then rebounded and sent her sprawling into the dirt. She got to all fours and heaved in a breath of dusty air. Then another. Breathe in, breathe out.

Stop crying.

She wiped away the last of the tears. Enough. She gritted her teeth and got to her feet. Checked her jeans pocket. The Glock was still there.

She took out the phone and checked the tracking app. The gray dot had moved, mercifully, about a half a block south of the Freedom Tower. Peter was on the move, and hadn't taken the bomb into the Tower. She had imagined having to go into the new World Trade Center, just like the emergency responders in 9/11, sprinting up the stairs, screaming at people to get out.

What would it feel like to be incinerated in an antimatter explosion? Probably like nothing. Here one moment, gone the next.

Nothing to fear.

The plywood she kicked had come loose. She wiped her face again, blood and grime from the cuts on her hands when she came down the ladder. Taking hold of the loose board, she ripped it back, making just enough of a gap for her to squeeze through.

Del popped up on Church Street, straight into a crowd of onlookers. She ignored them and began jogging and then running south, weaving and dodging through the chanting pedestrians waving American flags. People turned and saw her coming and parted, giving her space. She had to be covered in dirt and blood and looking wild. She scanned the faces, searching for that tan build she knew so well. Was Jacques somewhere here?

Or the gangly features of Peter Breedlove.

He might have dumped the bomb, hidden it. Given it to someone else.

She looked at the faces staring back at her as she sprinted forward. Nobody looked alarmed. Everyone except her looked calm and happy. Everyone still walking toward the Memorial.

"Go back!" she yelled and waved her arms. "Don't go any further."

"Shut up, asshole," someone yelled back.

They thought she was a political protester. Or just crazy. It was futile to try and warn the crowd that was walking toward what could be death, but then that was part of the reason for her getting in touch with Coleman.

How long had it been now? Maybe ten minutes since she made the call? She told Coleman everything.

Said to contact Dr. Ross Aringa, to verify her story about the possible antimatter bomb and Dr. Breedlove. To call her boss, Marshal Justice, to verify the list of stolen equipment. She pleaded with Coleman, told him everything she knew about Jacques. How he would hide from her sometimes, how he disappeared mysteriously. Coleman confirmed that the Red Notice from Interpol was for Jacques's links to Muslim extremists.

Del realized now that the IRGC woman—Anila—had really been trying to warn them. She still didn't understand why she had tracked down Del. Why hadn't she gone through official channels? Contacted the FBI or CIA or even the NYPD? It had to be something to do with CERN, with Del's visits there, with Peter's fascination with Del.

Jacques had silenced the woman, just as she was trying to reveal the truth. And he must have gone to the hospital and killed her. Finished her off.

She had his child inside of her.

Del wanted to vomit.

She was implicated in all this now. Her relationship with Jacques, that she was at CERN. She had even admitted to Coleman that she had aided and abetted a known terrorist, her uncle Johnny. She knew how all this must look.

They had to alert Governor Guthrie, she pleaded with Coleman. Stop the event. Evacuate the entire lower half of Manhattan.

She heard the cursing on the other end of the phone in the background when she told all this to Coleman. The officers at One PP were already making calls before she got off the phone, alerting emergency services, but why were people still walking toward the rally? Coleman said she still had to come in, and when she refused, said that there was still an all-points bulletin out for her arrest.

She had no time. She hung up on him at that point.

Could she disable the bomb? She didn't need to, but just needed to make sure it wasn't turned off, from what Peter had said. It needed to remain powered, but had Peter wired it to a remote device? Maybe she could get it as far out of the city as she could. Maybe a water taxi, a boat, take it out into the harbor.

That was her only plan.

She needed to find Peter, find the bomb, and get it as far out into the harbor as she could. There were ferries at Battery Park just to the south, and to the west docks with yachts and sailboats. She could take one of them.

Or a helicopter. Wasn't there a heliport right below the financial district? That was a few blocks farther, but would be faster to get away from the city. Or a drone if one was big enough to carry it?

She sprinted down Church Street, her breathing coming in heaving gasps as she passed the Four Seasons. The crowd thickened as she weaved her way to Fulton Street. One block west to the edge of the 9/11 Memorial park. Johnny would be coming down West Broadway and skirting around the Freedom Tower to the west, Dermot down Broadway almost to Wall Street before circling back from the south.

What was she forgetting?

Gasping air, she slowed to a walk and took out the phone to check the tracking app again. The gray dot had moved to Liberty Park, at the southern end of the 9/11 Memorial. That was where Guthrie was setting up the stage for the speeches this afternoon. A young boy held the hand of a man walking next to her. The boy looked up and smiled at her.

Del pulled a scrap of paper from her pocket and dialed Angel. He picked up on the second ring.

"I'm still tracking the woman," Angel said immediately. "She seems to be heading down at the rally at Liberty Park. There's another woman she just m—"

"Abort whatever you're doing, Angel. There's a bomb at the rally."

Silence for a beat. "Did you alert the authorities?"

"Of course I did."

"I'm already halfway there. These women, they just met four men and got in a taxi. I'm about two blocks back from them. We're coming down Broadway to you."

"Call Charlie right now. Get him to get Rodrigo, and get out of the city."

Another beat of silence. "What kind of bomb are we talking?"

"A big one."

"I'm still coming. These women are acting really odd. I'm sending you another picture."

"Get Charlie and Rodrigo and yourself out of the city, Angel, I'm not kidding."

She hung up.

She had reached the northeast corner of the 9/11 park.

Throngs of Guthrie supporters walked by, chanting and carrying banners and placards and balloons, music echoing from speakers set up on stands around the park. The people around her sticky hot in the warm spring afternoon, their elbows catching her in the ribs, and more than one beer spilling on her. Inch by inch, she squeezed her way through, moving as fast as she could. People everywhere, some cheering, waving flags, packed in tight, all of them waiting for Governor Guthrie to appear.

The dot on her tracking app kept moving around the park. She was close, but with every step she thought she was getting nearer, the dot moved away from her. Like Peter knew where she was, where she was going. Did he have eyes on her? Did someone else?

She was in the middle of the crowd now, barely able to move, being crushed by the mass of people, her eyes on the tracking app dot, when the music cut abruptly and a cheer rose from the crowd. She raised her head.

"Everyone, please," said an announcer on the stage, "we are very sorry, but the event has been canceled. I repeat, everyone must clear the area—"

Musicians dove for the wings as a scuffle broke out near the front of the stage. A wiry form broke from a knot of security guards. And there was Peter. Standing in the middle of the stage, his eyes darting from one end of the crowd to the other, holding up one of the black satchels.

A low wailing sound began, the noise echoing from the skyscrapers and buildings around them. The din of the crowd, the voices questioning what was going on, was eclipsed by the rising moan. It wasn't coming from the speakers for the event, Del realized, but it was the city warning system. She had heard it being tested before, it was supposed to be used for tsunami warnings, but it could be used for anything.

This counted as that.

Coleman must have finally gotten through to the city.

All around her, people's cell phones began screeching emergency warnings. They picked them out of their pockets and began reading the messages. Someone screamed. Peter was still on the stage, holding the black bag above his head.

"He has a bomb!" Del shouted. "Everybody clear the area!"

The people around her started screaming, pushing and shoving and yelling, the words "a bomb!" repeated over and over again, one person to another, before all sense was lost, and the crowd took on a life of its own.

The rising wail of the emergency warning system grated in her ears.

Del fought against the tide of people, battering her way upstream. Hands out, she pushed forward, her eyes on Peter. He held the backpack out at arm's length. A ring of security guards surrounded him, but no one made a move. The area around the stage had half-cleared by the time she reached it, people running in the opposite direction. A cordon of NYPD was trying to guide the crowd fifty feet away, but the officers were being swept away.

Del pulled herself up onto the stage. "Let me talk to him," she said to the guards, flashing her US Marshal ID.

The words had an almost magical effect.

One guard bolted, the two-hundred-fifty-pound man lumbered away without looking back. Then another. They had heard her screaming about Peter having a bomb. She glanced at the back of the stage. Guthrie's people had already cleared the area.

It was just Del and Peter on stage now.

"Dr. Breedlove," she said, holding her eyes steady on him. "Don't do this. Look at all these people. You're not the kind of man to harm anyone, are you?" She took a step toward him. "What about your daughter? And her mother, your girlfriend? What if they were in this crowd?"

"Our children are doomed to die anyway, Deputy Marshal Devlin. Yours and mine."

Another step.

Peter's eyes darted. He held up the satchel, looked away from it. Del jumped at him, knocked him to the ground. He collapsed under her with a crunch, his slight weight offering little resistance. She grabbed the bag, felt the weight of it—maybe twenty pounds—and held him down with her other hand. He twisted his head, writhed under her.

Del gasped, "Where's the other bag?"

"We are out of time, detective," Peter said calmly.

"Don't do this."

She pinned both his arms down with her knees and placed the bag down gently. Peter stopped writhing beneath her. She pressed her full weight against his chest and leaned forward and carefully unzipped the bag. Two NYPD officers had seen her come up here and advanced onto the stage, but she held up her US Marshal ID—still in her hand—and urged them back.

She opened the satchel.

It was the device her uncle Johnny had picked up the day before. The one he had stuck the tracking device into. No lights blinking inside. Just a pile of papers beside the device, which looked inert. It was cool to the touch. Didn't look like a bomb.

What it looked like was a diversion.

Peter must have known the tracking device was in it.

"Where's the other bag?" Del yelled over the noise of the bellowing sirens and screams from the crowd.

She looked down. Peter's eyes were open, but he stared vacantly into open space.

"Where's the other—"

Del stopped mid-sentence. His eyes were open but clouded. She swung one leg away from him. What was he looking at? She looked behind her in the crowd.

And found Jacques staring back at her. Fifty feet away. Not more than that.

"Get him," she screamed at the NYPD officers hovering at the edge of the stage. "He's the terrorist." She pointed at Jacques, then returned her attention to Peter.

He hadn't moved at all the last few seconds after squirming beneath her when she first pinned him. His arms were splayed out. She reached to put a finger to his neck.

She waited.

Nothing.

No pulse. Peter was dead.

34

Financial District, New York
May 2nd, 1:32 p.m.

Had Del killed him? Did she press down too hard on his chest? She hadn't hit him that hard. If anything, she had handled him with kid gloves. She hadn't wanted to damage the antimatter device. What was the last thing he said?

That we were out of time.

Del had to find the other bag.

A helicopter—no, two—overhead. Up the street, people poured out of the buildings in the area, the streets overflowing with pedestrians, cars, trucks, and bikes, everyone going every which way, what little order the security and police were managing to impose while corralling people out of the park dwindling.

Complete panic.

Del felt it, too. The groaning siren vibrated the plywood platform of the stage, the sound seeming to come up through her feet and knees into her bones and brain. The terrible moan, warbling now at a blaring pitch, screaming at her to get out of there.

"Marshal Devlin?" someone yelled. It was one of the NYPD at the edge of the stage. He had his weapon out and trained on her. "You need to come with me, ma'am."

Del looked down into Peter's lifeless eyes, bowed her head.

"Ma'am, please, you need to—"

She heaved the black satchel with everything she had, straight at the officer. He thought it was the bomb, so he scrambled back along with a knot of other officers behind him. Two of them fell off the stage in a tangle of arms and legs.

Del leapt off the platform and hit the pavement and bounded away.

A flash of tan behind a tree up ahead. That suit. Those brown crocodile leather shoes.

Jacques.

No way he was going to get away with this. She didn't yell, she didn't tell him to stop. A barking dog wasn't going to bite, and she intended to sink her teeth into him. She clamped her jaw and began pumping her legs with everything she had. The park had already mostly cleared by now. Why was he still here? What was he doing?

Was this a suicide mission?

No time to think.

She pounded the pavement, swinging her arms as she sprinted between the low trees dotted through the 9/11 Memorial park and swept past the granite placards naming the dead around the infinite pool. Jacques took a right and disappeared around the glass outcropping of the 9/11 Museum. A woman pushed a baby stroller as fast as she could ahead of Del.

Del cleared the edge of the museum and scanned the backs of people running away. She glanced up at the towering glass face of the Freedom Tower. Still running, she slowed and tried to find her target. Where was Jacques?

She stumbled to a stop.

"Delta," said a voice, loud enough to be heard over the siren.

She turned her head to the left. Her breath came in and out in heaving gasps. She would know that accent anywhere.

Jacques half-crouched behind a gray 9/11 Memorial kiosk, still open but abandoned, books and magazines spilling out onto the ground. A row of metal crowd-control stanchions and a ten-foot-wide bed of creeping ivy, set in a garden in the pavement, were all that separated them.

Del balled her fists.

Jacques held out his hands, palms outward in surrender, but held his ground. The lady pushing the baby stroller, both wailing, rolled by. The siren edged down in its warbling screech and then ratcheted back up. Del waited for the woman to pass.

Then launched herself forward.

One foot hit the middle of the ivy garden and slipped in the dirt as she tried to jump and clear the nylon web of the crowd-control stanchion. Her attempt to clear it landed her stumbling through it. The black nylon rope caught her left foot and she stumbled forward.

Fists up.

Jacques didn't even try to get out of the way.

Flailing, she went straight into him. He tried to catch her, but even off-balance, Del landed a swinging haymaker punch into the side of his head. Her momentum carried her into him, and they crashed backward into the pavement. She brought her right knee straight up into his crotch before they even hit the ground.

He convulsed and crumpled. Pulled his legs up and arms down and tried to protect himself.

Del skidded over top of him, rolled, and bounced back to her feet. With her left hand, she grabbed the collar of his shirt, and she punched straight down with her right. Then punched again, her fist coming away bloody this time.

Still, he didn't resist. Didn't fight back at all. Just balled tighter into a fetal position.

Still gripping his collar, she cocked her fist again, but held back this time.

"I know," she said. "I know everything."

"Are you done?"

"Where's the bomb?"

"Will you stop hitting me?"

"Why are you doing this?"

Cringing, he pulled his hands slightly away from his bloody face. "I love you, Delta, please, stop punching me."

The words hit her harder than any fist could have.

The fury boiling through her felt like it vented through her skin. Still gripping his collar, she staggered back against the kiosk and slid down against it into a crouch. A station wagon police cruiser rolled slowly up Church street fifty feet from them, its lights flashing, the officer inside telling people to clear the area over his loudspeaker.

"Why?" was all Delta could say. "Explain to me, why."

"I am trying to save you," Jacques replied.

"Save me? Like some insane religious way?"

"I mean your life."

"Where's the bomb? What did you do to Peter? Why did you kill the Iranian?"

"I did none of these things."

"There's no point in lying." Del spat the words out. "I know about your connections to Muslim extremists. There is an Interpol arrest warrant for you, a Red Notice. You've been changing records on the French national databases, hiding fugitives. Concealing terrorists."

"So have you."

"Excuse me?"

"Your uncle. You were modifying the Interpol database as well."

"That was different. I was trying—"

"Me as well." Jacques got to his knees. "I was protecting my family, too."

"Killing thousands of innocent people is not protecting anyone."

"I am not the one doing this, Delta. I keep telling you, but you are not *listening*."

The siren wailed and echoed. The police cruiser swept up the almost empty street. The park was deserted now.

"My brother is schizophrenic," Jacques said over the noise. "His threats are not real."

"I didn't know you had a brother."

"I didn't know you had an uncle."

"Just tell me where the bomb is. We can still stop this."

"Faith is very important to my family," Jacques said. "But my brother, with his mental problems, he imagines things. He posts fantasies on the internet. He's not dangerous. When I see him, I have to go along with his delusions, otherwise he shuts me out. When he posts crazy things on the internet, he gets flagged by search algorithms. I make small changes. I delete the red flags. That is all. You understand how complicated it is with family. I have seen how you protect your own."

Del let her breath come in and out, once and then twice before saying, "Give me your phone."

"Pardon?"

She dragged him toward her by his collar, then patted down his pockets and slacks. In one she found a cellphone, in another a pistol, a snub-nosed .38 special. He didn't resist. She released him, opened the pistol's barrel and pocketed the rounds. She threw the gun into a garbage can next to the kiosk, and the phone onto the ground. She smashed it underfoot.

Del said, "You beat your girlfriends. Don't tell me that's a lie as well? I've seen the police reports. Are those fake as well?"

He bowed his head. "It's not what you think."

"You've been gaslighting me this whole time."

"Are you not the human lie detector?"

"I can't tell when people are lying if they believe their own insanity."

"And you've not been lying to me?" This time his voice wasn't placating but took a harder edge.

"What's that supposed to mean?"

He looked away. "You are going to lie and tell me you are not carrying my child?"

The siren wailed.

"I followed you to that doctor's office in Paris," he added. "Your morning sickness? The way you've been acting? I am a detective, you realize."

Del let go of Jacques's collar and bunched her arms and legs together. She had shared a bed with this man, had looked into his face most mornings for months. Had she been able to see it? The lies? She had been fooled so easily, but then, she always seemed to fall for the same sort of man. The wrong one.

"I'm getting rid of it," she said.

The way his face crumpled, it was like she had stuck in a knife, and that had been her intention. Find a way to hurt this bastard as badly as she could. Twist and push deeper. "Tomorrow. I'm having an abortion."

"It?"

"Tell me where the bomb is."

"This is not an 'it,' this is a human being."

"He's dead anyway if you don't tell me where the bomb is. What's wrong with you?" Did she say "he"? The words tumbled from her mouth. She retreated into a ball, arms around her knees, tight against the kiosk.

Jacques got to his feet. "I am not who you think I am."

"We can agree on that. My uncle has been messaging with you," Del said. "He's been communicating with you at Interpol. I know everything. You've been directing him, buying lab equipment for Peter. Providing cover and profiting. I know you were waiting outside Peter's girlfriend's apartment here in New York. Are you working with her? Twisting Peter's mind? He's dead."

"Peter's girlfriend? Samira? I was never outside her apartment. Not here, anyway." Jacques paused. "Peter's dead? Did you kill him?"

"My friend Angel is tracking his girlfriend. Do you want me to show you pictures?" Del tried to focus on Jacques's face, but the grating wail of the siren made it difficult to concentrate.

Jacques ran a hand back through his hair. "I was never outside her apartment. Wasn't she staying with Peter?"

"Then what were you doing in Alphabet City?"

"Zoya, I found out that Zoya was here in New York," Jacques replied. "Did you bring her with you? I wanted to know what she was doing here."

"Zoya?"

"I have friends, too. I had someone outside of Interpol tracking her movements."

"Still stalking her? After all this time?"

"Stalking?"

"I know about you two. I know you were with her before me. You beat her."

Jacques laughed grimly. "Is that what she told you?"

"You think it's funny?"

"She is the one who beat me, Delta. I never touched her. Be careful of that one. She is a snake."

The venom in his voice was real. That wasn't faked.

Del rubbed her eyes, felt them stinging and still watering from the dust at the construction site. Her eyes. Stinging. Zoya. A snake. Del pulled her phone from her pocket. Angel had sent more pictures of the woman he was following. Not just one woman, but two. She zoomed in.

And there she was.

Zoya.

Was she here on Interpol business? Why hadn't she called Del?

And standing next to Zoya, she recognized that woman as well, from surveillance photos of Breedlove here in NYC—it was Breedlove's girlfriend. Samira. What was Zoya doing with her?

"Do not move," someone yelled.

35

Financial District, New York

May 2nd, 1:42 p.m.

The station wagon police cruiser must have backed up.

It was parked, lights strobing, fifty feet in front of Del and Jacques on Greenwich Street. One officer advanced toward them, his service revolver out and ahead of him and aimed at Jacques. The other policeman had his weapon out but remained behind the cover of the vehicle. Del heard him calling for backup.

"Don't move, Marshal Devlin," said another voice from behind.

Del rocked forward on her heels. It was the young officer from the stage, the one she threw the black satchel at. He had his gun out as well. Another NYPD officer behind and to the right of him. Lights flashed in the distance up Greenwich Street toward Midtown. Police sirens warbled under the groaning roar of the tsunami warning system.

"We're going to have to take you in," the young officer said. "Please do not force this." He advanced another ten feet toward Del and Jacques and stopped. "That man back there, he's dead. I'm sure you have an explanation, but we're going to need to hear it at the station."

"There won't be a station if you take us in," Jacques growled.

"I took his weapon, he's unarmed," Del yelled over the noise. "I have a Glock in my waistband, but I'm keeping my hands away." She held them up.

The young officer adjusted his aim to point at the Frenchman. "Sir, Detective Galloul, we have an arrest warrant for you on terrorism charges. If you so much as move an inch, I will be forced to shoot."

Where the officer didn't sound like he wanted to hurt Del, his finger looked itchy on the trigger when it came to inflicting damage on Jacques.

The Frenchman was standing but half-crouched as he had been moving toward Del. "She is pregnant," he said to the officer. "Do not hurt her, please."

"That is in your hands, sir. Please raise them, get on your knees, then lie facedown on the ground. Arms out. Both of you."

Jacques looked at Del. She glanced down at her Glock. He shook his head.

She needed to get out of here.

As the officers advanced toward them, screaming at them to get down, the truth began to blossom in Del's mind. Drips and drops at first, and then a rushing torrent that broke through the dam in her mind.

She gripped the Glock in her pocket.

They wouldn't shoot a pregnant woman, would they? Jacques jumped at her as she pulled the weapon from her pocket. A gunshot punctuated the siren's wail, then another.

"Stop!" screamed a voice.

Jacques staggered against her and then slipped to his knees. Blood spattered on the pavement below him. "Don't do it."

"Everybody stop what they are doing," said the voice in an Irish accent. "Or I will send us all to bloody hell together this sunny day, along with a million other people."

Johnny strutted past the kiosk and winked at Del, a black satchel raised above his head with a cord coming down out of it. "If I release this trigger in my hand, Manhattan and the five boroughs will be no more. Ten million people dead. So, lower those guns."

Jacques slumped against the kiosk next to Del. He began to tip over.

She reflexively put her arms around him and pulled him back upright. Her hands came away soaked in bright bed blood. He groaned.

Del yelled, "We need an ambulance!"

"No, no, I will be fine," Jacques grunted.

"Everybody put those goddamn guns down," Johnny yelled. "Do ye not know who I am? Have you not seen the pictures of the Bomber of Teebane?"

Del glanced up. Dermot with his eye patch approached from the other side, from behind the cruiser. The officer back there had his hands up already.

"You better listen to him," she said to the younger officer that was closest to her. "He has the bomb."

The young officer cursed and held out his gun, then motioned for his partner to do the same. "One PP is getting all this on live feed, Marshal Devlin. I'm advising you." He indicated the body cam on his vest.

He knelt and put his weapon on the ground. The other officers did the same.

"Over with your friends," Johnny said to the cops, and then to Dermot, "Cuff them up with their own around that tree there. Get the keys to the cruiser."

The young officer did as he was told, but said, "You can't escape, there are a hundred officers coming d—"

"Maybe I'm not looking to escape," Johnny said.

That quieted the officer down.

"Call them off," Del said to the young man. "Tell them we don't want another 9/11. There's no reason for anyone else to die. Dermot, don't cuff them to that tree, let them go." She got to her feet and pulled Jacques to his. "Can you walk?" she said into his ear.

"Maybe," he groaned.

"Help him," she said to the young officer. "You got a cruiser here?"

"On the other side of the park."

"You take Detective Galloul, and get out of here. That's something, right? You got one of us. I'll handle this from here."

Johnny still had the black satchel with the cord coming out of it above his head. "You heard the lady. Take him and run. Don't look back."

Del helped Jacques to the two officers closest to her. "Are you okay?" she said into his ear as she handed him off.

"Do what you have to," he replied.

"Go on, help them out of here," Johnny yelled at the two officers near the cruiser.

They ran to assist the man helping Jacques.

Del backed up toward her uncle and Dermot, who still had his weapon trained on the NYPD. "Is that really Peter's device? Tell me you found it."

Johnny leaned into her and said, "I found this in the dumpster in the next alley. Somebody's gym bag. Most dangerous thing about it is the way it smells. Now what's the plan? Is your man hurt bad? He caught one in the back."

"I don't know."

Jacques was managing to walk, helped by two of the officers. Blood soaked the back of his tan suit. She hadn't had time to check his wound. The best thing for him was to get help as soon as possible.

"I got friends on Long Island," Johnny said. "We get in the cop car here, ditch it up in Midtown—"

"Is Charlie getting Roderigo out?" Del yelled into her phone.

She had dialed Angel, who picked up on the first ring. She stuck a finger into her opposite ear to listen above the wailing siren.

"They are on their way out of the house now," Angel replied.

"On your way to joining them?"

"Still tailing those women. Six more have joined—all men—eight total. It's a party now."

"And where's this party happening?"

Angel said, "Straight against the traffic from lower Manhattan. Just got off the East Side highway before the roadblocks got up. On foot now."

"What street?"

"Wall Street."

"You're kidding."

"What do you want me to do?"

"Go to Charlie and Roderigo."

"No man left behind, Del, I'm not leaving you in this fight. I'm a New Yorker, too. I'm not letting this happen again in my town. No way."

Del gripped the phone tight for a moment before saying, "Then stick with them. Make sure they don't see you. I'll call you in two."

She hung up.

The warning siren wailed.

"I'm guessing this means we're not running," Johnny said. "I trust you know what you're doing?"

"I don't think there's a bomb," Del replied.

"You know, or you think?"

"Give me the keys to the cruiser. You two get out of here."

"So, you're not sure."

"Just give me the keys," Del said.

"You're not going anywhere without me, young lady." Johnny waved Dermot to the car and leaned in to walk with his man, who nodded a few times. "We're both coming with you. Come on, get in." He held the back door to the cruiser open.

"You get in the rear, I'm driving," Del said.

"Wouldn't be my first time in the back of one of these," Johnny grumbled and nodded at Dermot to toss Del the keys.

Del caught them. Hesitated. Turned to catch a glimpse of Jacques being helped across the 9/11 Memorial park between the trees. The lightning rod of new truth she had felt electrifying her seconds ago seemed to fade the further he retreated from her.

Did she believe what he said?

She had.

But now? Moments before she had believed him to be a Muslim extremist terrorist that had planted a bomb set to kill hundreds of thousands of people.

Yet in the space of thirty seconds being close to him, near enough to smell that lingering scent of musk and cardamon and feel his presence, he had convinced her everything was different. That it wasn't him.

She had looked into his eyes and believed—but she always believed the wrong sort of men, even if she was a human lie detector. Something about men she loved crossed every wire in her brain.

Was she doing it again?

"Give me my phone," Del said to Johnny as she crossed in front of the cruiser.

She opened the door and slipped into the driver's seat. The NYPD cruiser felt so familiar. It wasn't that long ago she had been making the rounds with Coleman out in Long Island.

She turned on the ignition, put it into gear but held her foot on the brakes. Dermot slipped into the passenger seat.

There was one way to find out if Del was right or not, to know who was lying. Del searched her contacts and dialed Zoya's number.

36

Financial District, New York

May 2nd, 1:52 p.m.

"Are we going, or not?" Johnny pounded on the cage that separated the front and back seats.

"Quiet, please." Del held her phone to her ear.

"That's a wee bit tough right now," he muttered.

The warning siren moaned and echoed across the now-empty park, the noise almost deafening even with the doors of the car closed.

The phone rang once. Twice.

Zoya was one of the leading financial cybercrimes experts at Interpol, a master in digital forensics. Stationed in Singapore, but she had just been in France, which was only a few hours' flight from New York. She was part of Jacques's interdepartmental team tracking the lab equipment thefts, and if Jacques was here, it made sense that maybe Zoya was, too. Even Boston Justice was in New York.

It made some sense Zoya might be here, but how did she have a team of people going into Wall Street right now? Tracking the bomb? Did she know something Del didn't? And what did Breedlove's girlfriend have to do with it?

Three rings. Four.

Zoya might not even hear the phone with all the noise, and Del had no idea what she might be doing. Five rings and then she heard Zoya's voice—but it was the answering message.

"Damn it." Del dropped her phone into her lap. She gripped the steering wheel.

"Making no decision is still making one," Johnny said from the back.

That was exactly what her father would say.

Maybe she should abandon this, drive the car to Presbyterian. Get her father, or at least be with him. There might not be much time left, not for any of them. Not for anyone.

"Whatever you're mulling, best to keep—"

Her phone rang, and then another at the same time. Two phones ringing—both her own on the seat and the burner her uncle had given her in her jeans pockets.

"You going to answer that?" Dermot said. "Or should I?"

The number on her phone's display was unlisted. Del picked up and said, "Hello?"

"Delta, it's Coleman. I've got both police commissioners, the mayor, the FBI bomb squad, and hostage negotiation teams screaming down my neck—"

"Hostage negotiation?"

"The whole city has been taken hostage by your boyfriend."

"He's been taken in. Four officers are coming to you with him. He's been shot. Question him all you want—if you can keep him alive."

"We saw the body cam footage from the officer. You need to bring that bag to the ferry port at Battery Park. Right now. We have a team waiting. They have eyes on you, Del. Not just CCTV cameras. Drones up high and down low, already sweeping the streets."

"Who is 'they'?"

"Snipers are heading into position. SWAT and bomb teams. Del, we're going to be cutting off all cell and commercial comms in lower Manhattan, only reason it's still on is for me to talk to you."

"I took Jacques's cellphone and gun," Del said.

Coleman continued, "Power will be shut off. The only people left down there are ones who aren't supposed to be by now. Only reason you're not already vaporized is they don't know how it might affect what's in that bag. That, and the commissioner is arguing for you."

He kept using 'they' but not explaining. "Bag?"

"That your uncle Johnny is holding."

"That's just a gym—"

"Did you look in it?"

The blood drained from Del's face. She switched to hold the phone against her ear with her left shoulder as she glanced at Dermot in the passenger seat beside her, his revolver out in his hand, watching her. She turned to look at her uncle in the back, clutching the black bag.

"Open the bag," she said to her uncle.

"Pardon?"

"Open the goddamned bag."

"Why? I told you—"

Del pulled her Glock out and held the muzzle at Dermot's temple. "Open. The. Bag."

Dermot didn't flinch and didn't even look her way. He must have had a lot of guns pointed at him over the years.

Johnny cursed in the back seat, but picked the black bag up and unzipped it.

Keeping her gun pointed at Dermot, she twisted her neck around to get a better look. A jumble of odds and ends, what looked like a radio, wads of paper and clothes.

"Delta?" Coleman said into the phone still balanced on Del's left shoulder.

It slipped away and fell into the foot well by her feet.

She stuck the Glock into her waistband, glanced back at Johnny's bag. There wasn't any of the equipment Peter had stolen or bought. She reached between her knees and picked the phone up. "I gotta call you back."

She hung up.

Del held her head down low and tried to see across the park. Couldn't see anyone. The warning sirens wailed outside the cruiser's windows. Had the officers taken Jacques away already? Her head still low, she craned forward to look up at the sky. Drones? Was there a Hellfire missile about to rain down on them?

Del released the brake and stomped on the accelerator.

The station wagon cruiser didn't peel out, but more hopped forward. Not quite the effect she hoped for, but at least she was moving. She said to Dermot, "Get Angel on the burner phone, right away."

37

Financial District, New York

May 2nd, 2:12 p.m.

"She went in the first entrance," Angel said.

To be sure, Del asked, "Zoya?"

"You work with her?"

"Sort of."

"She's law enforcement?"

"Not here, she's not."

Angel met them at the corner of Trinity and Rector, one block west of Wall Street and the New York Stock Exchange. They drove the police cruiser all of four blocks south before stopping and getting out after Angel messaged on the burner phone to tell them where to go. Johnny and Dermot crouched behind Del and Angel as they hid in the cover of a scaffolding beside the Pantheon-like hulk of the Federal Building across from the NYSE.

An iconic giant American flag adorned the neo-Gothic columns across the front of the stock exchange's facade, while six more red-white-and-blues snapped in the breeze from flagpoles set to either side of the deserted street. The cobblestone alley of Wall Street itself hooked off to the left.

Maybe half an hour since the evacuation order had hit lower Manhattan, and already the place was like a ghost town. Two people ran around a corner in the distance and came up the street toward them, but then disappeared into the Broad Street subway entrance.

The smell of hot dogs wafted past from an abandoned vendor cart.

Low black metal fencing ringed off the front twenty feet of the NYSE and blocked the westward section of Wall Street. A blue-topped tent stenciled with "employees" and "registered guests" occupied and covered the closest entrance to the stock exchange. Half of the street looked under construction, with an exterior elevator mounted against the building's far corner. Further down, past the soaring columns, was another entryway in blue plywood atop more scaffolding.

Del asked, "Another man went in the far door?"

Crouched beside her, Angel said, "That's right. They're all dressed in civilian clothes. Two went into the entrance of Deutsche Bank further up, then two more into 37 Wall Street, right across from the Trump Building and Tiffany's? You know the one?"

Del had been up and down this street a few times. She nodded and shrugged at the same time. It wasn't her area of town.

"You sure she went inside?" Del asked.

"As I can be. Didn't see her come back out, but I was keeping a few blocks away. Any idea what she's doing here?"

"Maybe the same as us," Johnny said.

Del fished her phone from her jeans and dialed Coleman. It didn't even ring once.

Coleman said, "Who's the other guy that just joined you?"

"Not important right now."

"The cavalry is about to be sent in, one armed with missiles and drones. Comms are going down any second, nothing I can do."

"Coleman, not yet."

"Then give me anything."

"Give *me* ten minutes. I'm the one that called this in, remember that. Is there anyone that's been authorized to come into lower Manhattan?"

"After our experts talked to Dr. Aringa, we evacuated the area.

Everything. Every single person, even law enforcement. We got volunteer bomb squad and SWAT teams ready to put down their lives, but Commissioner Basilone held them off. You got friends high up, Delta. If you have a plan, we need to know what it is."

"So, nobody else, no other cops down here?"

"Not that we know of."

"Do they have Inspector Galloul in custody?"

"The cruiser with him just made the barricade at Fortieth Street. There are alarms going off everywhere in the financial district. Don't hang up again. We need to—"

Del hung up.

And cursed.

Her headaches and blurry vision had started in Singapore, right when she had first met Zoya in person. Was it possible she had something to do with them? It was the headaches that had sent Del to the doctor in Paris, the one that Zoya had recommended.

She had told that doctor just about everything about her vision.

About her family.

But she had told about as much or more to Jacques. And he had followed her to the doctor's office, he just told her. He had been stalking her, even when they were dating. Of course, she had been hiding things from him, too.

"Angel, you go in the back entrance," Del said. "We'll go in the main where Zoya went."

"All the same to you, I'm going to climb the scaffolding and go in one of those windows up there. Sure the alarms will go off, but who'll notice? I'll work the upper floors and come down to you. Should be easy. Place should be empty. What's the plan?"

"Find Zoya. Call me if you do."

"And if I find anyone else?"

"Keep hidden. If confronted, disable them as best you can. You have a weapon?"

Angel nodded.

Alarms going off everywhere. That's what Coleman said.

No security at the entrance to the NYSE. The front gate was abandoned as everywhere else. "Keep your phone with you," Del said to Angel. She turned to Johnny and handed him his phone. "And you, too. We're going to need to split up."

She took off from cover of the scaffolding, checking left and right.

The warning sirens echoed through the concrete canyons. A knot of people scurried past two blocks down Wall Street, but nobody else visible apart from that. She ducked in the front flap of the security tent, then jogged down the steps into the stock exchange building.

Dermot and Johnny kept pace a few steps behind her. Angel kept with her as far as the front steps and then peeled off for the scaffolding down the other side of the structure. The glass of the entrance door was smashed, the door half-open.

She pulled the Glock from her waistband.

Eased the door fully open. A staircase led up and down inside the main doors. "You two go up," Del said. "And call me if you see anyone. Don't shoot anyone."

"I'm sticking with you," Johnny said. "Dermot can go up."

She didn't have time to argue.

His back to the wall, Dermot edged up the marble staircase.

Del pushed through an inside set of double doors into an expansive hallway that looked more like a ballroom. Fanlight windows topped ten-foot glass French doors that led into an interior courtyard. Gilt ornate molding across the ceiling with hanging chandeliers. A large wooden grandfather clock occupied a central archway at the end of the room.

The contents were more mundane.

About a dozen small circular tables covered with blue clothes, half-eaten sandwiches and papers and pens and water bottles strewn across them, gray metal-and-plastic chairs haphazardly left, some of them on their sides. Left in a hurry.

The exterior sirens warbled, the noise muted indoors. It smelled of new carpet and lingering cigarettes and coffee. She noted the urn on a side table.

The hallways at the end led left and right.

"You go left," Del said to Johnny, "I go right. We meet back here in two."

"No way. I'm staying with you. I still don't know what we're doing here."

"I don't have time to argue."

Del walked down the middle of the room, her weapon up and scanning the edges of the archways. Her phone rang. She released her double-grip on the Glock and fished the ringing device from her pocket. "Coleman, I don't have time to—"

"Delta," answered a female voice.

Del stopped and waved Johnny forward. He shook his head and indicated they should get in cover of the wall if they were going to stop. She nodded.

"Who is this?" Del asked. It was hard to hear over the noise of the siren, even if muted indoors.

"You called me."

Del backed up against the right-hand wall. Johnny beside her.

"Zoya?"

"Do you have Jacques in custody?"

"Ah, uh—"

"I had information from One PP they took him in."

"Zoya, where are you?"

"I assume you're not evacuating. Are you nearby? Still in lower Manhattan?"

Del asked again, "Where *are* you?"

"New York Stock Exchange building, lower level. In the main trading floor. Interpol had information on where Breedlove might have left the bomb."

Del paused a beat. "Who had information?"

"Suweil. He tracked one of his handlers. This was masterminded by Jacques, Del, he's very dangerous. I filed the Red Notice for his arrest myself. I tried to get in touch with you, but your phone was off. Where's Peter? We saw images of you talking to him. Anything he might have said?"

Del's mind skittered back and forth. "He . . . he was talking about a great evil. I thought he meant Governor Guthrie. He seemed to think he needed to kill Guthrie. He thought he was—"

"—getting messages back in time?" Zoya completed the sentence for her. "It was a psyops campaign. Peter had top-secret security clearance, access to strategic labs. Mentally unstable. They exploited him. Where is Peter? Do you have him?"

Pause for a beat. "He's dead."

Cursing on the other end.

Del asked, "Did you inform anyone at NYPD you came down here?"

"No time to ask for permission. Brought a small team, they fanned out in buildings down the street."

"You think this antimatter bomb is here?"

Johnny's eyebrows raised as she said that.

Zoya replied, "Call Suweil right now, I know you trust him. He'll back me up. We're going to need all the help we can get." A pause. "Did you bring Johnny Murphy with you?"

Del hesitated. "You knew about him?"

"Because if he is, I need him."

"Why?"

"You should get out of here, Delta."

"I'm coming down."

"Delta, please. Send Johnny down, but you need to leave."

"Why?"

"Please trust me."

Del indicated to Johnny to go back. A sign on a hallway to the back indicated the main trading floor. Head to the stairs down, she whispered to him, and then to Zoya she said, "Why do you want Johnny?"

"He's a bomb builder, isn't he?"

"And?"

"Because I'm st—"

The line cut off. The lights went out.

Johnny bolted the opposite direction that Del indicated, back out toward the entrance.

38

Financial District, New York

May 2nd, 2:25 p.m.

"I thought you said there wasn't a bomb," Johnny yelled from a flight up and behind Del.

When the lights went out, she headed straight for the stairs, but Johnny went the other way. She didn't have time to chase him. She thought he had bolted, but seconds later heard him clambering down the steps behind her.

Her phone lost all connections. No chance to call Angel or Dermot to find out if they'd seen anything.

While the ballroom they had been in when power went out was sunlit through the huge glass French doors to the interior courtyard, the interior staircase was illuminated only by the harsh thin glare of emergency lights.

If there was a bomb, what were they waiting for? Why had they not set it off by now?

Would she even feel it?

She wasn't afraid anymore.

Governor Guthrie had long since been removed from the area, so maybe he wasn't the target. The way Peter had beelined for the politician,

Del had assumed that was what was in the scientist's mind, but then, the man had been unstable.

Had he been stable enough to build a world-ending device? Genius and insanity were two sides of the same coin, her father always said.

Her mind raced to make sense of all the things Peter knew about her, all the tiny details. He was convinced he had been talking to Del and himself in the future, but now Peter was dead. He couldn't have been talking to himself in the future if he were dead, right? He was convinced some shadowy organization was tracking him and threatening her. Threatening their unborn children.

Why was her mind even trying to entertain that line of thought?

It had to be a ruse, pure misdirection.

One thing was certain. Del had been lured here, like a fish following a shiny bit of metal through dark waters. A little glitter here and there through the murk, enough to keep her on the line. Now she had been the last one to see the IRGC woman alive in the hospital, and Peter had literally died in her arms. Everything was pointed at her, but why?

"Zoya?" Del called out.

She exited the stairwell. Her sneakers squeaked to a stop on the wooden floor of the cavernous main trading hall. Thirty feet overhead, a gantry-webwork of tubular gray-metal beams crisscrossed below snaking ventilation ducts, all of it lit only by blue-white LED beams of emergency lighting on the marbled walls. Circular pods of banks of monitors, all dark, littered the trading floor, with walls of monitors to either end of the hall, all the way to the ceiling. Webs of wires hung down to support the circular pods and hanging NYSE signs.

In the shadows of the pods of monitors, it was near pitch-black.

But not quite to her eyes.

A faint red smudge crouched near the middle of the room.

The room should have been humming with machines, but she only heard a faint muttering from the crouched figure below the reverberating exterior sirens. Del pulled her Glock back out and held it out in front of her.

"Zoya?" she called out again.

A cell phone light flashed from the figure in the center. "Over here.

Do you have another light, something more powerful?" After a beat Zoya added, "Can you not point that at me?"

Del hesitated but put the Glock back away in her waistband.

Squinting into the semidarkness, she scanned the room. She began walking toward Zoya, who seemed to be talking into her phone. Zoya kept her back to her. Del heard her saying to hold them back, that they had found the device. How was she using her cellphone?

"Who are you talking to?" Del asked.

Without looking around, Zoya replied. "Head of UN Security, he's over at One PP."

A bright light clicked on and cast long shadows around Del. "Found this at the guard station," Johnny said from behind her. "They always keep flashlights at the security. Hey, how are you talking on your phone? Mine's dead, no reception."

"Satellite phone," Zoya replied, still with her back to Del. "They're bringing the bomb squad in. They'll be here in five minutes. I want you to get out of here."

Del cleared the first bank of monitor-pods and scanned left and right. "You found it?"

"You tell me." Zoya got up from her knees and turned to Del, exposing what her body had been blocking.

In the bright beam of Johnny's flashlight, metal flashed. Red lights blinked. A black satchel matching the one Peter had on the roof was under one of the workstations. Del recognized the chunk of metal of the radiation tracker stolen from CERN. It was wired into a mass of other lumps of electronics.

Johnny whistled behind her, obviously impressed.

"You should get out of here," Zoya repeated to Del, and then to Johnny she said, "But since we have a bomb expert already here, maybe you can have a look? Make up for past deeds?"

"I'll see what I can see," Johnny replied.

Zoya gave him space as he knelt beside the bag.

"I don't see a timer," Johnny said.

Del said to Zoya, "Did you come alone?" She squatted next to her uncle and inspected the device. Was this thing really a containment contraption for antimatter cooked up in a massive particle accelerator?

"I've got another man upstairs who should be down in a moment," Zoya replied. "Six more that went into other buildings down Wall Street. We intercepted Peter's communication. Suweil did. We knew he was coming into one of these addresses. This one made the most sense. The great evil was not Guthrie, but American capitalism. He wanted to destroy it."

Del leaned in closer to the bag and asked her uncle, "Turn off the flashlight?"

"I can't make heads of tails of whatever this is," Johnny said.

The light clicked off and cast the area under the workstation into pitch blackness, except for the winking red lights on the device. Del stared into the dark edges of the bag under the workstation. The device was warm and glowed a soft red in her vision, but the edges of it were smudged in fingerprints.

From behind her, Zoya asked Del, "Did Jacques have a phone with him?"

"I took it. The police shot him."

Zoya said, "He escaped. I assume he escaped."

"He what?"

"They just told me on the phone, just as you came in. When I was talking to UN Security. NYPD said the arresting officers didn't show up. Call them yourself. Use my phone."

"I'd like to speak to them." She nudged her uncle, caught his eye in the semidarkness as she turned to rise.

Zoya thumbed a button on her phone. "Did Jacques tell you I was the one who beat him? I tried to warn you." She held her phone out. "Talk to them."

A stuttering electronic beeping like an alarm emanated from the bag, the noise of it just audible under the moaning sirens echoing down the stairwells.

Johnny said in a rising voice, "Oh Jay-sus. I found the timer. It just started. Ninety seconds." A loud beep. "Eight-nine. Delta, honey, you need to run."

A shadow moved at the edge of the room and darted toward the center.

39

Financial District, New York
May 2nd, 2:35 p.m.

Del reached for the offered phone, but instead of taking it, she grabbed Zoya's wrist and twisted. Zoya anticipated and leaned back, leaving the phone to clatter to the ground. She swung out her right hand.

Del lunged forward to block, but the woman dodged back and away and fell to the ground, skidding away from Del's grip. She brought her gun up before Del could find hers in her waistband. Two other men appeared from the edges of the room, one from each side, flashlights blinking on as their handguns tracked Del and Johnny.

Another beep from the device in the bag.

"Throw your weapons on the floor, kick them to me," Zoya commanded.

Del had hers halfway out, as did Johnny beside her.

Zoya said, "Don't force me to shoot. We don't have time. I need to be sure what side you are on."

In the dim light, it was impossible for Del to get a read on Zoya's face.

Another loud beep from the bag.

"Then put your gun down," Del said.

Zoya jabbed the gun at her. "I don't want to hurt your baby."

Del squeezed the grip of her Glock and stared down the barrel of Zoya's pistol, hesitated just an instant, then dropped her weapon and kicked it over. Johnny cursed, but slid his across the floor as well.

Two more beeps.

Del glanced at the bag. Eighty-two seconds on a digital clock Johnny had exposed at the side of the device. Had he turned it on?

Her uncle clenched his jaw and caught her eye.

She looked away. The two men to either side didn't look like police officers. They were dressed in casual clothes, more like tourists, except for the weapons up and drawn and pointed at Del and her uncle.

Zoya got to her feet and kicked the two guns on the floor further away, then aimed her weapon at Del's chest from five feet away. "Zemya," she said to one of the men, "zip-tie them to the metal guardrail."

Johnny cursed out a stream of expletives and rolled to his feet.

Zoya pointed her weapon at him. "One more inch and we will put bullets int—"

Her uncle roared and launched himself into the air. Zoya swung her gun left.

An earsplitting crack, then another.

Johnny spun half-sideways as the bullets impacted his body, but he kept moving forward and crashed into Zoya and knocked her backward into a computer workstation and monitor. The men to either side of them swung their weapons to follow Johnny.

Del leapt forward and skidded along the ground toward the area where Zoya had kicked her pistol. Another crack of gunfire and Del cringed, expecting to feel a bullet impact her body as she scrambled on her hands and knees, searching for a weapon. She found it and spun around.

Two more shots rang out.

One of the men behind her fell to the ground. The other disappeared into cover.

Del rolled over to her right and brought her pistol up, swung it to point where her uncle and Zoya had crashed into the computer station, but the woman had already extricated herself from Johnny. Del glimpsed Zoya disappearing around the side of the workstation pod.

Dermot appeared from the shadows to her left and kicked the gun away from the man he just shot. He crouched using the cover of a chair and swung his weapon around. "Johnboy, you alright there?"

"I got her gun." Johnny coughed and managed to pull himself to a sitting position.

The bag beeped loudly again. The sirens echoed from the stairs. Del heard footsteps.

"They're running," Johnny said, and then to Dermot, "Get me that bag. There's a bomb in there we need to switch off."

Del kept her gun out and scanning the shadows. She dropped to her knees next to Johnny, quick-checked him. His white shirt was dark in splotches. She held her left hand down and felt the hot, wet slick of blood. "Don't move," she said. "I'll get help."

"You will get out of here, that's what you'll do."

"I'm going to get help," Del repeated.

"They're cowards. They're running. You'll get them."

"Did you just turn that bomb on?"

"I did not. I have nothing to do with that woman."

Del got halfway to her feet. Johnny reached out and grabbed her arm. "But I did bomb that truck in Teebane. I lied about that." He looked away. "It was a mistake, my head was full of foolishness back then, and I paid for it. God, I paid for it. Tell your dad I'm sorry for everything. But I had nothing to do with this."

Another beep, then another.

"You get out of here," Johnny repeated to Del. "Me and Dermot will turn this off. Get as far away as you can, mind you. That woman is running for a reason."

Del hesitated, then said, "I'll be back."

"Sure, you will."

She glanced at Dermot, who nodded back at her, before she took off at a run. The metronomic beeping of the bag faded below the wailing exterior sirens as she reached the staircase. She backed against the wall, then swung out, gun ahead of her. Scanned up along the edges of the railing, then back down.

Del edged forward and swung her gun up. She jogged up the stairs, one at a time, her head and weapon up. If that device went off, she wouldn't feel a thing, would she? And if she wouldn't feel it, then there was nothing to be worried about. She needed to stop Zoya.

Find out what the hell was going on.

Was Zoya the one planning this? It didn't have the feeling of wild-eyed extremists.

The lighting brightened as she reached the top of the staircase, natural sunlight streaming in through the French doors on the side of the ballroom. She swung around the corner, gun up and searching. Papers and coffee cups strewn across the floors. The room was empty, didn't look as though it had been disturbed since Del was there a few minutes before.

Through the hall at the end of the room, she had a view onto Wall Street. Lights flashed. Red and blue lights. Del crouched to get a better look. Police cars in the distance. At least three or four, speeding up the street toward her. She edged forward past two of the circular tables, next to a display case heralding next week's bell ringing for a new company coming onto the stock exchange.

Had Zoya gone up the stairs? Angel was there somewhere.

If she had gone up, then the police just had to cordon off the area, assuming her uncle could disarm the weapon. How long had she taken to get up the stairs? Thirty seconds? Forty? No time to bring in the bomb squad, and no telling how powerful the blast might be. She had to warn them back. The flashing lights grew in intensity.

Del was halfway down the hallway and she broke into a jog, lowering her weapon. Movement in her peripheral vision. A curtain to the back of the display fluttered.

Instinctively, Del dropped.

She caught only a glancing blow against the side of her head, but it was enough to knock Del off-balance. Her drop and roll turned into more of a flailing crash into a chair and tabletop that flipped over and tangled her in the cloth. Del kicked reflexively and caught a heavy weight dropping toward her.

The straight leg knocked the wind from Zoya and knocked her back two paces.

Del scrambled back on hands and feet, the tablecloth still half-wrapped around her. Zoya dropped into a fighting stance. Del swung her weapon around and fired. The shot went wide as Zoya anticipated and ducked. In the same motion, she uncoiled and launched herself, snarling, straight at Del.

The ground beneath them heaved upward.

It felt like a concrete wall slammed into Del's face and body at the same time, lifted her up and away in a gnashing inferno of shattering glass that sucked her away into a black hole.

40

United Nations Building, Midtown, New York
May 4th, 10:35 a.m.

Boston Justice adjusted his tie.

Morning sunshine glittered off the East River twenty stories below the glass wall of the UN Security conference room. It was going to be a long day digging through the debrief.

This mess had happened on his watch.

Coming straight after the debacle involving his predecessor Katherine Dartmouth in the Ukraine, a lot of uncomfortable questions needed to be answered.

The Israeli and Iranian ambassadors were due to arrive in half an hour. Having the two of them in the same room was like trying to arrange a date between a lit flame and a can of gasoline. Boston had to make the most of the time he had to prepare.

Still facing the glass and view out onto Long Island, he said, "Did they positively identify the remains yet?"

He turned to the conference table.

So far this morning, Suweil was the only other person there. The heavyset Indian man had flown in last night and brought with him all the case files from Deputy Marshal Devlin. He hadn't wanted to put any more information on servers outside of his own office, Suweil had said. He wanted—needed—to come here and do this in person.

"Yes, they have." Suweil replied. He had a stack of printed materials organized into what looked like a hundred manila file folders strewn around the chestnut conference table. "Will someone be informing the Devlin family?"

Boston turned back to look at the river and bowed his head. "I'll do it." That family had been through too much, lately, and this might be the final straw. "Have we been able to trace the internal messages at Interpol?"

Suweil replied, "Now that we know the actors involved, it's been possible to begin reverse engineering some of the phishing tactics used to gain access internally. It appears that Zoya Abramov was the one feeding misinformation regarding Inspector Galloul. The two of them had a relationship before she left the Lyon Interpol HQ for Hong Kong offices."

Boston nodded. It was about as much of a secret as Delta and Jacques' relationship. Which brought up his next point. "And the police reports charging Inspector Galloul with domestic violence?"

"We talked to the doctors and officers involved. Inspector Galloul vigorously denied any wrongdoing, but the officers who filed the complaints were erring on the side of caution."

Boston ran a hand through his hair. "The French police did confirm his story about his brother. Schizophrenic. Has been living in a kind of Islamic commune in St. Denis just north of Paris. He was committed into care this morning, at Jacques's request."

Suweil asked, "How is he doing? Inspector Galloul, I mean."

"Out of critical care this morning. On the way to recovering well. Wish we could say the same for everyone in that blast."

"Did anyone from our office talk to him yet?"

Boston shook his head. "We'll have to get his statement, but that can wait. Tell me more about Zoya Abramov. The Israeli ambassador will be here in"—he checked his watch—"twenty-five minutes. Give me everything you've got."

Suweil opened a different folder and then keyed his laptop. A projection screen behind him blinked to life and an image of Zoya filled the screen.

"Zoya Abramov was an Israeli policewoman detailed to Interpol five years ago, as you know. She had been cleared by the Mossad in a background check, yet there seem obvious holes in their coverage of her history. Russian father, Kurdish mother. Grew up in Russia in her early life before moving overseas and becoming a naturalized Israeli citizen."

"She served in the Israeli army?"

"Completed her service before she joined the Tel Aviv police department and made a name for herself in the financial cybercrimes division."

"Tell me about Dr. Aringa. You interviewed him this morning? What was his connection to Abramov?"

Aringa was the one who backed up all of Deputy Marshal Devlin's claims about the massive antimatter bomb being real. It was on Dr. Aringa's word that the NYPD ordered the evacuation of lower Manhattan.

"Tenuous at best. It appears Dr. Aringa was a victim of this graft as well. A review of the email servers at CERN revealed that the messages passed back and forth between Dr. Aringa and Dr. Breedlove had been spoofed. By that I mean, someone was faking the messages. Presumably to further push Dr. Breedlove over the edge. And to give credence to the bomb threat when Dr. Aringa was questioned."

"And that someone was Abramov?"

"We are working on this assumption, sir."

"So, no messages were being passed back in time?"

"This is a little out of my area of expertise."

"I was hoping I was joking asking that."

"Dr. Aringa had nothing but praise for Dr. Breedlove's work, even more so with his death. His experiments at the LHC do appear to enable subatomic particles to pass backward through time, however Dr. Aringa assured me that this does not break causality."

"Causality?"

"The chain of one event causing another. Passing information back in time creates opportunities for paradoxes, however not when it comes to time-like curves using Gödel metrics, according to Dr. Aringa. I'm afraid this is out of my depth, sir."

"But the messages Breedlove was getting, we've traced these back to Zoya?"

"It's not quite as simple as that. The messages were coming through encrypted channels. The American NSA is working on breaking the chain of distribution. I will, of course, keep you updated."

Bits and bytes created endless opportunities for obfuscation. Boston preferred bricks and humans. "Someone did talk to this clockmaker? In Saint-Genis-Pouilly? The papers that Jacques recovered from the man in the 'time capsule.' What was the connection?"

"They were from Dr. Breedlove, but it appears these were all part of the setup. It appears these were intended for Inspector Galloul to find, to draw him further into the web. The French police are still interrogating the clockmaker, but he seems innocent."

"Seems?"

"His background is harmless. No connections to extremist groups, no unusual activity—"

"I'm going to need something more concrete, Suweil. I've got the Iranian ambassador to Britain who has just flown in. They are standing by their claims that Anila Jalili, who they admit worked for IRGC counterintelligence, was trying to warn Deputy Marshal Devlin of an extremist plot involving an Israeli national, and that two of our own Interpol agents killed her for it. Do you understand the gravity of the situation? What have you got, concretely?"

Suweil stared at Boston for a few seconds before going back to his folders. "Gait analysis of the security videos at the LHC confirm that the hooded figure that stole the transition radiation tracker device, was in all likelihood Zoya Abramov."

"In all likelihood? That's not exactly 'concrete.'"

"It's the most recent information I have, sir."

"And what about Johnny Murphy? What were his—"

The door to the conference room opened. Boston expected to see a security guard, one coming to inspect the room before the arrival of the ambassadors, but instead, a set of crutches appeared.

Delta Devlin swung her body into the room.

41

United Nations Building, Midtown, New York
May 4th, 10:40 a.m.

Delta collected the crutches into one arm and angled her body to catch the table so she could sit. Suweil sprang for his chair to help her, as did Boston who came from the window and offered to take her crutches. She shooed both away and settled into the chair at the head of the conference table by herself.

Suweil returned to a seat halfway down the room, behind a stack of file folders and a laptop.

Boston hovered near her and rubbed his hands together, then clasped them, fingers interlocking, as if he was praying. "Are you okay?" he asked after a pause.

Del was about the furthest from anything resembling okay she could imagine.

After extricating herself from the rubble of the explosion at the New York Stock Exchange, even before they found the lifeless body of Zoya Abramov, Del had only one thing she needed to do. Coleman had appeared from the police cruisers and tried to calm her down, told her she was bleeding and needed a hospital, and she told him to take her right away.

To the Presbyterian.

To her father.

Coleman apologized and said he needed to cuff her, that she was still under arrest, but Del had barely noticed. Covered in dust, bleeding from her head, she had put on the handcuffs and gotten into the back of his cruiser. The drive uptown seemed to take hours, but she barely remembered it, just had memories of running into the ICU ward and searching for the monitor that tracked her father's heart rate—the one she always looked at when she came in, to see if he was calm or in fibrillation—and his name wasn't on any of them.

Still cuffed, still covered in dust and blood, she had run into his room.

But she was too late.

Her father had died that afternoon.

Her mother had been there by his side, despite Del telling her sister to take her away.

Del had crumpled to the floor of the ICU room, her world spinning away into darkness.

***

Her father always hated it when people hovered.

Boston was still doing it. Her friend Suweil had retreated to a safe and respectful distance halfway down the conference table, but Boston held out both hands toward her as if he wanted to make sure she didn't tip over.

"Are you okay?" he repeated.

She gritted her teeth. "I'm fine."

Truth was, she felt like she had been hit by a cement truck.

The explosion hadn't been an antimatter bomb. It had been a more mundane device, about twenty pounds of C4, but with a collection of lab parts stolen from CERN and other locations to make it look like something else.

Her ears still rang from the blast, so she had to concentrate to hear what people said, but she needed to be here this morning. She had no broken bones—except for a rib in her top right—a slight concussion, lots of cuts and bruises, and a badly sprained knee, but she was physically intact.

Boston said, "I didn't expect—"

"I came to tender my resignation," Del said.

Suweil raised his eyebrows but didn't say anything.

"Resignation?" Boston's hands came apart.

"Twice now in as many years, I've been targeted by an internal"—Del paused to find the right word—"operative inside of Interpol. Someone inside using resources inside the organization to go after me. Personally."

"This was hardly about you, Deputy Marshal Devlin," Boston replied. "I'm not sure 'personal' would be the right word."

"It certainly feels like it, sir."

"I'm sure I cannot even imagine how you are feeling." Boston dropped his hands, realized he was still hovering, then retreated a few steps to take a seat, giving Del some space. "First things first. How is the baby?"

Suweil looked away and down. At least he could sense the impropriety of the question. Del felt her cheeks burn. Just keeping her relationship with Jacques a secret had been critical to her in this world of men. She didn't want the gossip, the looks, the snide remarks behind her back, and now—now everything was in the open. That she had become pregnant in a casual relationship with a coworker, and worse, this had been used against her in a case.

She could almost hear the rumor mill grinding her reputation.

"Fine," Del almost whispered.

When the doctors at the hospital had brought up her initial CBC, they recognized she was pregnant, and that had spun a whole new cascade of emotions as her grieving mother realized her daughter hadn't even told her. Her father was still warm on his deathbed, and Del hadn't even been able to tell him.

"Good, good," Boston said.

Good? Del wasn't so sure. She had been scheduled for an abortion the day before, and it might have been merciful for her to have simply lost the baby in the shock wave of that explosion. Somehow, the fetus survived, even with Del cracking a rib. Del had to admit, the little life inside of her was tenacious. Just like her.

"I am afraid we have some bad news," Boston said. "We have a positive match on the remains found on one of the bodies in the explosion. From the lower level in the trading floor. It matches your uncle, Johnny Murphy. I'm deeply sorry, I know the two of you had only just reconnected."

Del took a moment to absorb. She wasn't surprised. Johnny had already taken two bullets before she left him down there. He said he could disarm the device, but obviously he hadn't been able to. A kind of irony that he had been killed by a bomb, probably one he would have appreciated.

In the end, he had confessed to her.

She finally believed him, in that moment. All the lies, all the deceit, had all washed away. He had saved Del's life, of that much she was certain. Of all the rest, she still had little idea.

Except a few tantalizing details.

When she logged into her personal email that morning, she found a message from her uncle. Detailing his accounts and messages. Some of the contacts had links back to Eden Corporation, he said in the message. Back to her old nemesis, Dr. Danesti.

"Thank you, sir," Del replied after a pause.

"We know you changed records inside the US Department of Homeland Security to allow your uncle to enter the United States without raising any flags."

"It was part of the case, sir."

Boston tapped the conference table with one finger for a few beats. "And that's what we're prepared to say, as well. As US Marshals, we do have a certain amount of leeway when it comes to national security. Enough we could argue it. Every three-letter agency out there is breathing down my neck right now."

"Which makes it easier to blame me, sir. Accept my resignation."

"I'm afraid to say that your uncle's DNA also matches the skin samples found under the nails of that body found in a bag on the East River."

"That was a setup, sir."

"And Zoya Abramov, she didn't die from the explosion."

"Sir?"

Del sat upright from slouching. This was new information.

"She died from the same poison that killed Peter Breedlove. A synthetic thiophosphonate compound similar to the nerve agent VX. We assume it was self-administered, the same assumption we are making about Peter Breedlove when he died after you made contact with him. VX is a nerve agent that we suspect was used against Iraq by Iran in 1988. So, you can see how this complicates the situation."

"Not my problem anymore, sir."

"But it is, Devlin. You were the last known person to be in contact with Anila Jalili, Peter Breedlove, and Zoya Abramov, all three of whom were killed by this nerve agent."

"You think I had something to do with it?"

He shook his head. "But I think you might be more easily protected from the inside, rather than being on the outside."

"Is that a threat?"

"Simply an observation."

"With all respect, sir, I do not feel like I can trust the—"

"Which is why I've been thinking of creating a new group, completely independent. Governor Guthrie called us to commend you on your work in uncovering this plot. You have a lot of friends in high places, Deputy Marshal, which is why I can make this offer. You pick your own team, totally independent, you decide what you want to investigate."

Del had expected to come in here and resign. "I'm not interested."

"Think about it. Do you have anything else?"

"Sir?"

"Because I have two ambassadors coming in this room in ten minutes. If you want to stay and answer questions—"

"I need to go. I have a doctor's appointment I need to get to. And my family."

"I understand. And I don't need to tell you not to go anywhere without telling me."

Del felt her cheeks flush again. She was still a woman on a leash, even as she told them she was done.

She felt like telling him exactly where she thought he could go, but that little Irish voice of her father was still inside her head and told her that if she didn't have something good to say, best not to say it. Instead, she said, "Yes, sir."

42

Long Island, New York
May 5th, 3:05 p.m.

On a white tablecloth, a picture in a black frame of Del's father in his NYPD uniform. It was from when he was Del's age, almost thirty years ago, when he had first come to America. He looked so young, his eyes clear and bright and looking to the future. Del had just been born, and he had just joined the force. His whole life had been ahead of him.

Del had selected the picture. He was so handsome.

His cremated body was in a gunmetal gray urn beside the photo.

Del had accompanied his body to the crematorium herself. It might have seemed grim to some, but she couldn't let him be alone on this final journey. Her mother and Missy had stayed behind at the house after they said goodbye to him at the funeral home, but Del had followed the hearse. She had asked to see him one more time before they put him into the crematorium's oven. As bizarre as the request had felt, she had just needed to see him one last time.

After waiting, she had collected his remains.

In the end, dust became dust. She had placed her father's ashes, double-sacked in plastic and seated in a neat cardboard box, and brought him home. Then transferred him into the metal urn for today.

It still seemed unreal.

A tent had been set up outside for the ceremony.

The gray Atlantic Ocean heaved in the distance beyond the green fields and oaks lining this corner of Long Island. He had always loved the ocean, and he'd said if he was ever laid to rest, he wanted the ceremony to be by the seas. To connect him back to Ireland.

The ocean wind whipped at the stacks of flowers people had sent in. One each from the police commissioners of Suffolk County and the NYPD. One from the mayor's office of New York. Even one from Governor Guthrie, whose special by-election for the senatorial seat was happening today.

Del's mother had reserved the event space, which was usually used for weddings. That was one thing nobody ever told you about funerals. That someone had to organize them, pay for the catering, and make decisions on the decorations. All this just at the moment when you felt incapable of even organizing your sock drawer.

The NYPD and Mayor's office had volunteered to pay for the event. At which point, Del had decided to make it an open bar.

He would have liked that.

The two-story cedar mansion toward the road was outfitted for the wake. No dour crying or sobbing, they were going to play some Rod Stewart and Rolling Stones and get properly drunk, just the way Del knew her father would have wanted.

But first things first.

They had to have his friends and family come and talk about his life, and Del was the last. She wasn't sure if she could get all the way through her speech, not before she started crying, as best as she would try not to. Part of her didn't even want to go up there in front of everyone, but what would her father think of that?

Get on with it, the Irish voice said inside her head.

He was still with her.

Del took some comfort in that.

Half of the First Precinct had shown up early, and already half of the whiskey was gone from the bar inside the event hall. But it wasn't just the police officers who were hitting the open bar—a whole contingent of family she had never met before had flown in from Ireland the day before.

And it wasn't just for her father, Sean.

Another photo was on the white tablecloth. A picture of Johnny from his younger years, but years in which he was already a full-fledged member of the IRA. He was just as handsome as her father, but with that unmistakable twinkle already in his eye, his grin the same as Del had seen just days before.

The remains of four men had been found in the rubble of the explosion. Two of them unidentified, another recovered with an eye patch which Del identified as Dermot, Johnny's longtime associate. The final body was Johnny's, but as he was right next to the bomb when it detonated, his remains had been scattered. As much as could be recovered had been collected into another urn and placed by Sean, on the table in front of Del now.

The two brothers, twins, had been born almost seventy years ago, just minutes apart. And they had died within minutes of each other.

Fate? It was hard not to believe some greater power was at work. That's what Del's mother kept saying. That these two souls had been connected.

At least Del had managed to bring them together, in the end. In some ways, they had reconciled. She laughed and sobbed at the same time. Johnny had even convinced her father into a last mad caper, giving him his badge and uniform to steal Del away from detention in One PP.

Del's mother squeezed her hand.

Amede was next to her, and Missy and her husband and kids along the rest of the front row of white wooden seats set up. To Del's right, Angel and his husband, Charlie, who nodded at her when she looked over. Their boy Roderigo waved at her.

She waved back and tried to smile.

A Catholic priest had agreed to come and minister the ceremony. Her father had never really liked churches. Religion and the fight over it had been the thing that had driven him from his homeland and split his family in half. But her mother was deeply committed and still went to Catholic church each week, while practicing her Louisiana Voodoo traditions more privately, even when her father hadn't been to church in twenty years.

As with everything in their marriage, it was a compromise, one based in love and respect.

The priest nodded at Del—were they ready? She held up her hand. Five more minutes, she mouthed silently. Already the seats behind her were filling up. Everyone was out of the house.

But Del was waiting for one more person.

She squeezed her mother's hand. "He'll be here soon," Del said. She looked up and away from her father's portrait at the rolling seas beyond.

Everything in Peter Breedlove's case had been explainable except one thing. That sports bet. He had won millions of dollars betting on a string of European football matches, but the email message telling him what to do had picked every single winner in dozens of games. The odds were one in billions. Nobody had been able to explain it.

Everything else had fallen into place in the past days.

His girlfriend, Samira, had not been pregnant. She had been part of the conspiracy—his handler—a honeypot that had helped push him over the edge. They were still trying to track the woman down. When he got a message saying his girlfriend was pregnant and had a baby girl, that wasn't true. It wasn't him in the future making a prediction. It was all part of the plot.

One led by Zoya Abramov.

It was in Singapore that Del had started to get the headaches. Zoya must have poisoned her, somehow. And she got the same headaches when Zoya and her went out in Paris soon afterward. It was the headaches that sent Del to the doctor in Paris, the one that Zoya had recommended. The police had raided the location Del had sent them.

They found nothing. No record of any doctor that had been there.

Del had opened up in that doctor's office, described everything about her special vision, had shared details of her family life. That was how they managed to get so much background about her, that they used to feed Peter misinformation and draw her into the web.

And it had never been about a bomb.

The antimatter bomb was a creation of pure fiction. But that didn't stop everyone from believing it was possible. Even Dr. Aringa had been fooled.

A conventional bomb of about twenty pounds of C4 explosive had been detonated in the bag that Zoya had revealed. Johnny had attempted to disarm it, and had mercifully told Angel to get out of the building when he came down. When the bomb went off, it had destroyed the entire trading floor and the ballroom Del and Zoya were in.

But that was a diversion on top of a diversion.

Boston had talks with the Iranian ambassadors. They were very close-lipped, but they said that their operative Anila Jalili was trying to contact the US Justice Department. That she had discovered a plot for a terrorist attack on New York that was going to be blamed on the Iranian Revolutionary Guard. The goal to try and tip the two countries toward war.

But even that wasn't the real goal.

The real reason all of this had been planned went straight to Zoya's main competence.

Financial cybercrime.

They had planned the whole ruse of the antimatter bomb, and used a psyops campaign to make Peter believe he was speaking with himself in the future, to create a perfect ploy to guarantee that all of Lower Manhattan would be evacuated when Del put out the call. The attackers had used Del, used her and her father's fame and notoriety in the NYPD, as a cover to convince the city to empty the entire financial district.

Exactly when Zoya's team had shown up.

They had entered the server rooms of dozens of trading offices and attached tiny devices onto fiber optic cables, something that would have been missed if Delta and Angel hadn't recorded all the men going into the offices as Angel was following Zoya into the area. All of the local area cameras had been shut off, the alarms in the buildings already going off.

It made no sense to bomb a financial center, and Zoya knew this. All of them had remote backups. It wouldn't have made any difference. The goal, which was still mostly guesswork, must have been to siphon off billions of dollars from the financial markets.

Siphon wasn't the right word.

The New York Stock Exchange had been recently criticized for constructing a pair of antennas on the roof of its data center in Mahwah, New Jersey. It gave an advantage of two millionths of a second over other trades to private companies.

Two millionths of a second advantage was all it took to change the world.

Zoya and her team had installed tiny devices to suck data and transmit wirelessly. It would have given them the ability to potentially alter data, move markets, create an exceedingly difficult-to-track chaos within the system. The NYSE wasn't really the target, but dozens of other data processors in the area. They might have been able to affect hundreds of billions or even trillions of dollars of trades, maybe even alter the course of political events.

The FBI and Interpol had begun tracking where the devices had been transmitting data, but it led into a myriad web of offshore companies. Suweil had decrypted the disk drive that Anila Jalili had given to Del. She had kept it to herself, hadn't told anyone else about it.

On the surface of it, the motives for Zoya's attack seemed to be a grudge against America, a desire to rip out the financial heart of the monster that had torn her family apart and killed her sister. Her mother was Kurdish, and when the United States abandoned the Kurds after they had fought side-by-side with American forces against ISIS—and her sister was killed by an American bomb—it spawned a whole new generation of young people with an ax to grind against the West.

That was the official line taken in the media.

However, in Del's opinion—and many others'—the attack was much more sophisticated than a single person could have carried out. The VX-like nerve agent was something only a nation-state might be capable of producing. Or an organization that was aiming for nation-state status which might have an ax to grind or an adversary to bring down a peg.

Suweil contacted the SETI Institute and conducted a forensic audit of their networks. They claimed they had been hacked, that someone had inserted the data into the downloads from the Allen telescope. The BLC1 anomaly was real, but the BLC2 and BLC3 were artifacts that were inserted into the data by a hack. They hadn't put much security up around the SETI data—after all, why would someone want to change data coming from a radio telescope?

Who would hack deep-space signals?

Some of the cyber forensic examinations led on a different and darker route. Suweil managed to decrypt files that led back shell corporations that Del suspected were linked to Eden Corporation, the growing conglomerate that was constructing an offshore platform it claimed was its own sovereign nation on the high seas. America had been blocking its application with the United Nations.

Boston had said she could pick her own team if she stayed. If Del was going to do anything in the future, it would be to investigate the Eden Corporation and her old adversary, Dr. Danesti. Somehow, he was connected to all this. She had no proof, but the thought tickled in the back of her head and wouldn't go away.

***

"Are you okay?" Jacques appeared quietly beside Del. He hung awkwardly in the middle of the aisle. "Do you want me here? Or should I go to the back?"

Del reached out and took his hand. "You stay here, with me. With the family."

She indicated for her family to move over a bit so that Jacques could stand next to her in the front aisle of chairs. "Mom, Missy, this is Jacques, who I was—"

"It is a real pleasure to meet you," Amede said as she swiped away tears.

Del's sister and husband said hello. She nodded to the minister that he could begin the ceremony. Music began playing in the background.

Tears welled but Del held them back. She leaned close to Jacques and whispered, "I'm going to keep our baby."

The Inspector's jaw clenched. He wiped his eyes. "I am very happy to hear this." He reached into his jacket pocket. "I forgot, but I had a gift for you." He gave her a pocket watch. "I had been meaning to give it to you sooner."

The last of the police officers were filtering into the final row of seats now that the music for the ceremony had started. She inspected the gold watch. It was beautiful.

Jacques said, "Sorry I was late, but there were new developments in the case. By the way, your Governor Guthrie, he just won his election. He's joined the Senate. The man can't stop talking about you, he said in a media post today that you saved his life."

Del didn't like the attention. If anything, she hated the man's politics. He was constantly talking about war with Iran. It might have been her own feelings about the politician that made her think that Peter thought he was the great evil. Peter had seemed convinced his target had been Governor Guthrie, that the politician was a future monster that would destroy the world.

"And another thing," Jacques added, "when news of Peter's death got into the news, a woman in France claimed to have had a child by him. She didn't tell him. She had a one-night affair with him some months ago, said she targeted him at a bar because she wanted to have a child with a bright intellect. She basically raped him after getting him drunk."

The minister appeared before the center of the table at the front of the assembly and told everyone to sit.

The tears flowed freely now.

Del stared at the picture of her father looking back at her.

Through her tears, she sobbed, and said, "So, Peter has a child?"

"A daughter. Born just a few weeks ago. At least it's his, according to this woman."

A soft chiming noise began. Everyone in the room looked toward Del. The minister stopped speaking and smiled. Put his hands behind his back.

"Very sorry," Jacques said, reaching into her hand. "This is my fault. There is an alarm on the pocket watch I just gave you." He opened her hand and clicked the top dial.

Del looked down at the watch.

Through her tears she could make out an engraving. Tiny flowers.

You will know I am right when you are crying and bluebells ring. That's what Peter's final words to her had been, what he said her future self had told him.

Bluebells were engraved on the back of the ringing watch. Bluebells. She wiped away her tears and felt a chill. The world seemed to tilt upside down, and the ground felt like it opened up beneath her as the memory of his warning filled her mind.

When you know that I am right.